# STEPPING
## INTO THE FAERIE RING

— WORLD OF PAERRIES SERIES | BOOK 3 —

## A NOVEL
## BY DAN SLONE

*For my father, James C. Slone,*
*my friend for many years.*

*And my mother, Patricia N. Slone,*
*because it's tough to step into a life already begun.*

*And for those around the world*
*who work tirelessly on behalf of wildlife,*
*sometimes even giving their lives.*

Stepping into the Faerie Ring
By Dan Slone

World of Paerries Series:
*Regretting the Rainbow Thieves*
*A Refuge in the Pandemonium*
*Stepping into the Faerie Ring*

Worldofpaerries.com
Follow the author through
Facebook at World of Paerries or
Daniel K. Slone

Book design by SparkFire Branding, LLC
Cover illustration by Gennady Sokolenko
Published Richmond, Virginia
Printed in the United States of America

ISBN (Paperback): 978-1-7326518-4-5
Library of Congress Control Number: 2021911362 Paper Edition

*"Any sufficiently advanced technology is indistinguishable from magic."*

— Arthur C. Clarke


*"… if a man riding in an open country should see afar off men and women dancing together, and should not hear the music according to which they dance and tread out their measures, he would think them to be fools and madmen, because they appear in such various motions, and antic gestures and postures. But if he come nearer, so as to hear the musical notes, according to which they dance, and observe the regularity of the exercise, he will change his opinion of them…."*

— Preacher Thomas Manton

*"When wireless is perfectly applied the whole earth will be converted into a huge brain, which in fact it is, all things being particles of a real and rhythmic whole. We shall be able to communicate with one another instantly, irrespective of distance."*

*– Nikola Tesla*

*"According to many English and Celtic tales, any human who enters a fairy ring will be forced to dance with the creatures, unable to stop until they go mad or perish of exhaustion.... Not all myth surrounding the fairy ring is quite so dark, however. Some legends say that fairy rings are, in fact, good luck."*

*– Ariel Kusby*
*The Myth and Lore of the Fairy Ring*

# CHAPTER ONE

## *Scene 1*

**Aran (Silth)**

Aran tried not to flinch as the jet of blue blood splashed his face, but he wobbled enough that the laser burned a stripe across his scalp. He smelled the singed hather through the room's stew of sweat, chemicals, solder, and ozone.

He slowed his breathing more and loosened his shoulders and wings, trying to relax past the surrounding chaos. The laser's beams crisscrossed around his head, wings, and body, just a leaf's breadth from his skin. He couldn't look down but saw them extend in his peripheral vision. He could also see the large wall monitor showing scenes of forests and mountains, while the captions said Antti Martikainen's *Lords of Iron* played. But the sounds coming from the speakers barely resembled either Human or Silth music. Powered by magic instead of electricity, the banshee wails from the speakers were beautiful in a way far different from normal music.

*Well, the bagpipes sound the same.*

Aran watched as the song changed to LEAH's *Do Not Stand at My Grave and Weep.* He blamed stress for the tears tumbling down his face, sizzling as they hit the heat of the beams.

He'd been sitting in this chair and holding this position for three days. The seat was big, designed for a large Human, and so he sat on top of a pile of books to bring him to the eye level of his Trow interrogators. If he fell asleep and his head nodded, he was burned. Lean back too far, and he would die. Once a day, they took him to a bucket in the corner. That had been a problem on the first day but with no food or water since he'd banged on the door, it wasn't anymore.

Each time when they strapped him back into the chair, they tightened the lasers. The process took time because the entire apparatus appeared to have been jury-rigged just for him, requiring substantial tinkering to both tighten the lasers and keep the whole thing from crashing down.

Through one half of a window, he saw the neon nighttime of Tokyo's Akihabara Electric Town, and he watched the corner of a big digital sign flashing its messages.

A Trow smashed back against the window, his size and waist-length black hair blocking it. This Trow called himself *Janku*, but Aran thought of him as *the Pirate* because of his eyepatch. One of the Steamtiki Crew, Blay, was hacking at the Pirate's left leg, as his sister Abney cut into the other. The third of siblings, 3 of 5, was trying to push a knife through the Trow's throat as he struggled to pull her away. *Tara, that's 3 of 5's actual name,* thought Aran through the fog that filled his mind. Tara had severed an artery and blue blood sprayed the room. It slicked down the feathers of her wings and the hairlike feathers—the hather—that covered her head, so the Trow was having trouble gripping her to pull her away.

Something bumped Aran and another burn joined the twenty or so around his head. He saw Temkaa fly backwards, narrowly avoiding a slashing short sword from an advancing Trow. Temkaa's mouth was open with a war cry Aran couldn't hear above the din of the music. He threw a club-like axe into the Trow's face.

*Temkaa, why is Temkaa here? He's not Steamtiki.*

Then Aran remembered Temkaa had taken leave from his leadership of the Africa Silth, to help him hunt for Trow enclaves.

Aran closed his eyes and blew out a long breath, letting the surroundings fade. He relaxed into the quiet of his mental clearing in the jungle but could still hear the noise of the Tokyo room. Instead of concentrating harder, he let go more.

An open space appeared, surrounded by deep green, and capped by tiny openings to a bright blue sky. The grunts and screams of combatants and the wail of the magically enhanced violin faded, replaced by layers of bird song and the distant growl of howler monkeys. A blue morpho butterfly bounced along the edge of the space, framed by the chatter of bugs. Moths and birds crossed through the shafts of sun slicing into the meadow.

The jungle allowed clearings only temporarily, and this one, created as an enormous tree had fallen and crushed the smaller trees and brush beneath it, was filling in with young trees and vines growing up around the carcass of the fallen giant. In the clearing sat three wooden, Silth-sized crates. Aran walked over and took the lid off of the closest, carefully laying it on the ground beside him. He paused to hold his concentration as a Trow voice bellowed in rage near his ear. He reached into the crate, pulling out a blanket covered in intricate scenes. The scenes, each a memory he'd placed there, moved on the blanket as he wrapped it around himself.

Aran closed his eyes in the mental construct, and Merit's face filled his mind. He caressed the thoughts he'd been cataloging onto the blanket for the last few days. His history with her. The time he'd spent with her when they first met; the way he'd broken her heart. The battles they shared. The way she looked—her reluctant smile, the curves of a body he'd memorized long ago, and the fierceness with which she carried herself. A thousand images flooded his mind with each thought. The thoughts continued in a long list of the ways she made him feel, the things she did that amused him or irritated him. Hours of cataloging. Then, a tally of why he wanted to spend the rest of his life with her.

*The rest of my life might not be that long,* he thought.

Another bump of his chair jostled him, and he brushed a laser, causing him to gasp and open his eyes. Something sticky and wet was sliding down his left side, so he inventoried the many points of pain in his body. Whatever it was though, it wasn't his.

A Trow backed into his field of vision, some kind of lab coat on with wires and electronic circuits woven into his dreadlocks and clutching a small dart in his throat. Aran watched another dart hit the Trow's sharp-featured face as Jules, another crew member, flew forward in pursuit, dodging the various appliances and tools the dying Trow threw.

*How does he keep that hat on in a fight?* Aran wondered.

Aran closed his eyes again, pushed aside the pounding headache, and slid back into the peaceful glen. He was at its edge again, the crates closed. He walked past the first crate and opened the second. This blanket brought back the last three days' memories—the chronology of how he'd ended up here in this chair, being tortured and awaiting death.

The map of his leadership failure.

Various clues led him and the team to Tokyo. He found the

Japanese knew more about the Silth than he'd expected. They told tales of beings from Mt. Horai, who had no knowledge of great evil, and consequently, their hearts never grew old, a reasonable interpretation of the Silth's 300-year lifespan. The Ainus spoke of a race of small people known as the *Koro-pok-guru,* and in the Ryukyuan religion, there were the *Kijimuna*—tree sprites. Any of these stories could be referencing the Silth.

But what drew his attention was an urban legend of a modern *Oni,* a Japanese ogre or troll, claimed to be roaming this district. This sounded more like the Trow.

He and the Steamtiki Crew, joined by Temkaa, began their search. Wanting a break from his administrative duties as leader of the African Silth, Temkaa sought adventure. For almost two weeks, from the moment they awoke to the time they staggered to bed, they scoured the city's back alleys and rooftops. Temkaa said this was the opposite of adventure. The crew stuck to the shadows, finding it disconcerting to walk the streets openly.

The Japanese appreciated their presence, however, and on the one night Aran allowed the crew to go out for recreation, they made many friends. The Silth crew rode through the streets on Mario-carts with Humans dressed as characters from the game. They stood in an art installation where the lights flowed like a waterfall crashing down on rocks. They drank—well, everyone but Aran—with the rows of light-saber-waving patrons at a Japanese burlesque show. The flashes of cellphone cameras went off around them like some mad, exploding swarm of fireflies.

But Aran's favorite part of that evening had been its beginning, as they watched the sunset behind the charming, shell-inspired spires of the Mermaid Lagoon in Tokyo's Disneyland. Their initial welcome faded as park personnel realized that the group just blipped in instead of paying. To close out the night, they'd explored elegant parks of blooming trees, iridescent in the light of a full moon.

Most days they roamed the streets, looking for signs of the Trow. Having few clues, they chose places to search at random. Then Vander glimpsed a Trow turning a corner, but there was no trace by the time he got there. The crew concentrated its search in the vicinity, and eventually—two days later, at 3:30 in the morning—they tracked a Trow back to this old office building.

Two more days of surveillance told them little about the Trow occupants. Only the one Trow, the Pirate, ever left the rundown building which appeared as though its rehabilitation had been abandoned years earlier. Scaffolding rusted along its facade, and most floors were empty. Black plastic covered all the windows on the tenth floor except for one. And it was through this window that they saw a mass of wires and electronic devices, not just computers and stereos but blenders, slide projectors, vacuums, robots, and other random electronic devices. Each time they looked, things had been moved, but they never saw anyone in the room.

Aran went in by himself, an unpopular decision. Since the elevator in the building didn't work, he flew up the dark stairwell to the tenth floor where a massive steel door blocked the only access. He tried looking through its peephole but saw only blackness. He could just blip to the other side of it, but that seemed like the wrong way to begin the conversation. So he knocked. Nothing happened.

He pounded on the door, but the steel and tight doorframe made little sound.

He blipped away, coming back with a hammer. For fifteen full minutes he beat on the door, swinging the hammer like a Human swung a sledgehammer or an axe. Then the door flew open, and strong, rough hands stuffed him into a bag. He couldn't blip out of it, and when they threw in a rag doused in something, he passed out.

Later, he awoke strapped into the chair surrounded by the lasers, the Trow asking him random questions. None could keep focused long enough to complete any task, including his interrogation. He asked them questions too, which sometimes they answered and other times ignored.

When he tried to blip away again, nothing happened.

The room's sporadic activity seemed directionless. Someone would come in, begin a task with a machine, and then walk away before the task had finished. Sometimes, they ran whatever the machine was by pushing magic through it. He'd watched as *Chains*, his unoriginal name for the Trow covered in them, put his gloved hands on either side of an unplugged computer monitor which then sprang into life, glowing in vivid fluorescents. At first, Aran thought the screen showed just static, but when he blinked his augmented eyes to reset them to the Trow spectrum of sight, he saw images moving across it of a strange, barren land. It was as though he was looking through someone else's eyes while they walked along a road.

Each day, the Trow adjusted the lasers a fraction closer to his head. He didn't know why. Was it to get more information from him? Did they simply enjoy torturing him?

Unlike the Human movies he'd seen, there was no evil laugh to give him a clue, just the methodical actions of a scientist or engineer. Today, each breath took him dangerously near a burn. Today would have been his last.

Could still be.

In hindsight, he hadn't led well. He had—and now he realized he did this often—made no contingency plans. He left no instructions on what to do next if he didn't return. He acted as though he was protecting the others, but he'd actually left them to fend for themselves. Now they were risking their lives rescuing him.

Picking at the blanket, he tested how hard it would be to reweave this set of memories to be more honest about his failure. Not enough time. He returned the blanket to the second crate and secured its top. Then he looked over at the third crate, the one on which he'd spent the most time. Not because it had the most information—as it had but a small fraction of the first or second crate's detail—but because the disparate thoughts within were the hardest to weave together. He wouldn't have the opportunity to explore that one again today.

Building these crates and weaving their blankets helped him meditate with absolute stillness. He might have balanced them on the edge of a cliff, to remind himself to hold still, but instead he'd built them in the jungle, a place he'd feared at one time.

He'd survived being awake and mostly without movement for three days.

From the diminishing activity around him, he sensed the fight was almost over, but he moved toward the last crate, hoping for one more quick review of its contents. He felt himself being shaken, moving past the point that would normally have brought pain, and his eyes flew open.

As Jules leaned in front of him and grasped his shoulder, Aran felt as though his head was full of cotton. Jules's lips moved, making sounds, but he couldn't focus on what Jules was saying. Someone turned off the music and Aran's eyes wandered over the surrounding scene.

Three Trow lay dead in the room, and he spotted the feet of another in the hall.

A smoky haze hung in the air.

Some of the crew moved around the room, staunching wounds or searching for anything that might be important. Presumably, the balance of the crew rifled through the other rooms. Although Temkaa and Jules continued trying to talk to Aran, he wasn't able to form a response. He didn't understand how he had been so lucid a moment ago, but now felt himself so fuzzy. Temkaa tipped him to the side, and with Jules, carried him from the room. When he allowed himself to relax, the muscles he hadn't moved for days spasmed. Pain arced through him and he gasped. Then, as he watched the broken ceiling tiles go by, he passed out.

***

Aran felt as though he was falling and cried out as he sat up in the bed panting, wings spread wide and tears streaming down his face. But no laser stung. Loana, always the most motherly of the Tiki Crew, shushed him and pushed him back on the bed.

"You're ok. We're safe. We're in a hotel."

As he sank back into the soft bed, he noticed the smoothness of the sheets and how Loana was stroking his hather. He looked around the luxurious bedroom, still confused, trying to resolve his last memory with his current circumstances. They'd spent their nights on the tops of high-rises since they'd arrived in Tokyo. He'd never registered and paid for a Human hotel room before, though he'd stolen nights in small, inexpensive ones once or twice.

Loana sensed what he was thinking. "Temkaa said since we're finished with the mission here, we should have some comfort." She pulled in her chin and imitated his voice, "I am a king, and would like to live like something more than a street minstrel for a day or two."

Dishes rattled and the murmur of voices drifted in from beyond the doorway. Aran recognized the smell of bread and fruit, and the deliciously overwhelming odor of warm maple syrup.

"I'm glad he's paying for the room service," Loana went on. "The bar bill by itself astonishes." She launched herself from the edge of the bed and flew gracefully from the room, returning with Jules and Temkaa.

"This was a stupid plan," Temkaa said.

"Beyond daft," Jules added. Loana giggled as Aran winced.

"You must have talked to Merit," Aran said, his nails-on-chalkboard voice even rougher than usual. "She calls all my plans stupid."

Temkaa looked at the ceiling and shrugged. "Merit, Storng, Nadara, and many others. There is a consensus on its stupidity."

Aran looked away, tightening his arms around himself. "It *was* a stupid plan."

Nick and Don pushed a cart covered with dates, almonds, avocados, and other food into the room, their wings flapping vigorously to keep it moving. Don filled a plate, carefully checking the avocado for any pieces of the husk or the center nut, and set it on the bed beside Aran.

"How long have I been sleeping?" he asked as he picked at the food.

"We came the night before last and it nears—" Temkaa checked the bedside clock, "—5:30 in the afternoon. Almost two days."

"Thank you all. Thank you. You shouldn't have had to do that. Tell me about the... rescue," Aran mumbled from behind a hand holding a fig.

"You first," Jules said as he grabbed food and sat on the bed. Nick called to the others. Some joined them on the enormous California king bed, carrying drinks in tiny plastic medicine cups, while a couple snatched food and perched on the dresser, squatting on their heels.

Aran used a small bread knife to spread apricot jam on a piece of croissant. He closed his eyes as the flavor flooded his mouth.

"Not much to tell. I was beating on the door one moment. Strapped into that chair the next. The leader—the others called him *Bosu*—asked me questions. He and one or two of the others talked to me from time to time, but they made little sense. He wanted me to tell him how I'd found them, and who I was working for; he was sure it was the Trow. All of them, I guess I saw five males and two females, thought my arrival meant a Trow squad would be close behind. They were packing to move when you came."

"What was that equipment?" Loana asked.

"The *Electric Trow,* that's what I called them in my head since they never gave me a name for their group." Aran stopped for a moment as his vision blurred and the room spun. "The Electric Trow experimented with what happens if you were to substitute magic for electricity. They ran everything in there—the music, the computers, the appliances, everything—on magic. And they'd gotten pretty good at it. I don't know if you've ever tried it, but that was some of the first magic I did in the field. It's hard to control. Not just to control the machine, but to avoid frying it out." Aran thought back to the police car lurching along behind the Dollar Store. "But they had a kind of energy dampener allowing them to flow magic smoothly into Human devices. The results sometimes went monkey scat, like the music, but it worked."

Temkaa said, "When you did not return, we assumed you could not blip out."

"I tried, but maybe something about the dampener kept me from doing it. They had a magic dampener... did I already tell you this?" Temkaa nodded. "They had a dampener that held the energy of magic in the room. I heard one of them saying it must be leaking and this might lead the Trow to them."

"Well, something in there screwed up magic," Jules said. "As soon as we fired the first bolt coming in, we knew we weren't going to be able to use magic. I think Don shot first, and the bolt just expanded into this big blue ball and exploded every piece of equipment around it. After that, everything was hand-to-hand—a dingo's birthday party."

"I saw some of the fighting." Aran nodded to Tara and Temkaa. "Thank you. I never intended for you to take those kinds of risks." Aran stared down at his hands.

"I kind of thought that was what we'd come along for," Vander said, Slatt nodding next to him.

"Did any of the Trow survive?"

Temkaa shook his head. "The twelve of them, you must not have seen them all, fought to the death. We looked around for papers or something that might tell us more about them or their mission. But we didn't find anything."

"A few cool toys," Don said.

"And the surge of magic through the equipment set the building on fire. We saw the flames coming from the windows as we left."

"Did you get any sense of why they broke from the Trow?" Jules asked.

"I think at one time they were scientists—researchers or something similar—working on a solution to the problem of the electrical machinery driving the Trow mad. They may have used themselves as test subjects."

"Well, I think they will not be helping us fight Thest when he returns," Temkaa said.

Jules frowned. "So, we got nothing from this group?"

The room fell silent.

Aran pulled at a thread on the blanket—and thought about the third crate.

*Maybe, maybe not.*

# *Scene 2*

## Thest (Trow)

Thest looked up as actual sunlight poured through the window behind the throne. The workers laid the bulky apparatus that had covered the window on the floor. This creature, related to the mind-reading threshold, projected its master's visions and moods to the mind of anyone else in the room. The source of Xafar's theatrics.

Moments later, the wall separating the throne room from the hall of the advisors crashed to the floor, sending a cloud of dust across the room. Workers rushed in, picking up bricks and plaster even as others began moving the enormous tables from the advisors' hall into the expanded room. They lifted the heavy iron chandelier that was now stripped of bones and body parts and lit with glow worms, back into the vaulted ceiling. The wall sconces glowed with the worms as well.

Servants had pulled paintings and tapestries out of storage and returned them to the walls, replacing heads and bloodstains, as rugs replaced the bodies on the floor. A group of Human slaves played soft music from an alcove, and incense burned on every table trying to chase the stench of death from the room. The smell of fresh food piled on a gigantic table mixed with the incense.

Instead of taking formal meals, Thest foraged the table when hungry. The advisors, workers, and slaves ate from there as well.

A general and two advisors walked in, deep in conversation. They paused and bowed. Thest waved them over to his table. They wore the white tunics required for anyone but guests to move about the room. Tunics left little room to hide a weapon.

The guards who had allowed in the knife he'd used to kill Xafar now patrolled the Faraway, the Land's remote poisonous grasslands, inhabited by nothing but flower fairies.

Thest had tried moving the mind-reading threshold so it hung above the throne room, but he found he could accomplish nothing with everyone else's thoughts intruding, so he moved it back to the only exterior door to the room and its attached chambers.

When he had first become King, there had been a rush of celebrations. Xafar had been insane and universally despised, yet Thest defied tradition and spared Xafar's wife, concubines, and children, binding their honor not to harm his children. In the Land, such a binding had no magical consequences, but breaking the promise was cause for instant execution. However, he did not bind them against him. Xafar's wife, barely saner than her husband, had objected on behalf of her baby son, claiming it was his right to take the throne through whatever means necessary. Thest had held his sword to the child's throat for a long minute, reciting the names of the heirs killed in prior transitions.

In tears, she agreed to the condition. The King's court spoke of the wisdom of his approach.

Then Thest dissolved the Queen's court, as there was no queen, before dissolving the King's court as well. He redirected the courtiers' pensions to the military, raising the wages for soldiers significantly. Stripped of their privileges and no longer under threat of death, the former courtiers became dangerous. But Thest did not care. He had no desire to keep the throne anyway and wanted only two things: to cleanse the Earth of Humans and Paerries, sweeping away Aran and Faelen in the process; and to protect his children.

"I remember when we held these meetings in places of whimsy," General Claibor said with hesitation. He had served in Thest's chain of command a long time, but like most of the kingdom, he was trying to figure out how to interact with their new King. The other two visibly tensed.

"We also lost to vermin," Thest replied. "Less whimsy, more victories now." Thest looked up from his work and stared deep into the general's eyes.

"More victories!" Claibor repeated as he broke eye contact and leaned over the map of the Earth spread on the table.

The map showed the portals and the population and governance centers for Humans and Paerries, as reported by the Trow spies. The advisors debated whether to destroy the Human governance centers first, attacking the national capitals and new protection zones, or move immediately against the population centers. Thest did not have enough troops and commanders to attack both simultaneously.

His generals pressed the enlistment of all able-bodied Trow into the army. Increased rewards helped, but the stagnant Trow population did not allow a large army. The Trow had no navy or air force, and with their transport ability on Earth, Thest saw no need for either. Their goal was eradication, not subordination, so they only needed to maximize death, not seize operations. Consequently, there was no need to control or preserve any of the infrastructure—they just needed to shut off communications and power to reduce coordination and response. Theirs was a simple mission—death.

"What about timing? Do we still need to wait because of the

psychic trauma of mass destruction?" Claibor asked, eyebrows raised.

Zep, an ancient adviser, hunched and gray, shook his head. "Yes, when we first set in motion our plan to activate the volcanos, we hoped the Humans would not know it was an attack. We believed that the large-scale psychic trauma of the murder of most of the Human and Paerrie population would contaminate the Earth for many years.

"This would interfere with our return by creating mental distortion for our Trow forces. The Humans learned we had activated the volcanoes, and the Paerries shut them down. Thus, only twenty-five percent of the Human population and almost none of the Paerries died from them. It seems their psyche stabilized and, according to the spies, they are preparing for our attack. I believe we can now proceed without fear of trauma."

"Now?" Claibor bounced on his heels.

"Yes, now."

"Our limitations? Besides troop numbers?" Thest asked.

"Not food, as we can eat the food of Earth. Because magic fuels us and our weapons on Earth, we do not need ammunition or normal supply lines—so long as we have magic. But its use will exhaust our troops. We need to carry non-magical weapons to use as their magic recovers, and we need to use the Humans' own weapons against them where we can. The Paerries also have magic, so we should rotate troops to ensure we always have some who have not exhausted their magic."

"As far as the backup weapons, we have some limitations," Claibor added. "We can only equip half of our troops."

"Make more."

"We have rounded up all the metal we can," Claibor said. "Your subjects were happy to turn in sculptures of Xafar but are less excited about giving us most of the utensils in their houses."

"Even so," Zep continued, "we can make swords for your forces. But swords do not do well against the guns of Humans or even the arrows of Silth."

"And biological weapons take time to grow. Twenty percent of your warriors will have them."

Thest looked at the map as he took a long drink from the tea glass his servants kept filled beside him. He sighed and shook his head a fraction.

"Then the first targets should be armaments storage. We will take the weapons we need."

Zep glanced at Claibor and the other advisor as if they'd expected this answer. "A good strategy, but our troops must train to use what we take. Humans do not use swords. They use rifles, drones, and tanks, not being intuitive in their operation. Working with our spies, we must identify other weapons or how to train for the ones we can get."

"I do not need my advisors to test me. Solve it."

"Yes, my liege." Two of the three turned to go, but Zep did not, instead taking a step closer to Thest.

"Your Majesty," he said, wringing his hands and lowering his voice, "many of your subjects question this undertaking. It will take most of our resources to wage this war. They wonder if we should attend to more important matters...." He trailed off as he saw the look in Thest's eyes. He saw the King's hand grip the sword at his side, the only weapon in the room.

All voices stopped and movement ceased.

Thest drew the sword so fast Zep did not have time to flinch.

He brought it smashing down on a piece of fruit on the table, sending one half flying in one direction and the other in the opposite direction. He stared at the trembling Zep and murmured, "No."

Zep nodded shakily, and he and the others resumed their work at another table.

Thest continued studying the map.

A few minutes later, a familiar voice interrupted him. "No more worries about meetings with the boss, My Lord?"

"Fod! Welcome!" Thest brightened for a moment. "Are you ready to return to Earth?"

"Always." Fod had squeezed himself into a white tunic at least one size too small and wore a new eye patch. He had been Thest's right hand on Earth for over a century.

"Good. You will coordinate the spies we send in the first wave. We have some there now, but we will soon send many more. You have one special task—find Faelen for me. This time, I will make sure he is dead." Fod nodded and hurried from the room.

When Thest saw Casius waiting with his appointed handler, his gaze slid past them as if he had not noticed. He must talk to the vermin, but first he needed to reset his thoughts. He had plans for this creature, and he must not let his emotions control how he managed him. He took a deep breath, trying on a smile but then returning his face to neutral. He signaled the adviser to bring Casius.

Casius walked across the room instead of flying. The first time Casius had flown in the Land, Thest had seen how the Trow looked on in envy. Many Trow missed flying more than other magic on Earth. From then on, Thest had Casius walk when around Trow. Casius, who translated everything here in the Land as steps on a mystical journey, smiled and complied. Still, even the presence of his wings galled Thest.

The King kept Casius and the advisor standing next to him without speaking for several minutes. Finally, he gestured to the far end of the table where the servants had placed a box that allowed Casius to sit, his wings and tail unencumbered, with his eyes lower than Thest's. The servants and staff had gotten used to Thest's frequent use of the table for his interactions. He rarely sat on the throne.

Casius pulled himself onto a chair and from there onto the table. He finally came to settle on the box.

"I trust you find the King's hospitality acceptable." Thest had never discussed the transition in leadership with Casius, and again, Casius seemed to see it as something done for his benefit—a hostile force replaced with a beneficial one.

"I'm honored at every turn, My Lord. Each day brings new learning of ways that I may be of service." The advisors had taught Casius several useful magics, but only in theory because there was no magic until he returned to Earth. They had also made up several complex and useless spells. No one would ever remember and perfect all the steps but even if they did, nothing would happen. But Casius would think he had taken a wrong step in the process.

"And you are ready for your mission?"

"Yes, my King. I'm eager to serve."

"Questions? Concerns?"

"No, my King."

"Then you go with my honor on your shoulders, succeed or do not return."

Casius stood, bowed, and clambered off the table.

As Casius followed his handler from the room, Thest leaned

back over the maps, making calculations on a piece of paper. He paused for a moment, feeling the weight of the preparations, the pressure building as they made ready for war.

Then he opened a mental door just a fraction, letting his hatred for the Paerries and for the traitor Faelen spill into his thoughts. Ridding the Earth of Humans was not a war. It was simply a chore—the eradication of a pest, like the Humans did with mosquitoes. But with the Paerries it was personal. And Faelen... Thest could not even complete the thought as his anger burned white hot, a super nova blasting away any other thoughts and leaving his teeth and fists clenched, shaking with a scowl so intense the Trow in the room avoided him for the next hour.

***

Hours later, as Thest stood in the main living area of his old house, he vaguely remembered a story of a Human general who burned his ships so his soldiers would not be tempted to retreat. Or perhaps it was to show the enemy he would only advance. He threw another handful of his medals on the bonfire blazing in the middle of the room's floor. He had already burned the few mementos of his children the house contained and tossed into the flames the relics of travels with Demest: a feather gained as they flew with the great condors; a piece of an ancient Earth tree with which they had shared thoughts; a perfect scarf, woven by an elderly Silth artisan. And now, the awards and honors he had accumulated over the years. The fire rose and licked the ceiling. He shoved furniture from the room into its heat and watched as the flames caught and coursed along the rafters.

He did not expect to return to the Land, and certainly not to this house.

He would kill Faelen, whose actions had led to Demest's death. He would eradicate the Human infestation and eliminate the Paerries. When he finished, he would rule the Earth and the Land from the verdant Earth, not from this diminished shadow world.

As he trudged from the burning house, he heard the sharp crackle and crash as the roof collapsed and oxygen flooded in to feed the marauding flame creature. He heard it tearing apart this memory of a prior life in its fury, but he did not look back.

# *Scene 3*

### The Hunter (Human)

*It's about how you hold your mouth.* His father had taught him that. As he slipped through the fence and crouched low, looking for the sensors and cameras he knew filled the woods, he thought about his father's lessons. He'd been hunting so long the physical moves were second nature now. Where to put his foot so his steps made no noise. He just knew where the most likely game trail wound through the trees, immediately recognizing the browse lines of the deer and the scat of the raccoons frequenting these woods. He heard the rustle and faint gobbles of the wild turkeys nearby. Similarly, he sensed where the best place to locate a camera or a vibration or sound sensor would be and avoided those.

The Hunter—that was how he thought of himself—wore night-vision goggles, but he was sure that he could've moved through these woods without them. He moved a few steps forward and then waited. Sensing. He listened to the others crashing through the woods ahead of him. They thought they were being stealthy but everything in the forest was aware of their presence and their location. That's what he was now, part of the forest.

The Hunter's father used to hold him back when they'd start a hunt. They arrived with a group, and he let the others go ahead. As a boy, the Hunter waited impatiently, worried there wouldn't be anything left, but his father said they didn't want to be near the ones hung over from staying up late the previous night. His father never missed the night-before-hunt camp prelude, always taking part in the campfire meals and the revelry. But he took his hunting too seriously to let that traditional ceremony impair the important day. After letting the others get ahead, his father took him in a different direction, all the while teaching him the world around him, the ethics of the hunt and its meaning for a man. In those mornings, his father trained him in self-discipline, the ancient competition of man against an animal designed to elude him, and how to honor the vanquished.

They hunted with bows, so his father taught him to be sure of his shot in order not to leave an animal suffering in the trees. He coached him to respect and appreciate guns and use them appropriately. He had no use for automatic weapons or high-powered rifles; these were not respectful, nor was there honor in that hunt. Maybe if you were hunting big-horn sheep or grizzly bears. But he didn't do things that way, refusing to hunt for things he didn't eat.

He didn't worry about the endangered species stuff they made up though. It was all fake news, and even if it wasn't, if it was time for a species to end, it was time.

That was what he taught his kids, and their kids too.

The Hunter stopped and leaned against a wide red maple. Fast movement through the trees told him that the others had triggered the sensors. They were the hunted now. He knew about that as well and knew all the tricks of the hunted.

He carefully began clearing leaf litter around him, digging out a slight depression in the forest floor. The sweet smell of the moist earth was so heavy he could taste it on the back of his tongue. As he lay in the hole he'd dug, he heard the first shot, and then a second. The guards were good. No wasted effort. No spare noise to mask a run forward.

The Hunter covered himself with debris, keeping his gun clear of the mud.

The Army had taken over where his father left off. The Hunter had enlisted, and his training had taken him into the special forces. He had learned to hunt Humans, sometimes smarter, but often not as smart as the prey he'd sought with his father. He used a high-powered rifle or an automatic weapon for this type of hunting because this prey shot back. While he didn't eat what he killed, he still honored the vanquished.

The Hunter also learned what it was like to be hunted, and to know someone wanted to kill you. He learned how to hide, evade, and mislead. He knew how to endure discomfort to stay alive a little longer.

But then he'd come home, and these skills weren't very useful in getting a job. Now this war, the war with the Trow, came from nowhere. He thought he might re-up, but they weren't looking for more folks who would survive in places no Human should. This was going to be an urban war. A technological war. A magic war. If he had been younger, he could still have gained the skills he needed for this war. But he wasn't young anymore. The Hunter was older than his father had been when they'd hunted together.

Now a different enemy wanted to kill him in a different way— to kill his way of life. They made it clear no one was going to take away his guns or bows. But hunting would be limited to those species that were missing predators in the ecosystems—deer, rabbits, and similar creatures. It would be managed and reduced as they allowed predators back into the systems. As the foxes, cougars, bobcats, coyotes, eagles, hawks, and wolves returned, hunting would be reduced. Priority would be given to hunters who needed supplemental food or were hunting on behalf of organizations that efficiently used the food.

He knew how to respond to a predator. He knew how to defend himself against an attacker.

The Hunter slowed his breathing and listened, part of the forest floor. He heard footsteps nearby. Mentally, he checked the readiness of his rifle and the pistol at his side, as well as the knife and other weapons he carried.

# Scene 4

**Joss (Human)**

Macho, a medium-sized black and white husky, followed just behind Joss as she walked from Administrative Building 1 to the Human residential quarters. *Waddled,* thought Joss, *not walked.* Though only six months pregnant, she felt it in her gait already.

Macho made a start after a chipmunk crossing the path, but it was in the bushes before the dog even got serious about the chase. The big dog stood above the bush, ears pointed, piercing blue eyes locked, poised to pounce. But the chipmunk wisely hunkered down. Macho glanced over at Joss for a second, looked back at the bush and then turned and trotted down the path, watching for more small creatures in need of discipline.

The birds were welcoming the soon-to-arrive sun with complex songs, and the frogs had not quite left their evening shift. Mockingbirds threw bits of melody back and forth from the edges of their territories.

Shots and shouting shattered the morning reverie. Joss ducked low, crouching in a bush beside the path, and called Macho to her. A siren wailed.

She turned back to the Admin Building, staying low and using the bushes as cover. As she crept down the path, Macho came to her side. The dog stopped and growled at the bushes twenty feet away.

"Macho, stay," she said, peering toward the bushes.

The sun came over the horizon, making it even harder to see in the shadows. As the hair on the back of her neck stood up, she realized she couldn't outrun a turtle. She jumped as two Silth guards appeared on either side of her. They said nothing. One of them just tilted her head toward the Admin Building. They escorted her the last part of the way but blipped away as she entered. Many of the Silth could not speak or even understand English. Once, one tried to talk with Joss and she didn't even recognize the sounds as language.

She flinched again as her phone rang, the head of security confirming her location.

"What's going on?" she asked.

"Three guys in camo tried to sneak in from the north side. When confronted, they started shooting."

"Status?"

"Two dead and the third being treated while the ambulance and sheriff come."

"Was that all of them?"

"Don't know. Stay in."

Joss wasn't surprised. Various groups had tested the perimeter for weeks. "Let me know when the police arrive. Do we know who these are?"

"No ID. But the live one has a tattoo that says *Wilddeath*." This was one of the several hunting groups that had declared themselves ready to fight over Joss's latest set of hunting mandates. "We need you to stay in place while we check the rest of the grounds."

"Okay."

She stepped into her office and sat looking at the James River, wide here and sparkling in the morning sun. The oranges of a marvelous sunrise faded to the east. Even though the airborne ash of the volcanoes had given them a cold, dark fall and a brutal winter, it had also given them gorgeous sunrises this spring and should offer a cooler summer this year than most.

Macho curled up on his doggy bed in the corner. Its empty twin sat a few feet away as Shadow was off with Tiny this morning.

The room's big window let in light, but not heat or cold. The buildings in the complex were green, which meant they functioned using less energy, ran on solar power, used rainwater for toilets, and avoided chemicals in the indoor air. The local university had constructed and used the core set of buildings for its big rivers program as well as other biodiversity programs. These still operated on a small part of the expanded campus, but most of the campus, and the extensive properties added to it, extended the various programs Joss operated. The university's name remained in small letters on the big sign that said *UN World Interspecies Directorate, UNWID* to most people.

Joss watched a pair of mallard ducks walking toward the river, their six ducklings toddling behind. *Spring. Everything has babies,* she thought. She ran her palm in a circle over her belly. Hers wouldn't be arriving until fall. She sighted another pair of Silth guards flying up from their patrol along the river.

She thought about her status as enemy number one for so many groups, with an actual price on her head, up to $12 million now. She hadn't cared when she'd first found out, but that all changed when she learned she was pregnant. She cared, but it wasn't going to stop her.

She did what she loved, with someone she loved. And she trusted the Silth to protect her. They would do whatever was necessary.

In fact, security reshuffled personnel so Humans patrolled the outer perimeter with Silth flying inside the grounds. The staff hoped to avoid the Silth having to kill a Human. They didn't want to make the already tense relations between the Silth and Humans in this region worse.

Today, things would be bad enough because UNWID had killed two trespassers. Two *armed* trespassers who'd cut through security fences of a UN facility and disabled other security devices. But it would have been worse if the Silth had taken the action.

Not long after the UN facility located here, forty-five minutes south of Richmond, Virginia, it had become a popular local sport to take shots at Silth flying along the River. One month ago, a twenty-something young man had succeeded in killing one of the Silth. The local Commonwealth's attorney refused to bring charges, saying they weren't Human, so it wasn't considered murder, nor were they protected wildlife. Congress had rushed through a law protecting the Silth and the Sohi, but that law was now tied up in litigation.

The pictures of the young shooter, a sneer on his face, went viral.

A radical wildlife group doxed him, sharing his name and address as well as the names and addresses of the online club of big game hunters that had made him an honorary member. The club members specialized in killing endangered species, and their website offered enormous sums to those who proved they'd killed Silth. Two days later, no one could find the young man.

No trace. No signs of what had happened to him.

One week later, a reporter pieced together that all the members of the club were also missing. The organization's phone went unanswered. Emails were not returned. Maybe they all went into hiding? They certainly had the money to do so, but families and business partners were sure they had not. Of course, suspicion centered on the Silth. But which ones? One or more could have blipped in from anywhere in the world. Legal scholars pointed out that even if it had been them, they had committed no crime since the authorities could only charge Humans with murder.

Joss wanted the Silth working with her to keep as low a profile as possible.

Her door opened, and Shadow rushed in, Tiny following. Shadow ran over to Macho, who sleepily raised his head to touch noses.

"Hello, baby mama," Tiny said as he slid around the desk to give her a hug.

She pulled the scent of his cologne and shampoo deep into her lungs and held it there, before releasing her breath in a sigh.

"You guys ready to go?"

"Yep, packed and racked."

Tiny and Shadow were on their way to Hawaii for two weeks' work with the Volcano Kilauea team. This morning had opened with gentle tension in their household as Joss accused Tiny of preferring the company of an active volcano to being home with a pregnant, recovering alcoholic as she dealt with one of the most stressful jobs in the world. He demurred, but not fast enough.

She had meant to be teasing but wasn't sure it had come out that way.

She was on her way back to their apartment to apologize when the attack began. He was just doing his job, or trying to in these odd times. Joss wanted him to stay under the shield of the Silth. She feared the rage over her work would be directed at him, and with the approaching war with the Trow, she just wanted him nearby.

He squinted, looking at her. "You ok?"

Joss ran her hand across her face and bit her lip before shaking her head. "Rough start to the day. Security just stopped some folks with guns sneaking in." She decided not to mention they'd killed two of them. "You sure you should go?"

"Don't worry. We're taking the plane. We're staying at Leilani's place, and you know she's got like a hundred ohana there. And Fetu's going with me."

The *plane* was one purchased by the Silth and kept nearby for Joss and Tiny's use, and Fetu was Tiny's best friend, as big as a moose and as close to a warrior from birth as Joss had ever met. Not only did he work with Joss and Tiny as a personal assistant, trainer, and bodyguard, but he was also a gourmet chef and mixed martial arts expert. Joss knew he didn't mind a trip back to Hawaii.

"You sure Shadow's going to fit on the plane? It's kinda small."

Tiny raised his eyebrows, too smart to take the bait from his increasingly large spouse. He came back around the desk, kissed her on the top of the head and began gently rubbing her shoulders.

"Maybe I should stay. Fetu and I can set up here in the offices and work remotely."

Joss rolled her neck and put her hand over his. "Well, if you were going to do that the whole time, I'd say yes. But I'm fine. Right now, other than the President, I may be the most heavily guarded Human in North America. You go play with your volcano."

Though he loved his work with volcanoes dearly, he wanted to quit it to stay at the center and protect her. Joss didn't want him to give up something important to him, and she didn't want to need protecting. It was one thing to pay guards, but this was different. This morning, he had felt a little whipsawed when she also seemed upset about him leaving to do his job.

He kissed her again. "Love you, hun. Video at 11?" he said, reminding her of their nightly ritual when he was away. He clicked his tongue and Shadow trotted after him as he left the room. Macho gave a disappointed *woof.*

"I agree," Joss told him as she pulled her keyboard toward her and opened her inbox. She sighed and rolled her shoulders, still tight before the day had really begun. The problem wasn't the amount of work. These days, she had an enormous staff led by Maria Luis and Tonho, who'd come with her from Brazil. It was more the number and size of the decisions making it to her desk and the complexity of trying to nudge Human behavior from centuries-old habits while not moving too slowly to satisfy the Silth. A quarter of the Human population had been lost during the *volcano attack,* as the media called it now, decimating most of the UN operations around the world. Thus, on top of being a new directorate, she competed with the other directorates as they restaffed.

Deeply committed to their work, her staff, a mix of Silth and Humans, developed the legislation adopted in almost every nation banning *sport hunting,* hunting for the thrill of killing something and displaying its body or parts on a wall or as furniture. Her group shut off world trade in endangered wildlife parts for their fake medicinal properties or for art. They had stopped the use of most animals for medical practice or experimentation. Each action was consistent with the commitment to the Silth, but each received an enormous push back.

Death threats, hacking, vandalism, and powerful organizations making existential challenges were a part of her daily life.

She opened another email. The Senator's staff member who had written it was rude and demanding, another example of a staff person acting as though they, and not their boss, had the power. She delegated the answer to the newest of her staff.

She had never thought that she would manage a bunch of people. Just a couple of years earlier, this would have driven her back to the bottle. But these days, between the ground root that Krackle gave her and the steady regime of meditation, exercise, and virtual AA, she was good.

*Besides, with the baby on the way, I'm not even touching cough medicine.*

The work her organization did on Human habitat was more important, and somewhat less controversial with the public than the work on hunting and poaching. And it had quieter, but far more powerful enemies.

UNWID moved forward with worldwide bans on pesticides and weed killers and elimination of predator eradication programs. They led the redesign of cities, suburbs, and farmlands to preserve fifty percent of the land for habitat and create safe movement corridors everywhere. The experts, both those paid by industries and those paid by advocacy groups, fought over the right steps to take. Additionally, UNWID sponsored local ordinances requiring bird-friendly glass, protection of birds and wildlife, biophilic design, and animal welfare protection. All required balancing investments in other controls, replacement technologies, education for the public, and substitute means of livelihood for disrupted jobs.

Her next email was from the president of a conservation organization supported by hunters. He was polite and expressed support for the general mission but reflected his members' general concern her agency was moving too fast. He warned she risked losing support by not allowing a more gradual change.

Navigating the Human side was hard enough. For decades in the US, it had been the hunters and anglers, not the general population, who had paid the costs of maintaining many natural areas and acquiring new ones. Many of them helped create the programs for avoiding species loss.

Those who supported the restrictions on hunting killed far more living things with their cats, cars, lawn services, and windows than hunters killed. Before the volcanos erupted, it had seemed that the debate would never end, and then the Silth forced Humans to commit to honoring *all life* as a condition attached to saving theirs. Now they worried Humans would renege on their promise. And the Humans worried they had misjudged the extent of change necessary to meet their promise.

In the meantime, not only did the Silth grow restless over the more extreme violations, but they also taught the animals how to recognize the consequences of Human actions and how to respond. Gorillas began setting traps for poachers. Farmers illegally clearing rainforests found endless poisonous snakes in their homes, and most worrisome, two planes crashed because of bird strikes when an airport destroyed a nearby rookery. Joss was racing to prevent a war.

Throw in the changes in Human society occurring after learning they weren't the only race occupying the world, the efforts to integrate the Silth in day-to-day society, and all the other disruptions, and she felt as if the wheels were going to fly off the cart. No, it felt more like the video she'd seen where the racecar crashed into the viewing stands and the wheels went smashing through the crowd.

"Sheriff's here," said the voice in her ear.

Her phone stayed on walkie-talkie mode into her earbud when here on the UNWID campus. She touched the earpiece to turn on the mike.

"Ask her to come to the office when she finishes with you, please."

Joss glanced around to make sure there weren't any classified documents lying open.

"Okay."

She continued through her emails for another hour and a half until there was a knock on her door, and Maria Luis escorted in Sheriff Anita Cade. Joss came from behind the desk and gave the shallow bow that had replaced handshakes after the last pandemic. She liked Sheriff Cade, a short and plump, caramel-hued ball of energy, goodwill, and quiet authority.

"Not the best way to start your day," the Sheriff said with a frown.

"Worse for them. Any idea who they are?"

"We got IDs from the fingerprints. Looks like they are for hire for the alt-right and extreme hunter groups. You can see where they cut through the wire. They had a Google Earth photo of the compound in their pockets with... certain places marked on it. One of them had a bunch of plastic explosive and detonators in his bag. The one who's alive isn't talking yet. I'll transfer him to Homeland. Anyway, they'll be here soon. I'll take care of the interface with them."

"Thanks. Did our folks handle everything right?" She watched as the Sheriff's eyes roamed the room. Though Cade had been here several times, the trappings of the UN and the gifts from the Silth filling the walls and shelves still fascinated her.

"I watched the video. It looks by the book, but we won't be able to answer for sure until we finish the investigation."

"How's Bayo doing?" Joss asked, leaning back to sit on the edge of her desk. "I see he's in the running for several scholarships."

"Doing great. Thanks for asking. Aren't you going to ask what they wanted to blow up?"

"I assume it's me and some critical stuff. I just can't get caught up in what these folks try to do."

"I'll leave a deputy in front for a while."

"You're stretched thin enough. We've got it. If you can deal with Homeland and the state, that would be a tremendous help."

"You look tired."

"Baby making isn't for sissies."

"Don't I know it." Cade had four children.

After the Sheriff left, Joss stretched out on the couch next to the mammoth smart window, which tinted as the sun shone on it. Her mind was back on the young man who'd killed the Silth. She tried to imagine any of the Silth she knew killing him in revenge; it seemed so unlikely they would do so directly, but then she could imagine them leaving him in the middle of a dark, forbidding jungle for nature to decide. She drifted into a sleep with ugly, violent dreams.

# *Scene 5*

**Joss (Human)**

Joss awoke to the sound of Macho's growl and the smell of soil.

"Tell your dog to shut up and lie down or I'll kill it. Scream and I'll kill you."

She slowly sat up, eyeing the middle-aged man covered in mud and scraps of forest. A rifle was slung over his shoulder, and a large pistol aimed at her.

"Macho, quiet. Sit." The dog sat at once and quietly leaned forward, ready to lunge.

"Dogs move fast from sit to attack. Make him lie down."

"Macho, lie down."

The dog whined as he lay on the floor, eyes aggressively focused on the man.

"What do you want?" she said through clenched teeth, instinctively clutching her belly.

"I want you to stop messing with my life. I want to teach my grandkids to hunt like my father did me. I want rid of you." He waived the point of the gun. "You're pregnant?"

"Yes. You know you won't see your grandkids again if you shoot me. You'll die in prison as a baby killer."

He stood between her and the door, his camouflage clothing and blackened face incongruous with the elegance of the room. Behind him, the door crept open, and Maria Luis ducked her head in and out, leaving the door ajar.

The camo-man glanced over his shoulder and back at Joss. "Don't think you can make it to the door before I shoot you."

"Is that what you want to do? Kill me and my baby?"

"You weren't supposed to be pregnant. And no, I don't really want to kill you. I just can't figure out how to make you stop."

"Your friends are mercenaries. Is that what you are? You don't sound like one."

"Hunting is everything for me. It is my peace—the sounds of war stop. I can talk to my grandkids and they'll actually listen to me."

"Good morning, Joss," came a voice from outside the door.

The camo-man put his finger to his lips and stepped back to an angle not visible from the doorway. He held the gun steady on her as Tonho came in with a cup on a tray. The steam coming off of the cup carried the coffee smell through the room instantly.

"I brought you your morning coffee," Tonho said, pushing through the door and walking toward her. His gaze slid to the camo-man and his eyes widened.

"Why is there a man holding a gun standing on the left side of your desk?"

The camo-man looked perplexed. When he spotted Tonho's earpiece, he growled and lifted the gun higher, squeezing the trigger. A figure appeared in the air next to his hand and knocked the gun upward as it fired. The camo-man was quick and backhanded the gun into the face of the attacking Silth. Macho leaped forward and grabbed the man's leg.

Before the camo-man could shoot the dog, another Silth appeared by the man's head and sent a stunning bolt into his temple. He collapsed, and Macho gave his leg an extra vigorous shake before letting go to walk back to Joss's side. The husky lay with a satisfied huff and stared at them, his bright blue eyes saying *I did my job, now you do yours.*

The Silth who'd knocked the gun upward had landed on the desk and was rubbing the side of his face. "How was I supposed to know whether that was the left side of the desk as you looked at it or the left side if you were sitting there?"

"Why would I say the left side as if I were sitting?"

As the two squabbled, Joss threw her arms around Macho, helping her heart to slow its hammering and her body to stop trembling. Maria Luis and the other Silth had rolled the camo-man on his side and were putting plastic ties on his hands and feet.

Another day began at UNWID.

\*\*\*

The camo-man came to in a small security office. He was sitting in a chair wearing a pair of metal handcuffs besides the plastic ties; his feet were cuffed as well. He looked around slowly before his eyes settled on Joss. He tested the cuffs.

"Y'all afraid of me?"

"Just being respectful of your expertise," Joss said. Behind her, several Human and Silth security guards were re-scanning the grounds by drone. "You've had a lot of training, Mr. Tangiers." She waved a sheaf of printouts.

"I just wanted a moment to talk with you before Homeland takes you away."

"I'm not going to tell you anything about the folks who sent me. Not so you can send those things to kill them." Tangiers nodded toward the Silth, who ignored him.

"I'm not interested in who sent you, Homeland will deal with that. As far as sending the Silth, I do not condone them killing Humans except to defend themselves. Two of the men who came here with you today are dead. But the Silth didn't kill them.

"They were mercenaries." She leaned in and looked into his eyes. "Are you a mercenary? As I said before, you don't sound like a mercenary."

"Why do you care?"

"A few months ago, Humanity was about to disappear. The volcanos the Trow set off were going to kill us. Your grandchildren had no future. The Silth agreed to save us, to save your grandchildren in return for a promise. And the promise was that we would change our relationship with the other creatures with which we share this planet. We made that promise, and they saved us. Now they're afraid that we won't keep our word. "

"I hunt with a bow; I eat what I kill. I'm no different than a wolf or a lion."

"Have you ever heard of fishermen who just keep catching fish to see how many they can get? Or bird hunters that just keep shooting, long past when they've shown their skill?"

"Yeah, but those are just killers. It's not my way."

"How about the trophy hunter who wants to get a snow leopard or a grizzly bear?"

Tangiers thought for a moment before answering. "Well, I understand the desire to compete. To test yourself. But it's not for me, and I don't respect these folks who kill a giraffe or a rhino for a trophy.

But what does any of this have to do with me?"

"Have you ever been on a deer hunt someplace where they killed all the bobcats and coyotes so they wouldn't compete for the deer?"

Tangiers was silent.

"It's a common practice. Same thing with wolves and sharks. Why do you think we get to kill these animals to make it more convenient for us to hunt? More importantly for your grandchildren, you tell me why the Silth should help us fight the Trow? For the Trow we are inconvenient, like the bobcats and coyotes. Or maybe the wild horses out West. The Trow want to cull the herd. Eliminate an invasive species. I do worry that Humans and Silth will fight over wildlife issues and there will be deaths on both sides. But I worry more that if the Silth decide they are better off standing with the Trow, my child has no future."

"Why tell me all this?

"Mr. Tangiers, you are going to have some time to think. A lot of time to think, I suspect. I believe you are a smart man. I believe you are concerned about your grandchildren. I would like for you to consider helping me figure out how to balance these things. How Humans can make their way in this new world.

"Is there a way for us to allow you to hunt with your grandchildren and to allow a tribe in the Amazon to hunt using traditional means and keep our promise to the Silth?

"If you decide that you really want to accomplish what you came here for today—create a future where your grandchildren can enjoy the peace that you find in the woods, you'll use this opportunity. Otherwise, you are just another nutcase with a bag of excuses for their behavior."

Joss stood. "When Homeland is finished with you, you'll be given an email to reach me. Misuse it and access goes away. Use it wisely and you may still accomplish something."

Joss left the room wondering if she had wasted her time. Did she give him too much credit? Or maybe she was just desperate for answers.

# CHAPTER TWO

## *Scene 1*

### MERIT (SILTH)

Merit felt the power of the place pulse through her feet when she landed for a brief rest. She took off again and flew ten feet above the ground, working her way over her part of the search grid they'd developed for Angkor Wat's grounds. Technically, she didn't need to be doing this. Her job was co-leading the combined Human/Silth armies. But finding the portals by which the Trow would come was a key part of the strategy for stopping them, and she had never been good at sitting around *supervising*.

Yesterday, she'd been working within the two hundred acres around the main grounds of the Hindu/Buddhist temple. Today, the team flew over another two hundred acres of active temple grounds around that core. Tomorrow, they'd begin on the jungle that obscured a maze of smaller temples and plazas built over eight centuries.

In the distance, she saw Silth flying their portions of the grid while Humans walked theirs. While she didn't see them, she knew four Sohi chanted in the enormous square next to the causeway into the main temple. They'd listened to the search plan offered by the joint Human/Silth/Sohi team and without comment walked away to begin their efforts to locate this Trow portal. Fortunately, the rest of the team had grown accustomed to the Sohi's directness. Aran tried to explain it to Humans by asking them how they thought they'd react if one day they had to coordinate, argue with, and even take instructions from their dogs and cats. The simile didn't work since most of the Humans, particularly the cat owners, claimed they already did.

They'd been searching for three days. The Humans complained about moving in the late spring heat and daily rain, normal weather for Merit, much like home. She looked around at the hundred different shades of green and breathed in the moist jungle smells.

As the sun set, she returned to the tents arrayed in a circle on the temple grounds with the headquarters and the cafeteria in the center. The government prohibited tourists during their search. She grabbed dinner, loading up on the corn she loved so much and taking a handful of raisins as well. She savored their sweetness, putting them in her mouth one at a time and rolling them around on her tongue before swallowing them.

She ate with her staff on the plaza, surrounded by the heavy stone buildings with their sandcastle roofs layering high above the occupants. Stone faces, many embedded in the walls, others on statues in alcoves, looked out at them. Eventually, she made her way back to the cafeteria for the evening recap meeting. Bowls of popcorn sat on each table. Portable lights gave the place a harsh brightness.

Her translator joined her, ready to supplement Merit's developing English skills.

The Sohi spoke first. Two members of their team had been alive and on Earth when the complex started in the twelfth century, beginning as a Hindu temple, and becoming the largest Buddhist temple, the largest religious facility of any kind, on Earth. Like the pyramids and the Taj Mahal, a wealthy Human leader had built it as a funerary temple. Merit wondered if the shortness of their lives caused Humans to spend so much of their resources on being remembered after their deaths. Building it on one of several portals to the Trow Land showed Humans were sensitive to the power lines, the ley lines of the Earth, connecting the powerful locations of the portals.

The Sohi team leader believed they would locate the portal the next morning. He expressed confidence it wasn't within the walls of Angkor Wat itself, but near one of the outlying temples—Ta Prohm. He also reported that, as they monitored the Earth's energies that day, they had become confident the volcanoes' eruption, though traumatic, had generated no major psychic event for Humans or Silth. He sat down as though this information had self-evident consequences.

A Human—they were less intimidated by the Sohi than were the Silth—asked what that meant. The Sohi leader looked confused for a moment and finally said, "It means there is no reason for the Trow to wait a measure of years for the invasion. We believe they might come at any time." This exchange resulted in a rush of text messages back to Human and Silth teams working around the world. The various team members talked among themselves until Merit stood to lay out the next day's search.

"We'll shift our search to the jungle around Ta Prohm. Make sure you mark where you ended in the Angkor Wat grounds so if we return to that search, you can pick up where you left off." She glanced at her translator to make sure what she'd said made sense. He smiled and nodded. "Remember, Ta Prohm is within the expanded *nature restoration zone,* with its aggressive rewilding program. An international group is trying to restore many of the species devastated by illegal wildlife poaching."

"What have they restored? What's there?" asked one of the Humans, her eyes closed as she rocked back and forth just a little.

"Not much water right now, so there shouldn't be cobras or crocodiles, but perhaps other snakes. Don't mess with the gibbons—they bite. Most of the reintroduced wildlife will run from you—langurs, sambar deer, muntjacs, slow loris, leopard cats, and civets. But recently tigers, elephants, bears, and clouded leopards have been added. You'd be lucky to see any of them but be careful."

"Elephants, tigers, and bears—oh my," one of the group said. Merit had gotten used to Humans reciting lines from movies and plays into their daily conversations. She assumed this was such a quotation.

"Are they *activated?*" someone else asked. The group grew still.

"You should assume they are."

"What does that mean?" This question came from a newer member of the international Human team. Merit knew he came from Uzbekistan, but she wasn't completely sure where that was.

Merit had been standing on the table to talk, but now she flew up a few feet, so she saw all the figures seated in the tent.

"*Activation* is a somewhat controversial program by which a few Silth are educating wildlife on the ways Humans hunt them and how to avoid being killed. They recognize guns and can work together to defeat hunters. They recognize trappers and can turn the traps on those who leave them."

"Why's that controversial?" the same Human asked.

Another Human spoke up. "Because the animals sometimes interpret the work of villagers in clearing for their crops as hostile and have attacked them as well. Something the Silth call fair, but the Humans don't."

"Back to tonight's briefing," broke in the Human team leader as Merit drifted back next to her interpreter. He addressed the Sohi. "Can you refresh us on what we're looking for?"

One of the Sohi stood, towering above the seated group. "It will not be a hole, a tunnel, or a cave, which is how most Silth and Humans imagine the portal. It will be more of a shimmering. A doorway that looks like a mirage on the desert, slightly translucent but unclear."

A man began passing around pictures.

"These just came from Newgrange, where the other portal is," he said.

Merit flew across the room and looked at the photos over a woman's shoulder. The first showed a glowing coin-like object, twenty feet in diameter according to a note at the bottom of the page, on the side of a grass-covered mound.

"Technically, they found this at Knowth Mound, near Newgrange," the Human said. "Similar to the relationship of Ta Prohm to Angkor Wat. Knowth is a secondary burial structure to the worship and ceremonial structure of Newgrange."

Merit looked at a picture of smaller green mounds around a flat-topped larger mound, including one labeled *Knowth*. The next photo label said Newgrange and showed a more refined mound with a white stone face. A closeup revealed engravings on the stone.

"Humans constructed *Newgrange* around 3,200 B.C., before Stonehenge and the Great Pyramids," the Sohi went on.

"Why's no one noticed this for 5,000 years?" Merit asked.

"The Trow protected this side with obscuring spells. The portal also becomes easier to see when recently used. The one in that picture had been used in the prior twenty-four hours, and we have removed the protective spells," the Sohi said as he retook his seat.

"Okay. We'll work in jungle tomorrow," said the Human conducting the briefing. "The Silth ask we do this *on foot* first before clearing the forest for a better line-of-sight search. It'll be hot, with plenty of snakes and bugs. Make sure your teams dress for the conditions." He raised his hand in a wave. "See you at Oh-Six-Hundred."

\*\*\*

Merit hummed as she slowly flew ten feet over the ground. She loved the morning in the jungle. Any jungle. Morning typically had the best temperature, and the sounds of the birds waking lent a certain optimism. The day began full of hope.

By midmorning, she dripped sweat in the humid air, overheated and drained of that hope. The dull thrum of insects replaced the sound of the birds. She squatted on a tree limb and reapplied the lotion that kept away the mosquitoes. The Silth didn't use the DEET products applied by the Humans since the smell made them gag, and the chemicals burned their skin, so they used an ancient blend of botanicals. These kept the bugs off their skin, but the swarm hovered in a dense cloud around them. After three hours, the first insect scouts made their way past the barrier and bit again.

In her peripheral vision, she saw movement. She turned and stared but saw nothing unusual. There, movement again. Slight and slow, but the leaves lifted and parted as something passed quietly through them.

Merit saw one of her team following his grid assignment. She gave a whistle that fit in with the background bird calls to anyone else, but for someone who'd practiced hearing it thousands of times, it was a bugle. When he peered through the trees and found her, she gave a few hand signals and then checked back to track the movement, not wanting to lose the trail. She flew to another branch. Perhaps it was just a tiger or a leopard, but she didn't think so. The whistle repeated several times in the distance. She raised her shield and flew toward the moving plants, stopping on a branch twenty yards from whatever was moving, before continuing forward to the next branch. She covered three hundred yards this way before she saw the portal.

The path of whatever was moving through the jungle was now heading directly toward a shimmering circle in the trees, concealed by the strangler figs growing on either side. The portal was only thirty feet away from the movement, which had picked up pace.

Merit gave a series of quick whistles and flew from the branches toward the movement. Her team members emerged from the trees, heading toward it as well. She spotted Human members on the ground following her team; they must have been watching them and recognized they were on the hunt. Two bright blue bolts shot from the area of movement toward the Silth warrior who'd taken a position in front of the portal.

Though her shield was up, the force of the two bolts knocked her out of the air.

Merit saw two Trow in the brush, no longer bothering to cloak. One rushed toward the portal wrapped in his shield while the other shot bolts in every direction. As the first one dove through the portal, the second fell in a rain of return fire from the encircling Silth and Humans. Merit gave a loud, shrill whistle, and the Silth stopped firing, though the Human gunfire continued for a second or two more. She advanced with her shield raised and arrived above the body of a Trow dressed as a Human, just in time to see it disappear.

Instead of fading away as Silth and Trow did when they died of natural causes, it dissolved as though covered in acid, leaving only the clothes and shoes behind. *Must be something special the spies can do,* she thought. The others gathered around the pile of clothes for a moment, and then the entire group walked the short distance to the portal.

The four Sohi appeared abruptly among them.

"A spy?" one of the Sohi mused.

"It begins this way," another answered.

"But how long have they been here? That would tell us more about when they will come," the first Sohi said.

"Why didn't they just blip to the edge of the portal? Why try to sneak back in?" asked a heavily armed man in jungle camouflage.

"They were afraid we would sense their movement," answered one of the Sohi. "We have been searching with a passive mental power, not performing magic. We would not have detected them with this method, but they did not know that."

The group clustered around the portal with the Silth and the Humans peering at it from different angles, trying to see through to the other side. A young woman moved forward and cautiously put her hand through the surface. As if in response, the surface exploded into movement as hundreds of flower fairies flew through the portal, driving the group away.

As Merit watched from a distance, she saw several Trow step from the portal within the cloud of little creatures and disappear as soon as they were out on the ground. A Silth-sized figure also came through, but she couldn't make out its face before it too disappeared

# Scene 2

*"The supreme art of war is to subdue the enemy without fighting,"* Aran quoted, skipping a stone across the lake surface and scattering the reflection of the surrounding snow-covered mountains. They glowed red in the sunset's light beneath orange clouds sailing a blue sky. He watched a mixed herd of llamas and alpacas wandering on a nearby hill, but otherwise, a scrub of small trees and underbrush surrounded the lake.

Faelen stared off across the lake where a speckled bear had emerged from the brush to drink water. "You quote generals a lot for someone who has never been in the military."

Lornix lay on the grass with eyes closed on the other side of Faelen, her round belly rising and falling as she breathed. Aran couldn't tell if she was listening to them or to the birdsong coming from the wetlands edging the lake.

"I've been in a lot of battles for someone who's not in the military. But I believe I only quote one general."

"The Sohi will not fight other Trow unless they attack here. They will defend themselves."

"I'm not asking them to fight. And I'm just asking you to take the idea to Tegrat."

The bear left, and a family of chinchillas came to the water's edge.

"I have learned more about Sohi governance, and Tegrat is the *speaker of the will of the Sohi,* so he is more of an implementer than a leader. The Sohi decide, and he executes."

Lornix turned her face toward Faelen but said nothing.

Aran leaned back and asked Lornix, "How's the pregnancy going?"

"Normal."

Aran waited, but she said nothing more, just turned back to watching the sundown paint the lake red. The grass was cool and gave off a faint smell of peppermint as it bent beneath him.

Aran told Faelen, "We still haven't figured out who's doing it, but the parrot nests around the world are full of baby Silth. We'll experience a population explosion in a few months as they're removed and taken into Silth villages."

"Have you told the Humans about the Silth pregnancies?"

Aran sat up and skipped another stone. Besides the traditional way Silth were born from parrot mothers, Silth females had begun to get pregnant, which had never happened before.

"Yes, we explained this as a gift from the Earth, just as it had given Humans the ability to bear young many centuries ago. It went better than we expected, given that so few Humans believe the Trow created them, much less brought them into the world unable to procreate. Humans have a special place in their hearts for mothers and babies."

"Do you think it has changed the way the Silth are thinking about their future?"

"I think it's too early to tell. Certainly, we're no longer just altruistically arguing for the animals' place in the future. We're fighting for our own as well. At the same time, we don't depend on the Trow for a future, so it makes it easier to oppose them."

Aran looked at his friends, reminding himself that they were Trow. Faelen dressed in the Sohi red robes with his head shaved. He'd put on some needed weight, much of it in muscle because the Sohi walked, worked in their fields, and honed their fighting skills. His skin appeared healthy, tanned around its many scars.

"I don't know how it will change our culture. We've never had to deal with pregnancies or anyone having offspring to raise except those who chose to do so. We've never had blood relations across generations, just siblings." Aran thought of his own terrible relationship with his brother. "That's been hard enough."

"Having offspring has unexpected consequences," Faelen said as he put his hand on Lornix's. "Protectiveness. Fear of the future. A wish to secure a safe place."

The chinchillas were shepherding their family back into the trees.

"I think you'd be safer with the plan I'm proposing. There is no safety here when the Trow return."

Faelen picked up a rock and threw it hard at the lake. It disappeared with a splash. "This place has survived for centuries with the Trow in the world. What has changed?"

"You know what's changed."

Faelen glared at him.

"Me. You think Thest will come here because of me. I am the danger to the Sohi."

"I think they'd eventually come anyway. But, yes, I think he'll know you're alive and will do anything to track you down. My plan is safer. But whatever the Sohi decide, you must keep it secret. *Let your plans be dark and impenetrable as night, and when you move, fall like a thunderbolt.*"

"You do not know the savagery of full-scale war with the Trow. Neither the Silth nor the Humans are prepared for a war with beings without empathy, without mercy for even their kind, much less for beings they consider vermin."

"Enough," Lornix said without raising her voice. "You came here to rest, Aran Shaman. Rest. Observe the sunset. This moment is the important one. The Sohi will consider what you have said."

## Scene 3

**Joss (Human)**

Similar raids were happening around the world. Joss hoped these appeased the rising anger of the Silth. Both Silth and Humans had miscalculated the lengths to which poachers would go in continuing their trade, and their willingness to sacrifice the national leaders who'd been bound to the oath with the Silth.

She was watching a raid on a seedy warehouse in Nairobi. The building showing on her monitor had a few windows located high on its brown brick exterior and a huge double door that admitted large trucks. The only sign of vegetation on its grounds was a forlorn tree growing from a crack in surrounding tarmac. Ten cargo containers sat in an otherwise empty parking lot on one side of the building, and a fleet of *Mad Max* style trucks filled the parking lot on the opposite side.

She watched from a new Homeland facility in Washington South, a new city located south of Washington, DC. The city was still being built around the train station at the intersection of the US east coast's major north-south track and the I-95 interstate. Many governmental agencies and contractors had opened either primary or secondary offices here, beyond the blast radius of a bomb detonated on DC itself. It was also the first city undertaking large-scale, Silth-friendly design—automatic revolving doors, door handles instead of knobs, automatic water fountains and countless minor adjustments in the sidewalks and streets.

Joss sat at a crescent-shaped table with several control pads in easy reach and three small screens mounted to the table, creating her own little room. Around her were multiple desks and consoles and walls filled with large monitor screens. Three more enormous screens dominated the front. Lead walls, and something they told her was called a Faraday shield—a mesh of conductive materials that blocked electromagnetic fields—surrounded the room. Intended to shield electronic equipment from an EMP, an electromagnetic pulse, the shield now also helped keep the effects of technology in the room.

Because of the technology, the Silth didn't enter the room but gathered around a series of small monitors in an adjoining one. Joss wasn't even sure she should be there four months away from her baby's birth. She wrapped herself in a cloth she'd gotten off of the internet that purported to block electromagnetic waves. Scam or not, it made her feel a little better about being there.

Twenty Humans sat around her, watching different monitors, and throwing feeds to the big screens in the room's front when there was something important. Joss laughed at herself as she realized how common it was now for her to note the species of a room's occupants. *What a difference a couple of years make.*

She had control of the monitors on her workstation, which she kept focused on Nairobi. A satellite view showed her the roof and surrounding fields of asphalt and concrete, already sending up waves of heat. Then she had a helmet feed from each of the co-team leaders, Dimba Tsango and *Zane* Taylor. While she'd talked extensively with Dimba, she knew little about Zane, except that he spoke French and Zane was a name he'd picked for himself.

The wall monitors showed raids in progress around the world, more or less coordinated among the countries and agencies leading them, so they'd maximize the capture of participants. Although they'd receive long years in prison, many locals still drifted into the illegal wildlife trade, responding to large amounts of money paid out of Thailand or Cambodia, whether it originated there, or in Hong Kong, or China. NGO's created counter-employment opportunities but could not compete with the level of pay the poachers received.

Suddenly, the cameras in Nairobi moved, the mixed international agency enforcement group rushing toward the building and soundlessly disabling the guards. They set explosives on the huge, locked doors at the front and back of the building, blew them within seconds, and rushed into the building. Joss heard the shouts of various agency names and orders in English and Swahili to put hands in the air before the gunfire began. She turned down the volume on her headset and caught herself as her fingernails returned to her mouth.

Many men worked in the room, three times the number of officials involved in the raid, and they lunged for their guns. Joss struggled to follow the flow of the fight from the helmet cameras. She glanced up at one of the big monitors that showed the heat signatures of the bodies in the room, but it was too confusing.

Dimba and Zane moved behind crates and shipping containers, trying to advance against withering fire from automatic weapons. The poachers headed toward one side of the house, covering one another as they concentrated there. Behind them, a large section of the wall dropped to the floor, revealing a hidden door opening directly into the parking lot. Remote starters had vehicles already coming to life. Once on the streets of Nairobi, the poachers would get away.

They rushed out the door into the lot, a few staying back to hold off the rangers and officers. Through dash-mounted camera feeds on the agency cars, Joss watched the poachers running toward the many pickup trucks, SUV's, and commercial open-sided trucks in the lot.

She leaned forward, face near the monitor, biting her nails again.

Three vehicles were moving. Then beside each vehicle, stopped or moving, a Silth appeared, firing a bolt into the driver before flickering and vanishing. Joss gasped.

The three trucks in motion continued forward and crashed. One began burning. The poachers shot into the parking lot, but the Silth had already disappeared.

Inside the control room, someone said, "I thought the Silth weren't involved in tonight's raids."

Someone else added, "They weren't supposed to even know about them."

Joss asked, "What is that the poachers are wearing?"

"Homemade Faraday cages?" one of the staff suggested.

"Those can't work," another said.

"No, the homemade ones have no hope of working. The military has tried to create a version of these, but they don't work with magical energy," added a contractor who worked with both the military and the international wildlife agencies.

The poachers rushed out to the remaining vehicles and began dragging the drivers out.

The Silth appeared again, this time blue-lit by their shields and right behind the poachers scrambling to get in the trucks. The poachers shot at them, automatic fire tearing into the trucks and their own colleagues. Again, the Silth disappeared. Dimba's helmet camera peeked around the corner of the hidden doorway at the chaos of the parking lot. Black smoke from the burning truck washed across the lot and gunfire spewed in every direction. Once more the Silth appeared, again each of them beside a gunman who collapsed from the bolt fired point-blank.

The Silth disappeared and an eerie quietness descended on the scene. Through someone's open mike, Joss listened to the crackle of the burning truck and the ticking of hot metal. Then came a scramble of voices as the agents searched among the bodies for survivors. A couple had bullet wounds but were still alive. Those shot by the Silth were dead.

Joss leaned back and exhaled loudly, rubbing her face with her hands.

As she convened her group and the agencies that worked with them, few mourned the poachers. They had killed far too many rangers and devastated species on the edge of being lost. Everyone had watched as the rangers opened the containers. Hundreds of tusks tumbled out of one and in the other, the flashlights reflected off rhino horns and imperial zebra hides stacked to the ceiling. The warehouse was full of the pelts of big cats and parts of hundreds of now rare animals, including hands and skulls of several gorillas. But they worried about the loss of operational control.

Similar Silth appearances occurred at the other raids. As long as the Humans had control, there'd been no intervention. But if they lost control, which they had in a third of the raids, the intervention had been swift and lethal. How did they find out about the raids? Silth, sworn to secrecy, served as part of Joss's group. Joss doubted they told anyone about the operations.

She called Nadara, a member of the World Silth Council, who said there'd been no official Silth involvement and no Silth had come forward to take responsibility. Nadara agreed to review the video of the scenes to see if she recognized anyone.

Because of the large number of dead in the operations, and because of the stories being told by the surviving poachers, there was no stopping the emerging narrative—that the Silth would kill Humans to save wildlife. While the intensity of their feelings surprised no one, many found it hard to believe that the Silth would be so aggressive. News commentators pointed out that with Humans about to go to war with the Trow, it was reassuring that their allies were not passive, but it added a new complexity to the joint efforts at preparing for war and designing a new world order.

The arguments immersed Joss's agency. Groups were angry about the deaths of the poachers because they didn't believe any animal deaths warranted the death of a Human. It did not matter to them that these species were only a few short years from being extinct. They came from a range of beliefs.

Some believed God had given Humans dominion over the animals, and that Humans—as the only animals with souls—should do whatever they wanted with the rest. Those that embraced the old testament cited Genesis's: *everything that lives and moves about will be food for you–just as I gave you the green plants, I now give you everything.* Only the Humans had value in God's eyes, never mind the notion of stewardship or Job's *ask the animals, and they will teach you, or the birds in the sky, and they will tell you.*

Others saw the animals as a crop, no different than corn.

Some groups professed to love the wildlife, but still labeled the death of the poachers inappropriate. They argued that because of the poverty or hunger in the surrounding countryside, turning to poaching was an economic decision that shouldn't damn the poachers.

The Silth had a particular disdain for that group. They believed all the apologists were *speciesists,* but that the last group was the most hypocritical. They would not have tolerated murder of Human babies by Humans on economic grounds, nor justified genocide as a rational choice because of poverty. The Silth took their point as proven when these Humans railed at the comparison, saying it was inappropriate to compare the genocide of Humans to Human-driven extinction of animals. It lowered the status of the dead Humans to the equivalent of animals. The Silth countered mass murder of animals and driving species to extinction only appeared different if you believed Humans were some special type of animal, which they didn't.

A very few groups believed death was never the solution, whether as punishment for the killing of Humans or for the killing of wildlife. The Silth said that while they respected this view, unless these people took action to force change, they were merely collaborationists, allowing continued speciesist attacks.

Penfield, with whom Joss spoke weekly, suggested beneath the surface of the debate was the question from the Silth—*is this how you see me? Something less than Human?* And from the Humans—*is this how you see me, no different from an oyster?*

While these public discussions raged, Joss knew that behind the scenes, the deaths distressed the Silth, and their internal debates were intense. None of the seven tribes had any version of capital punishment for actions by their own. They would fight wars but had little appetite for war over concepts or for a new territory. Rangi had been an exception, leading to a suspicion that perhaps her mercenaries, the Steamer Crew, were involved. When Joss asked Nadara about these rumors, she said she too had heard them. She reminded Joss that the Steamer Crew, along with the Tiki Crew, had saved Nadara's life, as well as Storng's. She didn't want to believe the speculation and refused to until there was proof. She'd been unable to reach Aran or the other members of the now Steamtiki Crew for several weeks.

After a couple of hours of follow-up to the raids, Joss returned to her home beside the river. She sat on a bench near the boat dock as the sun sank, and Macho climbed up beside her and lay with his head on her leg, since her lap had disappeared. As she looked at the trees across the river, she thought about the sensors and guards there, ever since the FBI had discovered a plan to kill her with a long-range rifle. She watched the boats pass and knew each time one came near, a Silth guard flew out to check it.

She remembered when she had turned her back on violence in pursuit of a cause. But non-violence is ineffective if it is just the position of bystanders, she believed. Where were the people marching in the streets for animal rights? She monitored the world of *huntsabs*, people who sabotaged fox hunts and other types of hunting. Was that a better way? Perhaps for fighting a legal activity, but how do you fight people who are breaking the law to begin with? She wanted a new world, without poachers and without people who killed for *sport*. But she had to achieve it with minimal violence.

She had this conversation with Dimba. He'd been in this fight a long time. His path was simple: pass the laws to protect the wildlife, enforce the laws, and use the courts to punish those who violated the laws.

The only problem was lobbyists watered down those laws for special interest groups, enforcers were sometimes bribed, and judges didn't take these crimes as seriously as violence against Humans. Joss sighed and ran her hand over her belly. She pulled her other hand away from her mouth and looked at her nails, chewed now to almost nothing.

Watching a flower fairy flying over the river, she thought about one piece of good news. As the scientists had studied them, trying to figure out the diets of this invasive species, they determined the flower fairies mostly consumed what Humans called *pollutants*. They ate plastics from the waters and strewn across the landscape. They gorged on industrial waste and sipped mercury from the air. When they fed on these materials, the flower fairies turned purple. One scientist argued this was an ancient form of photosynthesis, and the flower fairies were actually a form of plant using arsenic to create energy and convert the waste products to useful chemicals.

Joss shook her head, watching the last color bleed from the sky. Each day—new challenges and new opportunities.

# CHAPTER THREE

## *Scene 1*

**ARAN (SILTH)**

For weeks after the Tokyo debacle, Aran searched for the remaining Trow colonies. He decided one of the hidden colonies had existed but had ultimately disappeared or been abandoned. Rumors and local legends suggested the last enclave lay in the Pacific somewhere. He sat in meditation in many parts of the Pacific rim, conjuring the giant pneuma to scour the islands and walk beneath the sea, searching for any evidence of the Trow.

Finally, he'd gathered enough to suggest a colony existed somewhere around Tahiti.

Visiting the inspiration for so much Tiki lore excited the Tiki portion of the Steamtiki Crew, but left the Steamers unimpressed. Krackle joined them on this search. Unsure of his own leadership skills beyond piloting them into danger, Aran involved Temkaa or Krackle in each contact, wanting someone with the gravitas of a leader taking part. But he'd even screwed that part up in Tokyo, barging into the Trow hideaway instead of letting Temkaa lead.

Aran had already made a mistake on this foray as well by starting the trip in a resort. Housed in several bungalows on stilts out over the water, none of the crew wanted to leave their personal pools, cool sheets, and handy drinks for the cold and stickiness of diving in the salt water today.

At breakfast, a mix of fruits and nuts with some bread covered in apricot jam, he received the usual back-squawk, and he left it to Jules and Kirstn to roust the crew into action. He dreaded spending the day diving as well. Made for flying, swimming was an awkward undertaking for Silth. Wings weren't useful under the water, and their feathers just absorbed water, weighting them down. Just putting their shields around their faces wouldn't work because the air eventually leaked out. Some Australian Navy divers Penfield had connected them with had jury-rigged small oxygen tanks into workable scuba gear. They'd use their shields for wet suits.

"Stuff leaks out of them, but other stuff can't come in?" one diver asked.

"Mostly, that's true, living things can come in, unless you harden it," Aran said.

"Too bad," the diver replied. "No wettie warmers."

"What?" Aran asked, confused.

"Yeah, but you'd rather have that on if the men in gray suits come round," another diver added.

Aran gave up trying to understand.

Shields up, air tanks on, the four former Tiki Crew, eight Steamer Crew, Krackle, and Aran bobbed in the shoals next to a boat. These surrounded a group of islands on top of a sand coated plateau ringed by a drop-off into deep water. They floated over a sand desert amid forests of coral with bright schools of colored fish swimming within them.

Uncharacteristically subdued for the last couple of days, Krackle whooped with joy as she followed a sea turtle making its ponderous way past them. The others formed themselves into a circle to protect one another's backs.

"Great… we've turned ourselves into a bait ball," Don grumbled, eliciting growls from the rest of the crew.

After they'd been in the water around fifteen minutes, Aran made a series of high-pitched keening noises. The others squirmed, squeezing their eyes shut and covering their ears, as the sounds, a call the Sohi had taught him, spread out around them.

"You're sure the Sohi like you, right?" Nick asked. "This isn't a *shark call, is it?*"

"It's a *barracuda bellow*," Don suggested.

Half an hour later and down to just fifteen minutes of air, even Krackle had grown tired of being in the water.

Slatt tapped Jules on the shoulder and pointed.

Jules stuck his head under the water before reporting, "Well, it calls something."

The others saw a squadron of various types of stingrays making their way toward them from each direction. The slow, majestic procession moved with graceful flapping wings and before long, were on top of them. With no aggression, the rays flapped soft flippers against them and probed them with their gentle mouths.

The creatures parted and, in the distance, Aran saw three figures. They sat on saddled mantas, heading toward the group, emerging from the distorted distance as they arrived. The Trow rose to the surface of the water, towering above the Silth even while seated. Wrapped around the throat of each was a band of darker flesh inset with two sets of gills. Aran suspected these were Quitquots, the same creature that had given gave him eyes where his had once been. Each Trow wore colored plastic clothing made from various flotsam—bottles, fishing nets, plastic bags, straws, and children's toys—melted into sheets and cut into clothing. The original items still showed in the plastic.

"Why have you summoned us?"

"I am Aran Shaman—"

"We know you, and we are aware of world events, including the impending Trow invasion. Why have you summoned us?"

"We need your help."

All three Trow stared at him for a long moment, and then they moved beside the Silth. The rays surrounding them scattered.

The Trow who'd spoken said, "Take hold." Each Trow waited while the Silth found handholds on the saddle. "If you let go, we will not return for you." The Trow sped away.

Aran tightened his grip and watched the others struggling to hold on. Jules grabbed Krackle's wrist as her fingers slipped on the wet saddle. Because he didn't know how far they were going, Aran was tense. But the ride wasn't long. The three rays slipped over the underwater ledge, the deep ocean extending on three sides, and hugged the wall for fifty feet before entering a water-filled cave. Bioluminescent lights mounted on the saddles illuminated the way. They followed the floor as it slanted back up for a couple of minutes before emerging into the air of a grotto lit with the same bioluminescence Aran recognized from the cavern leading to the Sohi.

As he stepped onto the sandy shore, Aran turned off his oxygen, hoping there'd be enough to get him back to the surface. He helped the others out of their equipment and laid the tanks in a row on the little beach. He blinked to shift the spectra of his Quitquot eyes to see the room as the Trow did. His mouth fell open as the room filled with bright colors and splashes of sparkles spread like diamonds along the walls and floors.

The only Trow who'd spoken earlier held up three fingers before proceeding down a corridor while the other two sat on a grotto rock. Aran, Jules, and Krackle followed the Trow.

Behind Aran, Don said, "Hey, here's a bucket of fish chunks to feed the mantas."

The colors and sparkles continued along the walkway, resolving into mosaics of more complex design. The group emerged into a large, brightly lit chamber where Trow appeared to be farming, growing long ropes of algae in tanks along the walls, and raising fish and shellfish in pools.

*The light source must be something stronger than the glow worms,* Aran thought.

The path wound downward through two similar chambers before reaching a crowded market with stalls displaying fish, shellfish, fruits and vegetables, small pieces of art, and various implements Aran didn't readily identify.

"Whooeee, there're a bunch of these folks here," Krackle said.

"Did you expect so many?" Jules asked Aran, who shrugged.

None of the Trow paid attention to them. Not even a glance.

The next chamber had three- and four-story buildings carved into its walls. The upper levels were homes, and the first floor appeared to be public rooms of various sorts, mostly without doors and with windows cut in the fronts but no coverings. They proceeded into one of the bigger rooms, where three Trow sat in a raised semicircle behind a wooden, crescent table made of driftwood. They dressed much the same as the group's escorts, though Aran's *Trow vision* eyes discerned added patterns in their attire, signifying either an important position or perhaps just increased affluence. The Silth flew onto a low table in front of the Trow.

"Greetings, Aran Shaman," the Trow in the center said. "Welcome to Magh Meall. I am Tethra, this is Lir and that is Manan," pointing first right and then left. "We are the elected leaders of the Neirads, the *diaspora,* which is what our band of Trow expatriates call themselves. You have found us. We were aware of your search."

"You saw my pneuma as it searched for you?"

Tethra, brow furrowed, looked at Lir, who said, "No, we saw you on an internet video discussing it."

Krackle gave her donkey bray of a laugh and stepped forward. "Then you know why we're here. We're looking for allies in the coming war with the Trow."

"You discovered the Sohi. Are they allies?"

Aran said, "The Sohi are allies to the extent their religion allows. They'll only use magic as a defense, a last resort, and they'd prefer to avoid confrontation."

Tethra nodded. "That is what we understood. Have you found any other Trow enclaves?"

"There was another," Jules said. "In Tokyo."

"I take it from the past tense they are no more."

Jules said nothing, but Krackle answered with, "There were all sorts of crazy lights on, but no one was at home."

"Is that the choice you give us—join you or die?"

"No," Aran blurted out. "The Tokyo Trow took me to torture and kill. We never discussed anything. They left us no choice."

"You can't talk to a fist," Krackle told them.

Tethra sat quietly for a moment before continuing, "We thought their research on magical energy was useful and important, but they have always been a cyclone of bees in a hat."

Jules grinned at Krackle's gale of laughter, but Aran's expression was deadly serious.

"We ask that you join us in fighting Xafar. If we win, we're working to rebuild the world so all who live here can thrive."

Manan replied, "You will not fight Xafar."

"Yes, we will. The Silth have gained the shield and bolt, and we've joined the Humans to—"

"No, I mean Xafar no longer rules the Trow. Thest rules now. Thest leads the invasion of Earth. It has begun. He has a particular hatred for the Paerries, and even more for Xafar's son Faelen, who lives with the Sohi now." Manan's eyes softened. "His hatred rivals that of a Silth who assists him. The one named *Casius* has a deep anger toward you, Aran Shaman."

Aran's knees buckled. Jules grabbed him, and he and Krackle supported him for a few seconds while he recovered. "No, I'm okay," he mumbled before he spoke again. "Then your help is even more vital."

"We are conflicted. For many centuries, we have lived a good life here. The water protects us from the effects of Human technology. We follow the events on Earth's surface and in the Land, and we think our life has been better than either. But we fear that time, a time when we can ignore outside events, is gone. On the one hand, if the Trow control Earth, they will hunt us down. We have history. We thought we were *unfindable*. You have shown us that is not correct. On the other hand, we doubt you can win a war with the Trow, so linking our future with yours seems suicidal."

Tethra continued, "We work on an answer. But our way involves significant internal discussion before we act. It will be several days before we conclude. Until then, you are our guests."

"We have a war to fight," Aran said. "I bound myself to keep the Sohi's location secret and have done so. We will bind ourselves to secrecy, but we must return. Your news makes this even more urgent."

"And we will leave a hostage," Krackle added. Jules and Aran turned to stare at her in surprise. "I'll stay. We need someone here to answer their questions and advocate."

"It is your risk," Lir said. "We might eat Paerries for dinner."

"You'd have to be pretty hungry to eat this tough old bird. Besides, staying lets me avoid getting back in that cold water."

The three Trow huddled with their heads together, whispering among themselves. When they turned back to face the Silth, Tethra said, "We accept. Lir will be your host. We have grown tired of Lir's humor, and fear that with both you—"

Tethra lifted an eyebrow.

"Krackle."

"With you, Krackle, and Lir among us, our brains will leak from our ears. Nonetheless, we welcome you. If you cause any trouble, we will execute both you and Lir."

Jules gave a nervous chuckle.

Lir accompanied them back to the harbor. There they found Don, Nick, Kristn, and Loana playing with the manta rays, giving them fish treats and riding them around in the grotto. Slatt, Vander, and 3 of 5 talked to the Trow guards, almost as heavily armed as the Steamers, about the weapons each carried. The Trow good-naturedly shared information on the different weapons.

Jules told Slatt, "Give them back."

Slatt shrugged, his whole face a question.

"Give them back," Jules said to all three.

Each produced a small weapon once possessed by a guard. Although the guards tried to look angry, they mostly just seemed astonished by the skill of the thefts.

Krackle said her goodbyes and bound the crew to secrecy. Lir showed them how to manage the rays provided for the ride to the surface. The rays would return to the Trow after depositing their Silth riders. Meanwhile, Aran sat to the side on a nearby rock. He'd hurried to his mental clearing in the jungle and added some of what they'd learned from the Neirads to the third crate. But then he found himself immobilized by the news of Casius's survival.

Krackle joined him. "The news your brother lives must have blown your feathers off."

"Yes." Aran had his hands on the headband that allowed him to see, despite his brother's destruction of his eyes, but he lowered them upon Krackle's approach. He watched as the reflected light from the waves inside the grotto danced along the ceiling. "And Thest. I've met him. He hunted me. It's somehow different to fight someone I know rather than Xafar, who I'd never met."

"Oh, honey. Like he's coming after you and yours?"

"Yeah, maybe."

"Well, snap out of it. No time to gather mouse hairs."

"You're right." He pushed up from the rock. "We need these Trow to help. Counting on you to win them over. Good luck."

Aran walked down to the water's edge and learned how to mount a manta ray.

# Scene 2

MERIT (SILTH)

DC South, spread over 10,000 acres, had become a thriving town over the course of just a few years. People moved around it on foot, by bike, and by autonomous tuk-tuks—electrical, three-wheeled driverless vehicles. Other AVs zipped through the air, delivering packages. High-speed rail, and more recently the completion of the hyper-loop down the center of I-95 stretching back to DC, connected the town to Washington and Richmond.

Sensors in the cross walks recognized individuals and their abilities as they approached, adding features for the blind or hearing impaired as needed, or simply adding a little extra time for a senior to cross. Monitors in the street tree beds caused their drip irrigation to turn on only when needed. The town produced its own power using a geothermal well extended several miles underground, which also cleaned its wastewater for reuse in cooling the sprawling data centers.

Because of security requirements, particularly the restriction on proximity to streets, the federal government buildings were on a campus at the edge of the town, rather than in its hyperactive center. Merit made her way through the street market in the center as she inspected security.

Humans and Silth co-managed ten of the fifty governmental centers established around the world, including this one. They shifted the smart city's technology to security use. An AI presence called *Martha* monitored the ubiquitous CCTV cameras, the name coming from some acronym no one recalled. Martha watched for Trow presence and for someone blipping in. Security teams responded immediately with the assumption the intruder was hostile.

Martha recognized each permanent resident and registered guests of the town, dropping their identity from her records and blurring their faces in the preserved video. Any tampering with the videos or accessing information on them created a permanent record in the block-chain ledgers. It took this level of privacy protection to make the residents comfortable with Martha's oversight. The Human head of security had carefully explained these arrangements to Merit, and she could recite them, but she had no idea what a block-chain was, and an AI seemed more like a ghost in the city to her. While Merit understood little of the technology, she appreciated the instant awareness of the presence of outsiders.

She flew toward the government campus, about 300 acres with a river on one side and a former quarry turned into a beautiful lake in its center.

A Silth dome covered the facility, transferred there from one of the Silth refuges. Both the dome and the buildings within had an additional security feature that released what the Human military called *FD,* because the generals refused to call it Faerie Dust like everyone else. Automated equipment released this dust, an atomized version of the magically treated dust which removed the power to transport, outside the buildings or inside any one of them. It would permeate everywhere except a few safe zones created for any of the Silth caught there during a release.

The sun shone warmly on Merit in the beautiful Virginia morning along the parks and parkways linking the town center to the government campus. Early for her appointments, she meandered in the cooler air beneath the street trees lining the sidewalks. She stopped in a park with an ornate fountain surrounded by flowers and shrub-lined pathways weaving together art, specimen trees, and exercise stations.

The splash of its cascades of water reminded her of the waterfalls of her home, while the sweet scent of late dogwood and early mimosa blooms made the air almost festive. This Human habitat had its own beauty, and Merit loved the art, but she longed for the jungle's wildness. Here, no dense understory hid a browsing parrot. Despite birds, squirrels, and chipmunks gamboling about the trees and flower beds, the place seemed oddly barren to her, like a house mostly deserted.

"Merit!"

She looked toward the shout and saw a female Silth flying toward her.

It took her a moment to recognize Nadara. Gone were the blond tips to her hather and all the visible piercings except in her ears, which now had small gold spheres as ornament. She still had her tattoos, but far less of them were visible in the clothing she wore.

Soon after Humans realized the Silth were mostly wealthy by Human standards, entrepreneurs began deciding what they'd like to buy. An early bet had been they'd buy clothing especially designed to be comfortable with the Silth wings and tails, but more stylish than the handmade clothing or stolen doll clothes they'd historically worn. Nadara wore dark blue slacks, a white silk blouse, and a scarf that made the blue of her hather stand out. She moved as gracefully as ever—if anything, the clothes made her even more liquid.

As Nadara glided down next to her, Merit suddenly felt provincial and hulking in her Silth-made leather with her blunt wooden hand.

"Nadara, how are you?" She extended her arm for the traditional forearm-to-forearm clasp.

But Nadara slid past and hugged the stiffened Merit.

Nadara pulled back but took hold of Merit's hand as they stood on the walkway.

"So good to see you!" she said with such genuine enthusiasm that Merit's rising irritation melted away. "How are you? How long will you be here? Do you have a place to stay?"

She laughed as she saw the expression on Merit's face under the barrage of questions. "Are you heading to the campus? Mind if I come too?"

They flew along, and Nadara brought Merit up to date on her life. She lived in Washington South and worked with Penfield and others on the continuing integration of the Human and Silth cultures while realizing the fresh world they'd committed to. Other than a monthly blip to the meetings of the World Silth Council, and periodic meetings in other Human cities with other international organizations, she spent most of her time in Washington South.

"I see Storng every so often. He's more the *Storm Rider* than ever. There're so many things going smoothly and working right, but you can be sure Storng has ferreted out whatever isn't working and is advancing an angry solution." She jigged to avoid a tree. "In truth, he's a calm negotiator, but always begins with a bluster as though establishing the edge of his territory."

She was silent for a few seconds, and then continued, "I haven't seen any of the Steamtiki Crew in months."

"I think Jules will be here today," Merit said. "He's been with

Aran scouting for the Trow enclaves."

"Any success?"

"I'm sure you heard Aran almost died in Tokyo. Well, that enclave's gone. The rest of the story you have to intuit. You know Aran. He says they've had some success, but he provides no details. He no longer talks about Krackle being with them. Again, you have to read into the silences. Together, this means they've found something, and Krackle has stayed to work with the Trow, but Aran has promised not to talk about them until they're ready."

"Ha! Reading silence isn't one of my strengths," Nadara said.

"Reading Aran is a full-time, frustrating job."

"Yeah, I know. I got fired," Nadara said just as they arrived at the gate for the campus.

They showed their badges and after a few moments, the guard waved them in. They made their way through the tree-lined pathways of the place to the five-storied building in its center.

"What's Jules like?" Nadara asked. "He and the Steamers saved me from Rangi, but I didn't have time to speak with him much."

Merit thought for a moment before answering, "He is... becoming. He is not what he was and not what he'll be. Along the way he is polite, friendly, and deadly."

Nadara chuckled. "Intriguing."

They ran into General Cogbill, the son of the UN general who'd fought beside them in Indonesia. Merit asked about his father, and then they flew up the stairs to Penfield's office. Most of the government functions of the US had moved to the dome. Several other countries operated from here as well. Around the world, governments had moved their most vital functions into the governmental domes.

"Merit!" Penfield stood when they came to his office. "Good morning, Nadara." Her office was just down the hall. After some small talk, they moved to a conference room where a mix of Silth, including Jules, and Humans were waiting.

The meeting opened with formal presentations in a monthly format created by Aran, famous for his dislike of meetings. He called it a *truth meeting*. They would come together and share not just information, but also their fears and hopes, plans, and needs for cooperation.

This was the first time Merit had attended. Nadara reported the concerns of the WSC, which included the increasing violence against the Silth around the world and proliferation of efforts to develop defenses against the bolts and weapons that would penetrate shields. Although these measures focused on defending against the Trow, they would obviously affect the balance of power with the Silth as well. The WSC, disappointed in the speed of change in wildlife exploitation, was also concerned that the historic weapons of Humans, including nuclear arms, chemical weapons, and biological weapons, were too easily accessible to the Trow, available for use against them all. The Silth had run a test in which they looked for all they could find in the course of three days, without using their status as allies.

They easily found enough to end both the Silth and the Humans.

Penfield had a similar list of concerns. The Humans were wary of the Silth coordination with the rebel Trow groups such as the Sohi. They also worried the Silth were setting in motion a level of self-awareness by wildlife that couldn't be controlled, an experiment that could not be undone. The day before, a group of ravens had purposefully begun disabling the infrastructure supporting a small town in their nesting area, cutting off phones and power. A large pack of wild dogs had formed in Tanzania and systematically hunted down a trophy hunter trying to track game.

The Humans worried about the vestiges of New Faerie and whether the Silth had them under control. Others around the table spoke. This gathering identified the top concerns that might affect the war with the Trow and made their resolution a priority while shuttling the other concerns to appropriate committees. Merit spoke toward the end. She'd learned that if she remained quiet, others put most of her concerns on the table and she didn't need to raise them.

She walked them through the events at Angkor Wat and their implications. She said she considered all preparations woefully behind and security weak, given they now knew there were Trow spies on Earth. She reminded them the Trow might appear as Humans, so they needed to take this into account in their security. She expressed concern the field communications between Humans and Silth were slow and involved too many escalations and reports to superiors to authorize actions.

They all jumped when an alarm blared in the room and in the hall outside. Penfield touched the screen on the tabletop monitor as Merit flew to stand on a table by the window.

"Intruders detected," Martha the AI said from Penfield's phone. "Someone blipped in where they're not supposed to."

They heard shouts in the courtyard, and the others joined Merit at the window. Not long ago, she'd have dashed out to join the pursuit, but here she wasn't really in the command structure. Well drilled in response tactics, they didn't need her. The lights flickered.

"Intruders D and D—detained and dispatched," Martha advised them.

Penfield hit the button to turn on the ceiling-mounted monitor. They watched a video where half a dozen Trow warriors suddenly appeared on the street and then rapidly skipped through a series of blips, each time attracting the Martha's response. By the third blip, the guards had dusted all the Trow, eliminating their ability to transport. The Trow changed tactics and started firing bolts back at the defenders. In seconds, the Trow were down in a swarm of bullets and bolts, but not before they'd wounded several Silth and Humans. Because the Washington South residents wore biomonitors, Martha was able to tell the room two Humans and a Silth were dead.

"This is a change," Merit said, still facing the window. She turned, frowning, eyebrows drawn together in thought. "They don't seek direct information anymore. They're probing for weakness. Testing attack theories. Can they shut off the power? Could they overwhelm the defenses by sending in several warriors at once? A normal tactic. The same one the North Koreans and Brazilians used when they attacked our shielded areas."

She leaned her head against the glass. "We're at war. And we aren't anywhere near ready."

# *Scene 3*

## NADARA (SILTH)

It was just supposed to be a picnic. As they had finished the meeting on the government campus, Nadara asked Jules to join her for a picnic lunch. It was a whim. Nothing unusual about that. It felt like one last chance to catch a breath before the storm.

Jules was handsome, tall—for a Silth—very serious in his coat with tails, his boots, and top hat, but he had a dry humor when not in front of a crowd. The red hather on his temples stood out against his black clothes and wings.

He felt—dangerous? That wasn't it exactly, but there was an exciting edge to his presence. In fact, perhaps he felt the opposite of dangerous. Perhaps he felt safe. The opening was easy as she told him how much she appreciated him and the Steamers saving her life when Rangi tried to capture her. She'd never thanked him properly, and would he like to accompany her on a picnic? She never really entertained the idea that he might say no, and he hadn't.

Nadara questioned herself as the two of them left the meeting together. Had she purposely paused so that Merit would see her leave with him? Did she intend to send her a message? Or perhaps one to Aran? She wiped those thoughts away. This was nothing more than a chance to spend a few moments with someone she thought good-looking and who might be interesting.

Why a picnic? She ate in restaurants for meetings or from Silth-oriented food carts where she quickly grabbed something. But she was lonely, and a picnic sounded like a better way to connect with someone. Besides, it might be her last one ever. Whether they won or lost the war, and whether she survived, it was going to be a long time until she paused for a picnic again.

They stopped at a deli and picked up a pair of prepackaged Silth lunches with generous portions of fruits and nuts and a berry dessert without refined sugar made especially for Silth. On a whim, she grabbed a Silth-sized bottle of wine and a couple of small glasses. The shops in Washington South catered to the many Silth that stayed, worked, or visited there. They typically had plenty of money and knew how to use their phones to pay for things.

The two carried their bags to the park beside the river and sat cross-legged on the low, flat benches with no backs, especially designed to accommodate wings and tails. The river, this section little more than a big creek, burbled behind them.

She peppered him with questions, catching up on the lives of each Tiki Crew member and learning about the individual Steamers. He readily answered, happy to talk about his friends. He asked her questions about her work and her time with the Humans and laughed at her rude descriptions of working as part of the World Silth Council.

"It isn't as glamourous as it sounds."

"Still, you're the most powerful Silth with whom I've ever had a picnic."

"Have you ever had a picnic before?"

"No."

"Ha. You could picnic with Aran or Merit."

"Well, no flies on Aran, but you're much better company. And Merit... does she eat?"

Nadara rolled her eyes. "How is Aran?"

While his answers on the other crew members had come instantly, this time, Jules paused. "When I first met Aran, I thought him pretty simple. The longer I've known him, the more complex I find him. He has no desire for a title, yet he leads. He chooses tasks that seem extraneous to others, but then they turn out to be important, maybe pivotal. He runs a constant game in his head—I think that the Human game of chess may be the closest equivalent—and he uses the people and groups around him as chess pieces. Makes it difficult to tell whether one is being benefited or used." A breeze blew across the field, rustling the tree limbs around them and flattening the grass. "In the end, he's my friend, and I know he would give his life for me if he had to. Other than the Steamers, I've never had that much confidence in anyone."

Nadara watched the river as it wove in and out of the trees.

"You ok?"

She shook her head. "I'm fine. You just gave me a lot of insight into some things."

"What about you?" Jules asked. "What is it you want?"

"Me? I'm pretty happy. One gift from Aran is that I have a chance to lead far earlier than I normally would have. On any day, I make twenty decisions affecting the lives of thousands of Silth and Humans. I like that. I've never been sure whether it was his plan. In fact, I'm pretty sure it wasn't, but the time I spent as a *hostage* gave me insight into Human behavior like no other Silth. Now being on the WSC, infuriating as it might be, gives me a chance to use that insight. Working with Penfield on various Human-Silth projects has been incredible. If it weren't for pesky little things like impending war and recovery from a mass extermination event, it would be perfect."

"So, you have everything you want?" he asked as he picked up her hand. "War is here. As we saw today, life guarantees none of us another day. Have you done everything you want to do?"

She put her hand on top of his and looked him straight in the eyes, registering their slight dilation and the acceleration of his breath. She'd never needed a *smoldering look*. She bit her lower lip for a second or two before saying, "Oh no, not everything. But Silth pregnancy is a real thing now. One that I have no time for." She squeezed his hand before moving hers and looking back at the river. "I understand solutions are close. About three weeks away. So, for now, just a picnic."

Jules saluted her with a piece of tangerine. "And a fine picnic it is."

They sat eating for a few minutes. "Do you ever think about having children?" Nadara asked.

"I didn't. I mean, I never imagined taking in a fledgling from the nests and raising it. I could blame my lifestyle—I have always been on the move—but I don't think it would have made any difference. But when I learned that some Silth could have children, I wondered what being a father would be like."

Jules carefully folded the paper his lunch had been in and laid it on the bench beside him.

"Rangi raised me in a group. Our caregivers were mostly kind but raised us to be tools. They separated us into four groups and some of them were more aggressive about physical modifications than others. Constant training, much of it focused on desensitizing us, reduced our empathy for others. None of the groups had a mother or father in the traditional sense. Most of the fledglings who grew in these groups drifted into insanity or died in the training. Those left became the Steamers."

He took off his hat and let it play its little song before the top snapped open and a little clown bounced on the spring. "I think maybe I'm too warped. Not broken. More like a tree trained to grow in a particularly convoluted way that only later realizes this isn't how normal trees grow. I worry I wouldn't be a good parent."

"I'm not even sure what *good parent* means," Nadara said, adjusting her wings behind her and smoothing her slacks. "Humans have these roles, Mom or Dad, and some idea of whether someone is filling the role. It used to be gender specific, and often still is, but less so than they pretend. Sometimes, someone outside the nest fills the roles. Sometimes, many people." She inhaled deeply, bringing the sweet spring air into her lungs, and then letting it out in a sigh.

"For Silth, the act of deciding to raise a fledgling had no relation to gender. There were no birth mothers beyond the parrots. Villages raise most fledglings. Councils, mostly led by females, govern the villages. But the care and feeding depends on the desires of individuals, not gender. Will that change? Will birth mothers take a bigger role? And what about couples? We have been pretty fluid in our commitments. Will that change?"

Jules watched a couple walking in the distance. "I suspect that we have some say in these roles and commitments. We don't have hundreds of years of social design to overcome. We just have to be intentional in building in the freedom to fit the pieces together the way we want, so long as we keep the best interest of the fledglings in mind."

She slid her hand over her heart, lowered her head, and gave a little laugh. "You've given this a lot more thought than I have. I can honestly say that all I've accomplished is to say *not now*. There's so much to do. We may all die in the next few days. I'm not ready to be responsible for more than me." She crumpled the paper wrapping from her lunch and stuffed it back in the bag. "But I bet you'll make a good father."

This dome, like the refuges, was large enough to allow weather to form inside, and rain started to sprinkle. They said their goodbyes, and Nadara returned to meet with Penfield while Jules blipped off to catch up with Aran.

# Scene 4

CASIUS (SILTH)

Casius looked around the freshly constructed Brazilian Newfie colony. He should have been happy. He should have basked in the adoration of the Silth who surrounded him, eager for his leadership. Amazed at his Trow-given powers, most would follow him anywhere, do anything he asked. Uninterested, he focused on his mission.

*It was a mistake to come here.*

After Faelen's appearance before the UN, there weren't many Newfies left. Gradually, the videos of the event made it around the world, ridiculing the Newfies for believing the brutal Trow were angels. Then the Sohi emerged from their hidden retreat. They bestowed no powers and disdained followers. Finally, the WSC shared the ability to produce the bolt or create a shield with every Silth who bound themselves not to follow the Newfie way.

For several months, the only Silth not possessing Faerie powers were the Newfies. Eventually, they stole the knowledge through spies and other means. But it was never a gift from the Faeries. The remaining Newfies were ardent, but perhaps not the brightest in the Silth gene pool. Casius himself doubted the celestial nature of his alliance.

Thest's advisors had given him Faerie powers, but little more than Aran had. While he was with the Trow, he pretended to find everything aligned with his expectations. He had, however, quickly determined that they hoped to use him, and that was likely the only reason he was still alive. Caius believed it was his good fortune that

Thest had replaced Xafar since Xafar was insane. But Thest's contempt for Casius was palatable.

Since returning to Earth, Casius had tried every spell they'd taught him. He had a few more weapons, and a little more power in those weapons than did others, but most of what they'd given him was show magic—good for impressing an audience, but of little strategic value. Many of the supposedly powerful spells simply didn't work. He'd spent all of his life memorizing the Newfie creed and rituals. He'd forgotten nothing, nor made any mistakes in the spells. Why did they need his help to retake the Earth, anyway?

But he didn't question it too much—he didn't really care. He ignored the assignments they'd given him. He had one mission—to kill his brother. If he helped the Silth along the way, that was fine. He tried to imagine what he'd do after the Trow successfully destroyed Humans and much of the Silth population. Each time, however, he would get drawn back to Aran's death, playing this scene again and again in his mind. But not what happened next.

Inspired to see his powers and learn the Faeries actually had trained him, the Newfies were disappointed when Casius told them he wouldn't lead them. Even so, he thought he detected relief in some colony leaders, either intimidated by him or not sure they trusted him. Stories lingered of how he'd squandered the lives of Newfies in his prior fights. Tonight, however, they celebrated in his honor, and he felt adored by the surrounding crowd.

A bonfire rose high into the inky darkness on the village's central green. Speakers heaped praise on him. They dragged three Silth in front of the high seat they'd built for him, and two adolescent females and an older male stood with heads bowed between him and the roaring fire, hands tied and wings cuffed. To keep them from blipping away, each wore an elaborate headpiece that would drive a stake through their head if separated from the warden connected by a leash. The evidence showed all were spies, or at least sources of information to the WSC.

Casius wasn't sure quite what the crowd expected, perhaps some grand sacrifice by tossing them into the bonfire. He ordered the traditional punishment of clipping their wings and casting them out into the jungle. Now that the Silth interacted with Humans and had the power to transport, this fate was unlikely to lead to immediate death, but there was a level of shame for Silth who couldn't fly. Another reason to be wary of the Newfies as a force—they were rife with spies.

In the evening's closing ceremonies, Casius stood in front of the crowd spread out in the bowl-shaped green. The gold-threaded ceremonial robes furnished to him by the Trow sparkled in the dying firelight. As the fire went out, the interwoven bioluminescent threads made him stand out ghostly in the darkness.

"Children of New Faerie. You few remaining. You few who still stand strong. The best of us!" He raised his arms above his head. "You have kept the torch of faith burning as tremendous storms extinguished all other light from the world. I salute you!"

The crowd's cheer echoed off the giant trees of the rain forest around them.

"Now comes the time for the ultimate test. Do we stand by the Faeries who would save us? They're on their way! I have seen it, and they are imminent! No longer judged by the standards of Silth, soon the Faeries themselves will judge you."

A breeze stirred the bonfire embers, and he looked at the faces reflecting their glow. "How will you be found? Will you be worthy? Will you be wanting? Are you sure? Are you ready to give your all to assure your place in the Land?" A cheer of affirmation.

He spoke louder. "I have one last task for you. One last burden before paradise. Are you ready?" The crowd shouted its approval. "I need you to spread out in all the colonies you can reach. I need you to go into the places where Humans and Silth are working together to stop our Faerie host from its task. I need you to infiltrate these places and destroy all you can. Do whatever you can to disrupt and interfere with the efforts to stop that which will save us all. Do this last thing and all the rest of your days, whether on this side of the veil of life or the other, will be in paradise, with the powers of Faeries at your disposal."

The crowd's roar split the night air as birds took to the skies from the limbs around them and animals dashed away in panic. Casius stepped out of the dim circle of light surrounding the fire's glowing coals and transported away.

*** 

Casius appeared in front of a small administration building next to an enormous church. He flew in through the front door and down a long hall before arriving in the reception area of a plush office with late afternoon sunlight still streaming through its windows. The room smelled of harsh cleaning chemicals. There was no receptionist, nor anyone else in the room, and he hovered to look at a few pictures. Reverend Tobias with this important government official at a ribbon cutting. Here with a celebrity, shovel in hand. The door opened behind him and Tobias entered the room.

"I didn't believe it when Sister Rochelle told me you were still alive. Imagine my surprise and honor when you reached out." After stacking books on the table in a small conference room, he poured water from a pitcher into a tiny cup. "Sorry, I thought she had set this up for us before she left. How have you been? *Where* have you been?"

"My brother sent me away after our confrontation. The experience was uncomfortable, but I've learned a lot. I don't have long. I'm just stopping to see how you are." Casius stood on the conference table to see the glorious sunset over a carefully maintained Zen garden. "And *where* you are."

"We're doing surprisingly well. Our international ministry is expanding faster than ever. We're in thirty-seven countries." Casius turned and looked at Tobias again. "We keep a low profile. Technically, nothing we did was illegal. Now that the Silth have saved the world, calling you *demons* isn't very popular.

"We even have Silth outreach programs in three countries. No effort to convert, of course—just helping them assimilate into contact with Humans. We also started a project to help them preserve their oral history. Many times, these histories evaporate when groups come into contact with a culture with written history."

"I assume you're still interested in money?"

Tobias's smile faded just a little. "We're always interested in the resources that allow us to expand the Lord's work. But these days, federal officials closely monitor all traffic in jewels and gold. It's because the Silth are already so intertwined in the economy, and so many of these things have appeared, that their value has become unstable." His mouth open and closed as though he was searching for the right words before he continued.

"If we suddenly had some additional source of such things, we'd have to explain why—and what we're doing for it. Homeland has gotten very aggressive in monitoring the flow of funds. Besides, as I say, the world has changed. My flock no longer believes the Trow are angels. We've become very patriotic now as we support the preparations for war."

"I see," was all Casius said.

"Sorry, I can't help you this time. Would you like to join me for dinner at least?"

Tobias faced Casius for the exiting bow.

He gave a quick gasp as Casius's face melted away to be replaced by Aran's.

The bolt hit Tobias in the chest, flinging him backward against the conference room wall.

"Then what use are you?" Casius muttered as he flickered and disappeared.

\*\*\*

"I don't understand," said the young Lieutenant standing in the strobing blue lights on the lawn outside Tobias's suburban headquarters in the morning predawn. Penfield stood next to him, and Aran perched on the back of the police car.

"There were cameras everywhere." He looked down at his tablet, watching different replays from the evening. "Here he is coming up on the building, and he looks like you." He touched the screen, fast forwarding the images. "Now here he is in the lobby and he has his own face on, or at least I assume that's his face." Once more, the images jumped forward. "Here, in the conference room, he changes to look like you, and that's how he looks as he leaves." The officer lowered the phone. "What was he trying to accomplish? It took about twenty minutes for us to find they scheduled you for a briefing with Dr. Penfield's group, and fifteen more to confirm you'd been in sight the whole time and couldn't have left, even by transporting." The officer closed his iPad and tucked it under his arm. "Seems like a pretty lame effort to put the blame on you."

"That was not the point of this." Aran sighed as he turned to face Penfield. "He probably realizes they saw him coming back into this world from the Land. Casius knew I would likely have an alibi, and while he might not be familiar with the technology of cameras, I suspect he knew cameras would likely capture some part of this."

"He knew it wouldn't work?" Penfield asked.

Aran frowned and shook his head. "Oh, I think it worked exactly as he wanted it to. Silth can tell when the Trow are pretending to be Humans because the Silth can see a blue glow around their glamour. Tell me, though, after watching this, the next time you're in a room full of Silth, how likely are you to trust they're all who they say they are?"

"He wanted to cause confusion and make it harder for Silth and Humans to work together."

"Tobias may have been the only Human who'd trust him enough to meet with him, and Casius found one last use for him."

# CHAPTER FOUR

## *Scene 1*

**THEST (TROW)**

Fod finally located the Sohi. Thest had searched the world for them. He started by looking for the holes, the places where he could not *see* who was there. But the Earth had many of those. His spies passing as Humans inquired, but the popular media did not have actual information, and the speculation by Humans ranged from *they're in Area 51* to *they're not real, just CGI made up by the media for a provocative story.*

On the Earth for a week since he too had come in with the flood of flower fairies, Thest expected to have killed Faelen already. When not looking for Faelen, he supervised the Trow battle magic training and oversaw the search for Human chemical and biological weapons. While doing a poor job securing the conventional weapons, the Humans had hidden the chemical and biological ones well. In some ways, Thest believed the Trow would be more comfortable with weapons based on nature rather than technology. Many of their own weapons were biologically based, though they had never developed tools for the indiscriminate death of large numbers like the clever monkeys had.

Thus, it was a bit of good news when Fod appeared, telling him he had followed two Sohi as they left a meeting with Silth and

Humans. The Sohi would not use magic, so the Silth escorted them back to the Andes. The Silth took them through a series of quick blips, designed to throw off anyone trying to follow them or identify such pursuit if it was successful.

Because Fod had followed Silth on the Earth for many years and was aware of all their tricks, they did not realize he successfully tracked them to the foothills of the Andes. The Sohi continued on foot without the Silth, not realizing Fod was close behind. After walking for three days without stopping, the Sohi reached the frozen slopes of a tall mountain and disappeared into a mountain crevice. Fod flew over the mountain rather than going through it. He lost two fingers and three toes to frostbite, but now knew the Sohi's location.

Thest paced on the Andes' slope outside the valley entrance with fifty well-trained warriors. He'd been unable to sleep the night before and had decided they would go through the passage, sending one scout ahead to look for traps, but quickly marching through the tunnel in case of any alarm. He had only heard rumors of the Sohi, most of which he did not believe. Some sort of religious cult, they modeled their lifestyle on a group of ancient Humans. No sane Trow would do such a thing. His advisors told him that Xafar avoided the Sohi for several hundred years because their fighting skills were so great. The only time they used magic was in battle, but then the power of that magic astonished. Other advisors claimed the Sohi invented these stories to dissuade attack.

*Advisors are useless,* Thest thought. *Every piece of advice they provided was so caveated and laden with bits of counter-advice that it conveyed nothing useful. They floated in a sea of qualifiers.*

The squad encountered no problems as they rushed through

the glowworm-lit cavern. Thest appreciated the warmth of the hot spring accompanying the last part of their passage. His warriors bunched together behind him at the valley entrance. Through the doorway, he saw a beautiful, sunshine-covered landscape. Peaceful. Quiet. Warm. No one in sight. His scout walked through the doorway and immediately vanished. The squad muttered behind him. Night would come soon, so Thest waited until a starlit darkness settled on the other side of the door and sent two more scouts through, only to watch them evaporate without a sound a few steps across the threshold. Thest waited. A few moments later, two of his warriors came into the cavern mouth from the valley.

"Report."

"A Sohi fighter hid above the cave entrance," the warrior said, long dreadlocks pulled to the back of her head beneath her helmet. She and the other warrior wore heavy coats. "We dispatched him easily as we came down from the mountain above him."

"Very good."

The squad spread out in the cover around the mouth of the cave. He saw the red-robed figure slumped on the hillside above the entrance and shook his head. He had no desire to kill Trow, other than Faelen.

"Lord Thest!"

Thest looked in the shout's direction. A distant yellow glow came toward them along a path winding next to the stream on the valley floor. The glow resolved into a single tall figure, red-robed like the first and also shaved bald. He walked along with arms raised to chest height, hands hidden in the folds of the robes and surrounded by a soft light.

"Watch him carefully. The sleeves of those robes might hide anything."

Though he seemed too far away to have heard, the figure held his empty hands up even with his face and let the folds of his robes fall to his elbows, showing he was unarmed. He walked forward with the glow still surrounding him.

Thest did not move. "Close enough. Speak your purpose."

"I am Tegrat, I speak the will of the Sohi. Why have you come with warriors into our home?"

"You house the traitor called Faelen. Deliver him and no one else need die."

"Wait here, and I will inquire of the will of the Sohi."

"No, we will not give you time to prepare to attack us."

"Prepare? We have known you were coming since your spy came over the mountain a few days ago. We have no need to further prepare. Wait here." He turned and walked back down the path.

Two hours later, Thest realized he had no intention of coming back, and in fact he had never said he would. Tegrat had merely instructed him to stay there.

"Proceed," he instructed the squad leader. "Kill everything, but if you can, leave Faelen to me."

The squadron took to the air, spreading out to search for the Sohi. They followed stone steps up the side of the next hill and on the other side, the trees gave way to the beginnings of the Sohi fields, most growing crops but a few occupied by llamas and alpacas. Thest stopped as they approached the seemingly empty village, then led twenty-five warriors, advancing warily through the sky while the rest landed at the village edge.

Two Sohi stepped out of one building and thrust their arms toward Thest and his airborne group. The wave moved so fast they had no time to react before it tossed them about and knocked them down like small children on the edge of a rough sea. Thest hit the ground hard. Stunned and waiting for his vision to clear, he sat up. Some of his warriors also sat trying to gather their shaken wits, and others struggled to stand. Three did not move, their heads at odd angles to their bodies.

"Get up. Move forward. Fire bolts into the dwellings. Flush them out."

The group moved forward, firing. Thest sent ten warriors back into the air above the village. They fired down into the roofs of the buildings quickly, before disappearing and reappearing in a new location. They repeated the shifts, never staying long enough to draw fire. He sent another group to the top of the hillside of buildings where they sighted down the street, waiting for anyone to emerge.

As Thest and his group drew even with the first buildings, a figure suddenly blurred among them, appearing next to each of Thest's warriors, or between two of them where they bunched together, and striking or cutting them too fast to even discern a weapon. While normally when a Trow or Silth transported they lingered for a moment, flickering before disappearing, this one seemed to disappear even as it struck. At least twelve died before any bodies hit the ground, and the remaining warriors raised their shields.

Tegrat appeared in the street in front of the remaining force.

"Leave now or die," he shouted with such force each of them took an involuntary step back. To the credit of their training, however, the front warriors quickly banded together with their shields up and another group stepped behind them, dropping their shields and firing bolts toward Tegrat. Or rather, toward the space where Tegrat had stood.

A shout came from the top of the hill as a group of Sohi appeared behind Thest's warriors. Not only were bolts flying and the Sohi appearing next to any unshielded warrior, but the dust of the road, small stones, and anything loose was being swirled around them, confusing and disorienting them. Thest recognized the tactic.

He did not see Faelen, but Faelen would be there.

"There! Attack."

All the remaining warriors on the ground blipped to the hilltop, the ones in the air redirecting their bolts to the hilltop fight. The ground force ignored the Sohi fighters and focused on Faelen, still recognizable, though he looked quite different from before with his shaven head and red robes.

By the time Thest got there, a grim-faced Faelen leaned into his shield, bolts lashing it from all directions. Fod, the closest to him, fired inches from the protective barrier.

But the Sohi used this opportunity to decimate Thest's troops in the air. As the Trow fired down on the Sohi fighting alongside Faelen, one or two Sohi would run out of a building below, leap high, and pull a warrior to the ground, where others rushed out and dragged them inside. If the target got their shield up in time, the Sohi pulled them down, shield and all. Soon, there were no more warriors firing from the sky. Thest realized the remaining dozen warriors plus himself and Fod were not enough to subdue the Sohi colony, but he did not care.

The only Trow he wanted dead was Faelen. The rest were simply in the way.

Thest saw Tegrat at the edge of the fight, his shield down as he lashed the sleeve of his robe around his arm to staunch the blood coming from a deep wound. Thest pulled a slim dagger from his cloak and transported to stand behind the ancient Sohi. He grabbed him by the forehead, sticking the dagger point just far enough into his throat to draw blood.

"Move and die," Thest said. As Tegrat stiffened, Thest pushed him farther into the street. "Faelen!" Thest shouted again over the noise of the fight. "Faelen!" The fighting stopped as the others saw Thest with the knife at Tegrat's throat. "Lower your shield and yield or he dies."

The Sohi fighters on the street looked stricken. Faelen snarled, looking around for some leverage. Fod moved closer, his hands forward, ready to fire as soon as the shield lowered. Faelen looked at Tegrat. Thest did not see Tegrat's face, but he tightened his grip on him. Faelen shook his head slightly, as though disagreeing with Tegrat.

"Now! Drop your shield now or he dies!"

Faelen dropped his shield but ducked below the bolts fired by Fod and came up with his hands on both sides of Fod's head. He fired his own bolts, and Fod dropped.

But Thest did not see him hit the ground. As Faelen moved, Tegrat transported from the valley, taking Thest with him. When they reappeared, Thest floated in darkness beneath a crushing pressure. He activated his shield, relieving the pressure, and in the shield's blue glow, he saw Tegrat floating dead beside him, the dagger driven into his throat. He realized they were deep beneath some ocean and he transported away while he still had enough air.

# *Scene 2*

Aran (Silth)

The Sohi stood in the sunset's glow, red clouds sailing like ships on the dark blue sky and the red snow-capped mountains reflecting in the glacier lake next to them. The summer air was full of different flower scents, and the temperature, already cool, dropped as the sun dipped below the rim of mountains. Besides Faelen, apparently now accepted as one of them, Aran was the only outsider. Tegrat's recovered body lay in a shroud on the pyre with blankets of flowers hiding the wood stacked beneath.

The Sohi silently covered the hillside in their red robes.

No songs.

No sermons.

No testimonials.

No tears.

As the sun slid further behind the mountains, darkness replaced the sunset, but it was the high mountain darkness of the kind that wasn't darkness at all. The sky was awash in the light of tens of thousands of stars.

Lornix took a torch from the fire ring burning next to the pyre and tossed it on the pyre's base. Other Sohi repeated the action. As the wood quickly lit and the flame rose high, its crackles and pops were the only sounds. The sparks flew up to join the stars. After a few moments, the flames turned dark blue and then green and finally, dark red.

Aran watched the reflection in the lake until the pyre fell in on itself, leaving burning coals. Buckets of water doused the coals, and a group laid fresh blankets of flowers on the ashes. Then the edge of the gathered crowd melted into the night.

Aran flew beside Faelen as they wound the circuitous path back to the small house Faelen and Lornix shared. He and Faelen sat at the table splitting some fruit, avocado, and nuts Aran had brought, when Lornix arrived. She settled in, awkwardly adjusting to accommodate her now enormous belly. Faelen pushed a generous share of the meal in front of her, and she ate.

He and Aran had been talking about the state of the world, but now the three sat in silence, simply eating. From his bag, Aran pulled several small, sweet cakes, made with honey. These were Faelen's favorites, and the three of them consumed the cakes in the flickering light of the vegetable oil lantern. When their eating slowed, Lornix leaned back.

"I am sorry I was delayed. The Sohi met to make several decisions."

Aran saw Faelen flinch a little, presumably because they had not included him in the deliberations.

"Faelen, they have accepted you as one of the Sohi. This is an unusual honor, as usually many years pass before they accept a novice."

"They probably recognized he's so old he wouldn't make it that long," Aran joked before he could stop himself. Faelen lifted a brow. "Sorry," Aran said, failing to hide his smile.

Lornix went on. "They also decided we will prepare to leave this place at once. These preparations will take three days, and we will need to be on our guard, as we expect Thest to return soon. We will temporarily occupy another valley similar to this one, but quite a distance away."

"Temporarily?" Faelen asked.

"There, we will prepare for the next phase." She took a mouthful of cake, and they waited for her to finish it and the drink from the cup of juice. "Aran, we will follow your plan. We will move to occupy the Land while Thest is here in this world."

Faelen sighed and leaned back in his chair, frowning.

"There was much discussion on this, as there has been for many days now. If we do not do this, will Thest win in his attack on Earth? Our conclusion is *yes*. If he wins, what will this do to our way of life? This is harder. The likelihood is that when Thest has destroyed the Humans and the Silth... and killed Faelen, then he will ignore us.

"But we have developed many spiritual ties and personal affections with the creatures on this planet. We do not believe we would be happy in such a world. We also discussed whether this action constitutes violence as aggression or as defense. Whether we will still be the Sohi if we invade the Land. How will they receive us? There have been many questions and discussions, but we have resolved we will do this, with one condition."

She looked directly at Faelen. "You must assert your right to the throne."

"What! The Trow throne is the last thing I want. What makes you believe there is any circumstance in which I would govern them? I have spent my entire life distancing myself from that fate."

"I did not say you would govern. The Speaker of the Sohi Will shall tend to governance, but we believe the Trow are more likely to peacefully accept this circumstance if it is under your claim of right to the throne."

Faelen was up and pacing the tiny room like a tiger in a small cage.

"Tegrat is dead, and why would my claim matter in installing the Speaker?"

"Because the Sohi made another decision made tonight. As Tegrat instructed, I am the new Speaker of the Sohi Will."

The argument crescendoed from there, and Aran excused himself to walk in the night air. When he returned two hours later, Lornix had gone to bed, and a sullen Faelen was staring at the cup of juice on the table.

"Right now, I am questioning whether sobriety is the best course for me." But he picked up the juice and drank. "It was a forgone conclusion I would lose this argument. And yes, I will hold you personally responsible if anything happens to her or my child." He pushed a smaller cup of juice toward Aran. "And you must sit here with me late into the night as we pretend to get drunk and find the courage to do what lies ahead."

# *Scene 3*

Aʀᴀɴ (Sɪʟᴛʜ)

Aran and Merit arrived at Magh Meall on the backs of the huge manta rays again, but without the Steamtiki Crew this time, hoping to conclude negotiations for support by this band of Trow. Aran called the Neirads, as Faelen had instructed him, and they collected the two of them.

For over an hour, they sat on benches in the cavern with the farms. Merit seemed to sleep while sitting straight up on the bench, but Aran was bored. He decided to amuse himself with a minor act of revenge.

Recently she'd seen the two movies Humans made about him and his efforts to stop the Trow from blowing up Yellowstone. He had to admit each portrayed him as bigger, more muscular, and frankly, more heroic than he was. But he didn't think the movies deserved Merit's gales of laughter. She must have mentioned them ten times over the last week, each time laughing so much she had to catch her breath afterward.

"You know you're what the Humans call a *stereotype,* don't you?"

Merit opened one eye but said nothing.

*"The beautiful, brave fairy warrioress, armed with a bow."*

"I'm not a Faerie." She closed her eye again.

"To the Humans you are. Maybe an elf. Look." He held up his phone showing her a Pinterest site featuring nothing but beautiful female fairies and elves with bows, images from artists and games, and cosplay Humans dressed as these characters.

Merit had grown familiar enough with the screens of phones that she touched her finger to the screen and scrolled down through the pictures.

"Stereotype? You think I am like these?" She frowned and scrolled further. "I shoot bolts from my hands, but it's true I still carry my bow for when the magic is exhausted. These females are not even credible. Look what they wear. You could never fight in this attire. Look at their hair. It's so long it would constantly catch on branches, and their enemies would simply grab it and control them. Their hips are so big I don't see how they walk. And their breasts so large! How would they even hold a bow, much less hit the side of a strangler fig?"

She scowled at Aran, who thought this joke was not working as he had hoped. "Is this how you think I look? Perhaps it is how you wish I looked?"

Merit, who did not wear a glamour, transformed before Aran's eyes. Her short hather turned from its red, blue, and green to long, blonde hair, and her clothing shrank, barely covering her exaggerated hourglass figure. The yellow tattoos below her eyes disappeared, as did her scars and artificial hand. Her orange eyes turned blue and her wings shifted from their green with a red spot to a color matching her hair.

"Is this what you long for? The one who would finally hold *Heartless?*"

"No, no, that's not what I meant," Aran stammered. "I—"

As she started laughing, the glamour melted away. "You're an amateur. I've lived my entire life in the company of warriors and the daily teasing of that culture. You'll need to do better than this." She waved his phone at him before handing it back.

Krackle flew into the room and landed in front of them.

"Hello my friends. So good to see familiar faces!" she shouted, leaning forward to hug Aran. She looked at his expression. "I'm not interrupting something, am I?"

"Just my daily ration of abuse from Merit."

"Ho! Well, no time for that right now. We're off to see the wizard." She leaped back into the air and flew back the way she'd come.

Merit looked at Aran, who shrugged and followed toward the council chamber.

"Welcome back, Aran Shaman," Tethra said.

"Good to be in your company again."

"We have appreciated the great gift you gave us of Krackle's company."

"You are rare connoisseurs of that fine wine then," Aran said.

Krackle shook her head in mock dismay. "Here I've been working hard under the sea, while you've been up playing—"

Aran turned serious. "May I introduce Merit, Dawn Guardian. She leads the Silth in battle and co-leads the combined Silth/Human Defense Force. She came with the hope you would join this force in resisting Thest. The invasion has begun. I'm sorry, but we must press for your answer." He didn't say the reason the Steamtiki Crew had not joined them was that they waited on the island above in case the answer was *no* and they needed to mount a rescue.

"Welcome Merit, Dawn Defender," Lir said.

The silence stretched on.

Finally, Manan spoke. "This is... unusual for us. We are an ancient splinter group of the Trow society, members of the Queen's royal court. We were in the highest strata of Trow society beneath the Queen's family. The Queen who Xafar overthrew. Tradition demands the death of the prior court upon such an event, so we fled here. The water protected us from detection and shielded us from most of the harmful effects of this world's technology. We followed that technology, though, and we have a room containing televisions and computers, tracking what is going on in the world."

Lir continued. "Although we have followed the technical advances of Humans and the reintroduction of Silth into Human awareness, for us, your arrival was disconcerting. Until then, none of us had communicated directly with Humans or Silth in centuries. When we did, most groups we spoke with held us in awe as gods or mystical beings. Your arrival was as though your pet parrot and his friend the monkey entered the room and talked to you as an equal.

"And then you left Krackle here."

Merit gave Aran a sharp look, like *what have you done.*

Tethra said, "We assume not all Silth are like Krackle. So, how would you know she was the perfect representative to stay and discuss our course of action?" Aran took in his first breath since the Trow had begun speaking.

"Before Xafar, the Trow were mostly a happy, whimsical race. One reason he could take power was he and his followers were so much more brutal than the rest of us, a product of the technology madness. Of course, these are relative things. As we said, tradition long before Xafar was the execution of the court. I am confident that you would also view the enslavement of Humans and Silth as brutal, as we do now as well. As I'm sure cats and horses will one day say as well."

"Krackle, so brave to stay with an unknown group, met with

us as an equal, showing great wisdom and insight, but also humor and whimsy," Lir said. "She is no pet. And she convinced us to take your side in this war, even though it may well threaten our existence."

Manan leaned forward to speak. "Remember, we were the court, not warriors. We are good at hiding. Quite good at it. Consequently, we are not yet sure *how* we might contribute to the fight, but we will be on your side and do what we can. In the meantime, a few conditions. Krackle must stay and assist us. Two more individuals, who do not have to be Silth, may join her here, but you must be sure of their loyalty, and Krackle must vouch for them. Neither you nor anyone else may come or go from inside our caves. Trow are very good at tracking.

"We mostly move beneath the sea where they cannot find us at all. Krackle says you use phones. We have a phone, very difficult to secure and arrange an account, but we have a telephone number we will give you. You may call or send texts. Within the next three days, we will advise you on what we think we can contribute to the cause."

Merit spoke for the first time. "We may lose this war in three days."

After the three Trow briefly whispered among themselves, Lir said, "You may be right. The best we can promise is day after tomorrow. We will reach out to you if it is faster. Before you leave, you will tour the weapons and resources we have, and you will meet the leader of our militia. Join us for lunch and then you can leave."

Tethra stood. "It may not seem to you we respond with urgency. Please understand things move slower here, and this is lightning speed for us. The very idea of coming out of hiding terrifies us. The last time we had any direct contact with the Trow, they almost exterminated us."

An aide, young, with dark, waist-length hair and green eyes, escorted the Silth to a sitting room and showed them the restrooms before telling them someone would return in one half hour to lead them on their tour.

"What do you think?" Aran asked Krackle.

"I don't know. I like them and they intend well, but they move so slowly it's hard for me to imagine what good they'll be. It takes twelve of them in committee to decide which shoe to put on first. They make all major decisions by *consensus,* which means they talk everything to death. I've never seen anything like it. If they start now and work through the night, perhaps they can decide on how to take part."

But Aran was thinking he'd seen something like it, just recently.

"They're an odd people," Krackle went on. "I still can't figure out the gender of most of the ones I've interacted with. There are no clothing, hairstyles, names, or other markers for gender.

"And you remember the name of the place—*Magh Meall?* It's Irish. Means *plain of joy.* This place connects to Ireland somehow. I mean physically connects."

"What do they call themselves?" Merit asked.

"They told us when we first arrived. Later, they told me it meant the *dispossessed,* but that turned out to be a movie reference that I still haven't gotten. It seems they call themselves the *Neirads,* which means the *diaspora*—the people who traveled into the wilderness."

Aran spoke up. "Ok. Merit, you need to identify someone in your organization who can help assess how they can assist. I have someone in mind for the other position."

"I know that look. That is the *Aran has a plan* look. And all your plans are coati-scat crazy."

As Aran gave Merit an enormous smile, Krackle clapped her hands together in excitement. "Oh goody, this'll be fun!"

# Scene 4

### Joss (Human)

Less than five minutes after leaving Richmond, Joss arrived in the Washington South hyper-loop station. The drone flight down the James River from her center to the station took ten. She would have taken the drone straight to Washington South, but the required flight paths were so convoluted it would have taken more time.

In every step of the journey she felt like an impostor, someone pretending to be important, even though she'd made this trip several times. The shiny, new hyper-loop stations had only been open a few months. The air inside the transport still had a *new car* smell that surely had to be an artificial scent. Manufacturers no longer used the plastics and foams in the seats and molded plastics that off-gassed the volatile organic compounds that made the smell.

She laughed at herself for knowing that.

When she arrived at Washington South, she grabbed a new Tata sidewalk drone. She and her bag sat in the drone as it moved along the sidewalk, monitoring the crowd and other vehicles—moving at their pace. When it detected an open sidewalk, it zoomed along. Images from an old movie with overweight Humans confined to such chairs always occurred to Joss when she rode these. She constantly struggled with weight, but now, as a *pregnopotamus,* she felt huge. Then she let it all go as she enjoyed the sunshine on the way to the government campus.

Once she cleared the security check, she walked up the stairs, just for the exercise, to the third-floor conference room where she met Nadara and Penfield. After the usual hellos and catch-up talk, they discussed Joss's international programs.

The alarm sounded at midmorning, at first generating eye-rolls as everyone assumed it a drill. But immediately, Martha's voice came from each of their phones, announcing that three or more strangers had blipped into the building.

"Level 2 personnel should evacuate to the *FDP rooms*," the AI announced. This was Penfield and Nadara's designation so they left the conference room.

"Wait, isn't the dust room in the other direction?" Penfield asked as Nadara headed the opposite way down the corridor.

"It is for you two," Nadara shouted over her shoulder.

"That's right," Penfield said to Joss. "Immediately after Casius killed Tobias, they segregated the lockdown rooms with Silth in some and Humans in others. None of the Silth in Washington South wear glamours anymore, but that just means they can recognize a spy who comes in glamoured. The Humans can't tell the difference. The Silth lockdown rooms are also dustproof, so they won't lose their ability to transport."

Joss tried to take deep breaths as she followed Penfield. She flinched at each loud sound in the corridor as the sirens wore on her nerves.

Turning the next corner, they stepped into a firefight they hadn't heard over the din of the alarms. They crouched behind three Silth, using the cover of desks and doorways to fire at another half dozen Silth down the hall.

Aran looked back over his shoulder at them. "Quick. They're

after Nadara. Where is she?"

"Heading back down the hall to the Silth dust room," Penfield said.

"Take me. Hurry!"

They began running down the corridor with Aran flying beside them, urging them to move faster. Penfield had to stop and leaned over to catch his breath.

"Are you alright?"

"Yes, but go on ahead, I'll catch up."

"Fine. Let's go," Aran said.

Something in that response, in the lack of concern for Penfield, jarred Joss.

"Wait. Do you know who he is?"

"What are you talking about? Of course. Penfield."

"What's my name?"

"We're wasting time," Aran shouted. "Nadara is in danger."

Joss knew. "You're glamoured. Aran is one of the few Silth who's distinctive without his. Drop the glamour."

A group of Silth guards came flying around the corner the three had just turned. They fired at Aran.

"I don't have time for this." He flew to Joss, putting one hand on her and the other on Penfield.

She felt the world go out of focus with a twisting feeling inside, and suddenly, she and Penfield stood in the jungle, a now unglamoured Casius holding up his hands ready to fire a bolt.

"Well, that didn't work the way I'd hoped," he said.

Joss looked around, taking in the Silth colony hanging from the jungle's trees. Several Silth rushed forward.

"What do you want us to do with them?" one asked Casius. "They're too big for any of the buildings."

"I don't care. They're bait. Tie them to a tree in the commons."

"What if nobody comes?"

"Someone will come. The real question is, will it be Aran or someone he cares about? I don't care about the rest of them, but I want Aran." Casius paused as he walked away. "Prepare. Just in case he brings a force."

The Newfie guards—Joss assumed this was a Newfie colony— led them to a large tree forming part of the commons' edge. The guard told them to sit. Joss quickly checked the area for snakes and soldier ants before helping Penfield sink to the ground, his back against the tree base. Then she began the laborious process of doing the same.

One Newfie told her to hurry, and she snapped, "Look, as you might be able to tell if you had your head anywhere except up your butt, I'm pregnant. It takes a few moments for pregnant hostages to sit, okay?"

When she finally made it to the ground, the group of Silth lashed them to the tree.

After the Newfies had left, Joss asked a pale Penfield, "Are you alright?"

"I'm fine," he said, though Joss noticed his hand was shaking as he pawed at the rope holding them to the tree. "Where are we? And what about you, are you ok? I should've been the one helping you sit."

"Unnecessary. I'm in that healthy stage of pregnancy where nature gives you lots of energy, to make up for having to maneuver with a watermelon strapped to your stomach."

She assessed the trees and the structures they held. "If I had to guess, this is in Costa Rica, near where I worked. Where Casius gathered the Newfies before... well, before he *died*. I'm still not clear on why he isn't dead." She continued staring at the jungle. "But frankly, one jungle looks kind of like the next to me." Joss squirmed, trying to find a comfortable position on the hard ground with the bark of the tree digging into her back.

"Are we in danger?"

"I don't think so right now since we're hostages. But if Casius is working with Thest, he has no reason to keep us alive after he's gotten what he wants. I'm sure the Silth will report that Casius took us and someone will come to get us. I just hope it doesn't take them long to figure out where this is." Then she remembered she was wearing two trackers, one provided by Homeland and the other by the Silth. "I'm sure they'll find us quickly."

Penfield looked toward the edge of the rain forest.

Joss followed his gaze and noticed how quickly the jungle turned to darkness once away from the clearing. Howler monkeys growled in the distance.

"Not what I meant."

"Those guys would only be a danger if you were wearing a hat covered in ficus fruit. But keep an eye out for ants. And spiders. Oh, and snakes."

"Thanks, very helpful."

# CHAPTER FIVE

## *Scene 1*

**CASIUS (SILTH)**

The last thing he'd wanted was Humans. Penfield was important, and there were surely people who cared about his return. He'd seen Penfield in some online responses to his broadcast exposing the WSC. But he wasn't sure whether Aran would care about him or whether Aran even knew the female Human. As Casius recalled it, his brother didn't particularly like Humans. Ironic perhaps, as now he was trying to save them and had exposed the entire world of the Silth to do so.

Despite everything, Casius still had trouble breaking the taboo on talking with Humans. While it had been hard enough to overcome with Tobias, it was harder still with these. But there was something more. He paused his pacing in the room the colony had given him. It was something akin to how you look away when there is an accident about to happen, and there's nothing you can do about it. Humans were all going to die. Thest would see to that. Faelen was going to die.

Casius still had some hope Thest would spare the Silth. Perhaps appeased by Aran's death and execution of a few of those who'd killed his wife, Thest would not hunt down all the Silth. For this reason, and for Casius's personal ones, Aran had to die. But he had to find him, to kill him. He couldn't even catch Nadara to lure Aran here. He swept the water pitcher off the table, smashing it against the wall.

He would wait to see if anyone came for the Humans by morning. Other Humans wouldn't come, as they wouldn't think to look at this colony, but Aran would—the whole reason Casius was here. If no one showed by morning, they'd smear the Humans with fruit and release them near the herd of white-lipped skunk pigs that had congregated here when it was part of the refuge. There'd be nothing left of the hostages by evening. In the meantime, he needed to set the trap, just in case. He flew from the balcony to find the colony leaders he wanted to enlist for help. He figured he had until nightfall to set things up.

If someone was going to come, it was then.

That night, he was in the tree above the hostages. He'd arrived quietly and was sure they were unaware of his presence, just as they were clueless about the ten Newfies in the surrounding trees and balconies of houses. The Newfies dressed in black with no metal to reflect the moon.

All had the bolt, the shield, and the blip. The hostages were quiet. Just before dark, they had led the hostages into the edge of the jungle to relieve themselves. They gave them some water and some nuts and fruit and then lashed back to the tree. The Newfies attached little bells to the hostages' bindings and these tinkled quietly in the warm, moonless night.

The night wore on, and in the early hours of morning, long after the sleeping hostages had stopped moving enough to generate much noise, the little bells suddenly tinkled. Casius was instantly awake and blipped down to the tree base, afraid the rescuers would loosen the bindings and transport away with the hostages. He flipped on the bright penlight he carried.

In the bright circle of its light was a single Silth figure sawing at the bindings.

They dropped away just as Casius arrived. He caught his breath as he saw the shaman robes and the hather colors he and Aran shared. But the face that turned toward him was older. Storng! Casius raised his hand to shoot a stunning bolt as the waiting Newfies appeared all around them, but Storng was no longer there. There'd been no flicker of transport—he'd simply become invisible in the night. Casius fired a bolt. Tree bark smoldered where it hit. Still no Storng.

"Keep the circle tight," Casius cried out. "He's still here. You two, go hold on to the prisoners. If they move or he tries to transport them, kill them."

He raised his shield just as the bolt came down from the tree. Several of the Newfies returned fire to the general area of its origin. "Storng, you don't need to fight!" he said. "I'll be glad to trade them for you." Another bolt hitting his shield from higher in the tree was his answer.

Casius called to one of the Newfies. "Raise your shield for me!"

She did, enclosing both of them within it. He lifted his arms and shouted "Reveal." A bright light emanated from his hands and shone up into the trees. In it they saw Storng, his glamour stripped away by the magic light. Casius was pleased. This was his first effort at this spell.

Storng put up his shield as the Newfies fired at him.

He flew from the tree into the surrounding forest and out of the light. They followed the glow of his shield for a moment, but then he dropped it. Casius cast the light like a spotlight around the rain forest, but it didn't penetrate the dense trees and vines.

"There!" A Newfie pointed to a different part of the jungle canopy. Something bright was emerging from the trees, but rather than Storng, it was a giant, grinning cat face. It spoke with Storng's voice, "How fine you look when dressed in rage."

The Newfies fired at the glowing image, but it just smiled.

"Casius, why are you working for the Trow? You've seen what they really are. They are not divine." Bolts smashed through the projection into the surrounding trees.

But Casius ignored all this and tried to sense where Storng was.

*Ahh, there you are. In a completely different direction, trying to draw us the wrong way with your silly games.*

After telling the two Newfies guarding the Humans to keep firing into the trees, he took the others into the forest toward where Storng was hiding. They flew quietly between the trees. Casius signaled to them to slow and circle the tree where he knew Storng was hiding. He waited until they were in place and blasted the tree with the magic light.

Hundreds of bats immediately burst from the tree, flying in every direction. The Newfies fired randomly into the storm of wings. Storng had apparently slipped into the center of a resting bat colony, and by the time they cleared, he was gone. Casius stood still and searched for him, probing the surrounding jungle. He wasn't there. And then he realized his mistake.

"Back to the Humans!" He and the others transported back to the colony square, but the Humans were gone. The Newfie guards lay on the ground, still breathing. The projection was not the bait to lure them away, Storng was. Someone had been with him and freed the

Humans while Casius chased Storng through the trees.

The jungle seemed restless around them. Casius listened to the yowl of a cougar not far away, and the sound of monkeys moving through the canopy far later than they should have been. The Newfies slunk around as though afraid he would burst into flames at any moment. But he didn't really care about the Humans or even Storng.

He paced beneath the tree where the Human's scent still lingered. He wanted Aran. He slowed his breathing, and his mind was on to the next idea for finding him.

# Scene 2

THEST (TROW)

Thest attacked the combined UN and Paerrie force around Angkor Wat in the early morning hours, well before dawn. Human armies expected any attack to come at dawn, when there was enough light to see, but the defending camp was most likely changing the guards, breaking camp, or eating, all while half asleep. The attackers might use the cover of night to get in place and might even use the rising sun to blind the defenders. But the Trow saw fine in the Earth's starlit darkness, and because of their power to transport, they needed little time or cover to take their positions.

Thest preferred to attack in the middle of the night when natural biological rhythms rendered the Humans most vulnerable. He did not have many of his warriors on this side of the portal yet, so his attack would be more of a harrying action, a guerrilla assault. Still, his warriors, well rested, would fire their bolts to exhaustion and carried an array of conventional arms to continue the fight when they ran low on magic.

They began transporting into the fields around the portal at Ta Prohm. This was inside the security fence, but outside the immense structure the Humans had constructed. They tried to take out all the sentries within a line of sight at once so no one would raise the alarm. After eliminating the tower guards whose lights swept across the open areas, they left Trow to continue the sweeps so none would notice. But the alarm came faster than Thest expected. The Humans must have put monitors on the guards, so their deaths triggered an alarm. No matter. Paerries immediately appeared and attacked the towers, but the Trow destroyed the tower weapons and disappeared. Humans and Paerries poured out of their tents around the temple.

Thest had known King Jayavarman VII, who had built the temple on top of the long-used portal. The portal was one of many, and the temple did not interfere with its operation. The King sensed the power of the place. In the almost nine hundred years since its construction, the strangler fig trees had drawn on the place's power to create their own form of a temple.

Thest kept his force on the edge, making the defenders come to him. His Trow warriors would appear in clusters of eight, and half would erect their shields, while the other half fired their bolts and then ducked behind the shields. Within moments, Thest adjusted as he realized the Paerries were attacking from above. He added two more Trow to each cluster, and the new members used the same tactic to block attacks from above.

The effect was devastating. None of the fire from Paerries or Humans was reaching them.

When Humans tried to wield larger weapons, other Trow intercepted them and took them. Mostly, they could not determine how to use these, so they destroyed them. But some, like the big machine guns, they would turn on the Humans and Paerries until the ammunition ran out.

The Paerrie put up their shields, but the heavy fire was exhausting them, and they couldn't fire while their shields were erect. The Humans simply died in large numbers. Thest saw some Humans trying to establish a new perimeter line closer to the building around the temple.

His warriors transported behind that line and immediately disrupted its formation.

Then, right on time, Trow began emerging from the gigantic building. In seconds, they overwhelmed the line the Humans had been trying to establish. At first, they emerged by the dozen, but then by the hundreds. They spread out, wiping away any defenders standing in front of them. But something was wrong. *Why are they walking, running, and flying—but not transporting?*

Thest watched Humans shoot down one flying warrior when he could have transported himself from harm. Thest blipped closer to the action, surrounding himself with a shield. One of the newly arrived lieutenants came forward, also shielded. Behind him, Thest watched as the Trow coming out of the building fell to a trickle. It only appeared that about half of his force had arrived.

"What is going on?" Thest nodded toward the building behind them.

"It was a trap. When our forces began arriving, a dust fell from the ceiling. When it touches you, you can no longer transport. There were guns and Paerries all around the portal. They mowed down about one third of the force before they had time to raise their shields. It took several minutes before enough were through and alive to overpower the guns and the Paerries."

Thest knew immediately what it was—an ancient and well-known method of stopping the magical power of transport, achieved with a handful of dirt. The Humans had created a device to turn it into dust and cover a room with it. *Clever monkeys!*

"Send someone back through and stop the group going through

the Irish portal. It will have the same trap. Then organize the force and clean out the Humans and Paerries around this area. Use the warriors who can still transport to remove the tanks and heavy weapons. Begin treatment of the ones who touched the dust. It will take three days before they can transport again."

The officer spun and rushed away to execute the string of commands.

Losing so many warriors was unfortunate, and they would have to be ready for similar traps. But they were through and would soon control this portal. Thest needed at least three days to train these troops fully in the magic they had in this world. He also needed them to train with the Human weapons they had captured. He would keep a few of the Humans alive for training. Maybe another five days. Two more days to rest.

In this time, he would also remove the Humans from around the Irish portal so his troops would arrive there unharmed. He could divert them here, but he wanted to control both portals. He needed to get the rest of his troops into the world by tomorrow to keep them close to the same schedule for those already here.

*One and a half weeks, then. We begin the attack in earnest in one and a half weeks.*

He also had other missions for them. He sent a group to attack the Sohi and other groups to probe the leadership centers around the world. His spies had located each of them. His goal was to destroy them within a few days of the beginning of a proper engagement. He was confident he would break the back of humanity in two weeks. It might take one week beyond to end the Paerries.

Thest had quickly realized a miscalculation regarding the

Paerries. They had not had transport abilities when he'd fought them before. Now, with the ability to disappear instantly and reappear some place far away, the Paerries were much harder to pin down and exterminate, another unpleasant gift from Faelen.

He remembered Faelen telling him he had changed the world, right before Thest shot him. Thest knew what he meant now, though he still did not know how Faelen had eluded death.

A mistake not to be repeated.

Thest wandered through the mop-up operation. Dead Silth and Humans lay everywhere. Very few Trow. While his losses had been heavy in the trap, the Trow had controlled the battlefield.

Thest looked up when he heard a shrill scream, and twenty jets appeared over the horizon. They swooped down in five quick waves of four planes each and dropped their bombs. The ground shook as though it would come loose from the Earth, and everything burst into flames. A few Trow warriors had not gotten their shields up in time and writhed in pain in the flames, but most were safe in the bubble of their shields. Waves of helicopters came over the trees, firing missiles and bullets that took huge clumps out of the ground. Some struck with enough force to send the shield bubbles rolling across the ground. Tanks appeared at the edge of the moat south of Ta Prohm and lobbed shells into the temple grounds.

In seconds, the Trow that could transport had done so into the cockpits of the planes and the helicopters and killed the occupants, transporting out of the machines as they dropped to the ground. After that, they took out the tanks.

Again came the screaming from the sky as shells rained down on the site from long-range artillery. From the way they avoided the portal, it appeared the Humans knew it would be catastrophic to destroy it. Fire roared and debris rained upon them, but the shields protected the Trow, and soon, the artillery stopped as the Trow determined where the guns were and transported in amongst the gunners, killing them all.

Finally, it was quiet.

Thest's ears still rang from the bombardment, and his hearing had not returned enough for him to hear the crackling of the surrounding fires. He looked around at the Trow digging out from the debris, no other living things anywhere within sight or sound. He walked into the building the Humans had constructed around the portal, now cleared of dust. He watched as wave after wave of Trow warriors came through the portal and immediately transported away to their hidden base.

He would leave the Trow who could not transport here, together with a squad which could. The rest would begin their training.

His advance spies had told him that after the planes, helicopters, tanks, and artillery would eventually come gases or enhanced radiation tactical nuclear warheads. Both were designed to kill the Trow but not damage the portal.

His warriors could modulate their shields to deal with the gas and the initial radiation. His problem was that his troops would be vulnerable to ground assault because they would have to keep their shields raised. But if there was still radiation when the ground assault began, it meant they would come in protective suits, which his troops who could still transport would quickly take from them.

It was not a perfect plan. He would adjust it over the next few days, but one of his favorite Human General quotations was, "A good plan violently executed right now is far better than a perfect plan executed next week."

He eyed the pile of Human and Paerrie bodies and the ten living Humans standing numb nearby. Then he called one of his lieutenants over and gave him his orders. The seasoned veteran swallowed hard and pinched his lips closed as though locking in his tongue.

"Afterward, we will allow a few of the living to escape, they will spread the stories, and our enemies will stampede in fear before us. This will cause them to make mistakes."

The warrior did not meet Thest's eyes, but nodded and trudged away.

As visions of Xafar's old throne room rose in Thest's mind, he kicked a Human radio aside. His goal was not to have the Humans or the Silth live in terror. It was to destroy them all quickly and efficiently, and this was a means to that end.

# Scene 3

THEST (TROW)

The buildings of Angkor Wat had withstood centuries of Human wars, many commemorated on the walls around the temple. During this last day, the Human artillery obliterated most of those walls. Thest sat in one of the Temple libraries, an outbuilding still standing. While the shelling had ceased for now, it would start again as soon as the Humans moved new weapons and personnel into position. Every so often, a drone passed over the field, firing missiles at them, and a soldier would fly up and blast it from the sky. The only weapons causing them any damage were the periodic and powerful long-range missiles, fired from too far away to locate and coming in too fast to disrupt.

He was receiving reports from messengers sent from the various field operations. The first was disappointing. When the squadron arrived at the Sohi enclave, it was deserted with no evidence of where they had gone. But as he thought about it, Thest was not worried. There was no way Faelen would stay out of this fight. He would appear, and Thest would kill him.

Another messenger arrived to update him on the attacks on the Chinese, European, Indian, and American leadership centers. These were mere probes, not expected to be successful but designed so the Paerries and Humans would show their defenses. All the attacks had begun in the same way, with the Trow raining down the body parts of Humans and Paerries on the centers.

They then probed the defenses. Few of the parties had received significant injuries in the exploration. In several cases, the probes had inflicted more damage than Thest had expected. But the group sent to Washington was almost completely wiped out by Storng, Merit, and something called the *Steamtiki* according to the Paerrie they had captured.

Thest remembered Storng well, thinking of him as the precipitator of all of this. If he had not taught prohibited magic to Aran and prior students, perhaps Thest would have allowed the Paerries to survive the extermination of the Humans.

He also remembered Merit. She was an intelligent warrior from a primitive people, out of place in an actual war. She had been effective against him only because Xafar had forced him to hold back. He was not holding back this time. Also, Faelen had helped her. But this Steamtiki group was worrisome.

While they might fight among themselves, the Paerries had always been defensive fighters when it came to the Trow, like a dog defending itself from aggression, slinking away when it can.

The Steamtiki were different, mercenaries who stalked their prey. This would be a problem if the attitude spread among the Paerries. *But then there will not be time for it to become a problem because they will all be gone within a month.*

The strategy used in the US leadership center had been like the one he had seen at the portal. A dome covered the primary members of the leadership, and if any Trow transported in, dust automatically released, and the warriors lost the ability to transport again. Inside the dome were only armed Humans. Outside the dome, the Paerries fought his warriors.

They had better communication than before, and if they ran out of magical energy, they defaulted to Human weapons. Of course, now they fought with bolt, shield, and what they called the *blip,* but otherwise they were still just Paerries, harassing his warriors more than engaging them. Thest paused. He knew he needed to be careful about his assumptions.

*In truth, the Paerries have already gotten better at tactics using the Trow weapons than my new warriors who have never been in this world before and are still learning its magic.*

An aide had moved a chair into the library where Thest awaited the messengers. The library was barely *inside,* as it had no doors in the doorways or windows in the sills. It provided shade and the big stone pillars and thick walls would absorb the heat all day long, keeping the inside much cooler than its surroundings. Mostly, the roof of the place kept the rain off him, good since it seemed to rain all the time. The moats woven through the complex had been full before the shelling, but broke into large ponds in the barrage. The sound of the raindrops on the ponds was soothing, and Thest dozed as he waited for the next messenger.

When the messenger came, she brought more good news. The squad he had sent to clear the entrance to the Irish portal had been successful, removing both the Humans and Silth guarding the portal and the heavy weapons located nearby. They dismantled the *dust room* so arriving warriors would not lose the ability to transport. Now, warriors were pouring through that portal and dispersing as instructed. All was going well, and Thest was pleased.

Reports came back that the troops he had sent into the large nests of Humans in the cities had also been successful in causing havoc. They had killed those they easily found, but more importantly, they destroyed the power stations, water treatment facilities, and communication centers and their towers. They blasted holes in interstates and runways.

As an experiment, they had released biological agents created in the Land in two cities. The results were impressive. Thest was not ready to eliminate the Humans yet, but he wanted to disrupt their ability to respond to attack. He needed some time for his troops to train, desiring the Humans distracted during that time.

But when he tried similar attacks on the Silth settlements, the Silth simply transported away as soon as the Trow appeared. The one exception had been a Silth city in Brazil, where the Silth had rushed out to welcome the Trow warriors. The Trow slaughtered them to the last. Otherwise, the raids on the Silth were so unproductive Thest moved these teams to attacking the Human cities.

His teams would create chaos in the fifty largest Human cities and then stop until the final push. He was not too worried about the Silth. There were far fewer of them than the Humans.

Thest's two best teams had been searching for more weapons. The advance spies had identified the armories and secret storage locations of major Human weapons, and the two harvesting teams were quickly moving through them, bringing all manner of armaments to the Trow encampment. Two-thirds of these were indecipherable to the Trow, so they kidnapped Humans to show them how to operate the weapons.

Night was falling when the last messenger arrived. The frog chorus, as the different species vied to get their voices heard, seemed out of place in the day's violence. The library was lit with bioluminescent lanterns, and Thest was by himself, his advisors having just finished a meeting with him. Many were experiencing difficulties venturing out into the world after being held so long in Xafar's palace. When every sound made them jump, meeting Thest in a zone still periodically being shelled was traumatic

Finished with the meeting, they were happy to transport to the staging camp where the bulk of Thest's warriors were resting and training with their magic and Human weapons. The Trow had only brought a few of their biomorphic weapons onto the Earth because these needed careful feeding and handling. It was easier to steal new weapons.

Later, Thest was not sure whether he had heard the high-pitched sound of the air parting or felt the change in air pressure from the projectile's rapid approach. Whatever it was, something caused him to raise his shield just before the missile stuck the building. He regained consciousness about two hundred feet from where he had been sitting. He shoved pieces of the former building off his legs and used the back of his hand to shovel off the parts of his messenger that had fallen on him when he closed his shield.

# CHAPTER SIX

## *Scene 1*

TINY (HUMAN)

Tiny always said he never wanted his name in a newspaper article that began with the word *apparently*. His friend Bill Browning had taught him that. *Apparently, she believed the ice would hold her. Apparently, he leaped on top of the buffalo, hoping to ride it.*

Tonight, however, he felt relieved to tell Fetu, "Apparently, we were the last private flight out of Honolulu before the Trow destroyed the airport."

Fetu nodded, his expression unchanged. He was watching the fourth in the Independence Day line of movies to get some ideas for fighting aliens.

The luxurious interior of the Bombardier Global 8000 contained everything Tiny needed to stay in touch with Joss and monitor events globally. Besides the captain, co-pilot, the two crew, Fetu, Shadow, and Tiny, they'd taken on nine passengers. Even though the full load reduced their range some, everyone left anything bigger than a small carry-on at the airport, so they still could make it to Richmond in one jump.

A couple of the passengers slept, but most were talking or staring out the oversized windows, watching for any sign of the Trow. They'd all seen the reports the Trow were crashing airliners around the world. Maybe a small private plane would be too insignificant. Maybe.

They flew at 40,000 feet. When they were over the ocean, they'd flown lower, but as they reached the mainland and the smoke rising from the Trow's fires began, they moved higher. The clouds now obscured the destruction below. They were half an hour away from the Richmond airport, at last report still undamaged by the Trow, too small for them to have targeted yet.

When Tiny had spoken earlier with Joss on a video call, they had tried to keep it light. Both had been watching the news, seeing the war had started, and the Trow were attacking Human and Silth cities around the world. They exchanged *I love you's* at the end of the call, with the implied footnote, *in case I never see you again....*

Although Joss had returned to Washington South after her rescue from Casius, Tiny wanted her to leave immediately. But the Trow had destroyed the hyper-loop and the Amtrak rail line. Interstate 95, too, lay full of holes and the wreckage of trucks. With traffic stalled in the surrounding countryside as people tried to escape the cities, there was no way she could safely return to UNWID yet, so she had to stay inside the bullseye.

Joss wanted Tiny safely out of the sky and with her. He wished he hadn't left on this trip but even without the war, it felt as though it was his last chance to study volcanoes. Once, he'd thought he would be one of the volcanologists who would lead a life of adventure—who wrote books and joined the Explorers' Club. He still held that lifestyle in awe, but knew it wasn't for him.

He wasn't sure what he wanted, but whatever it was, it didn't live on the edge of a volcano.

As they dropped below the cloud cover for the approach, they saw smoke rising from the airport, multiple fires burning across the horizon. Two figures flying above the field began moving toward them, and a large jet dropped from the clouds next to them seconds later.

The Trow fired on it, causing it to burst into flames and plummet downwards.

Tiny's plane pulled back up into the clouds.

Tiny staggered to the cockpit, working against the plane's ascent, and a steward quickly dashed out of the galley before Tiny filled the small hallway. The ceiling was high on this plane, so Tiny barely had to crouch.

"Bad news," the pilot said as Tiny stuck his head into the cockpit.

"I saw."

"We wanted back in the clouds so maybe nothing would come after us, but there are a lot of planes up here. Everyone's stuck in the air and circling. Trying to figure out where they can go to land."

"Ok, coordinates in," the co-pilot said. "We're going to a small local landing strip. Unfortunately, no one's answering the phones there, so we're hoping it's still intact."

"It's got a long enough runway?"

The pilot and co-pilot exchanged glances before the latter answered, "We'll need every foot."

"Crashing a sixty-million-dollar plane off the end of a runway wouldn't look good on my resume," the pilot said as he began the descent again.

"Maybe not our biggest problem." The co-pilot turned back to Tiny. "Get everyone buckled up back there." He picked up the mike to explain crash landing procedures to the passengers.

Tiny helped the crew get everyone awake and in position. He

buckled Shadow into his special dog seat. As he sat, he chuckled at the instruction to put his head in his lap. He crossed his arms on the table and lay his head there, listening to the wheels go down and the engines strain as the pilot slowed the plane as much as possible without stalling.

It wafted up and down before the wheels hit the ground hard and bounced. The contents of the cabin slammed forward with the hard application of the brakes, and someone cried out. As the plane shuddered like an angry animal trying to escape, Tiny waited for them to lurch off the end of the runway. But they came to a smooth stop, and the pilot turned the plane.

Tiny looked out the window as the grass and runway's end passed beneath the plane's wing on their turn. Nervous chatter filled the aircraft as they taxied past several gray hangars. Fetu began packing up, wireless earbuds still in place.

Tiny tried his phone but got no signal. The plane stopped in front of the small airport's office, and he rushed down the plane's steps and into it.

"Hello?"

The office was unlocked, but there was no sign anyone was there. He stuck his head into a few rooms but found nothing. He picked up a landline phone and listened. No dial tone. Because plenty of light came through the windows, there was no need for overhead lights, but he flipped a switch anyway to see if they were working. Nothing there either. He walked through the office to the parking lot, empty of cars. The road was close by, so he hurried over to it and looked each way. No cars. No signs of life.

The parking lots of the surrounding industrial and warehouse buildings were also empty.

Because of their official UN status, Tiny had a walkie-talkie with a dedicated band for their team.

"This is Tiny. Any UNWID team out there?" He repeated the call several times before a crackly voice answered.

"This is Maria Luis. Where are you?"

"Hanover County Municipal Airport," Tiny read from the parking lot sign. "Not a soul around, and no way for us to get to Washington South."

"Yeah, we were waiting for you at the Richmond Airport. To take you to Washington South. Hold on, I've got to look at a map to see how to reach you. GPS isn't working."

Tiny heard the stress in her voice and remembered the smoke they'd seen rising from the airport. "Are you ok?" No answer but plenty of static. "Maria Luis? You ok?"

"No. Because Tonho's an idiot!"

"Hey!" Tiny heard Tonho say in the background.

"Looks like we're about twenty miles from you. We'll be there as fast as we can. You're right next to I-95, but it's bumper-to-bumper for the stretches between the holes the Trow have made. Just hang on, be there soon."

Tiny stepped back into the building where Fetu was sitting in the waiting room.

"TV, radio, and internet are all out," he said.

"Maria Luis is on her way. Probably half an hour to forty-five minutes away."

Tiny and Fetu walked the few blocks to 95 with the crew and the other passengers, some of whom wanted to head north and some south. Traffic inched along in each direction. To the north, they saw several trucks overturned on the interstate with cars weaving between them and crawling up grassy shoulders to get around.

After the others caught rides, the pair walked back to the airport and raided their plane for food.

When Maria Luis finally pulled up in UNWID's electric Toyota Highlander—it had taken closer to an hour and a half—they were standing in the parking lot with a bag of food to share with their rescuers. Tiny climbed into the front passenger's seat and Fetu pulled himself into one of the middle captain's chairs. They looked at Tonho lying on the back bench seat as he raised a weak hand in greeting. He was holding his shirt, balled up against his eye and the side of his face. Blood had soaked it red.

Maria Luis shoved a map into Tiny's hands. "You're responsible for getting us to Washington South. It's only 25 miles away, but we can't use 95."

"Yeah, we saw. We walked up there. Traffic was barely moving."

"If it was moving at all, it was doing better than most parts. The Trow just flew down it blowing up trucks, and if they didn't find any, destroying overpasses and bridges. If they didn't find those, they just blew enormous holes in the road."

"It looks like we just cut over to Highway 1 and it's a straight shot north."

Fetu looked over his shoulder. "But all the interstate traffic is going to be dropping over to 1 every time they get blocked. If we go up 301 and double back on 207, it's farther, but I bet faster."

Tiny nodded and pointed to the right. "Tonho, what happened?"

Maria Luis answered for him. "He's in a lot of pain. We were waiting for you in the small aviation parking lot when the Trow attacked the airport. There were only a couple, but they were pretty efficient. We saw them blowing up planes, empty and... full. We watched the tower explode, and there were other explosions as well. I guess they were fuel trucks and storage. They blasted a line of holes in each runway. When Tonho saw that, he ran inside to see if the counter could reach you to tell you to divert. I tried to stop him, but just as he entered the building, the Trow got around to it. Caught a face full of glass, including his eye. He needs a doctor. I've called the emergency center at Washington South, and they're ready for him."

She gunned the motor and sped through the nearly empty roads. When they reached 301, the bumper-to-bumper traffic brought them to a full stop. Maria Luis pounded the steering wheel in frustration. Fetu checked on Tonho, who had stopped answering questions.

"Guys, he's not doing well. We need to hurry."

Maria Luis growled and shook her fists at the traffic.

Tiny checked the map for nearby hospitals or emergency centers but found none closer than Washington South. They inched down the road so slowly that Tiny watched a young woman dressed in fatigues exit her house and walk up to the road even with them, a backpack with a duffle bag slung over her shoulder.

Tiny rolled down his window. "Need a lift? Where you heading?"

"Just over to AP Hill." She frowned at the long line of slow-moving traffic. "But it might be quicker to walk." She looked past Tiny to survey the other occupants of the car. "Sure, I'd love a ride." She opened the passenger door, nodded to Fetu and got in, tucking her pack and duffle around her. As she climbed into the captain's chair, she glanced at Tonho.

"What's wrong with him?"

"He was next to the windows when the Trow blew up the Richmond Airport. I'm Maria Luis, this is Tiny, and that's Fetu. That's Tonho in the back."

"I'm Bian. Bian Dang."

"Unusual name."

"Actually, pretty common in Vietnam. That's where my folks are from." Bian rummaged through her duffle bag, ultimately pulling out a small box that reminded Tiny of a tackle box. She undid her seat belt and spun the chair around so she was facing Tonho. "I just finished my medic training out in San Antonio, Tonho. Do you mind if I look at your face?" When he didn't reply, she reached over and gently pulled the blood-soaked shirt off his face.

"He's out. Is it okay if I turn his face so I can see?"

"Go ahead," Maria Luis said.

Bian took a closer look. "You can't see it from where you are, but the seat is soaked. He's lost a lot of blood." She took his pulse and broke open a big bandage and some tape. "Looks like he's in shock. Pulse is weak." She removed a syringe, a couple of small vials, and a stitch kit.

She carefully worked on Tonho's cheek cut, covering it with what Tiny assumed was an antibiotic, closing it with steri-strips, and taping on the bandage. She asked Maria Luis if he was allergic to any drugs before giving him two shots. Fetu, who'd watched plenty of triage ringside in his mixed martial arts career, narrated for them until she got to the shots.

"All I can do is make him more comfortable. One shot is an antibiotic, the other morphine. I can't do anything for the eye. He needs to be in a hospital fast."

The traffic was now moving at a steady, moderate speed. Bian said she'd been on leave, and her CO had called her back to AP Hill that morning. When she heard their proposed route, she said, "You can drop me in Bowling Green. Short hop to the south gate from there."

"I'm surprised they let you leave with everything going on."

"Yeah. They weren't really sure about it, but my mom got sick, and I'm her only family in the area. They let me go take care of her until my aunt arrived. That's why I have my go bag—so I could come straight back. They were supposed to call me back if things got messy, but I think someone forgot. I kept waiting for a call when this started yesterday. This morning, my aunt got here—she drove down from New York—and I packed up to head in. She's super glad to be out of New York. Lots of casualties there. Also, glad she didn't take a train or a plane. In the last twelve hours, they've destroyed the railroads and the airports around the world. She had to get off of the interstate though when she heard on the radio they were attacking that."

"Is there any pattern to where they are striking?" Tiny asked.

"The last I heard, before my internet went down about five hours ago, was they were attacking any gatherings of people they found, mostly in large metro areas. They went after the transportation networks, and the infrastructure of many cities—the water, power, communications, sewer, and internet. I also heard they'd started attacking the armories."

After a moment, Maria Luis asked, "Does A. P. Hill have armories?"

"Oh yeah. Regular ones plus tanks and artillery and helicopters. It's where all the armed forces come to practice with the big toys."

"Maybe that's why so much of the traffic seems to have disappeared," Tiny said. "No one else is driving toward a lightning rod."

As though in response to the comment, they heard the distant rumble of titanic explosions as they drew even with the sign for the Bowling Green town limits. They pulled up to the intersection where they needed to head south and Bian needed to head north. They saw black smoke roiling into the skies above the trees to the north.

Tiny looked at the dark sky. "You sure about this?"

"It's what I signed up for."

"You need for us to take you closer?"

"Nah." Bian dragged her backpack and duffle from the SUV. "Gonna be a beautiful day."

They headed south again for the couple of miles that separated them from their destination. Fetu and Tiny scanned the skies for Trow.

"There!" Fetu shouted from the back and pointed.

A helicopter was speeding over the treetops, followed by two Trow. They flew with one arm down by their sides and the other extended toward the aircraft. The helicopter dodged and juked to throw off the shots, though smoke was already coming from its tail. Then one warrior disappeared, and the helicopter stopped, lurched to the left, and dropped toward the ground.

The Trow reappeared next to the other, hanging in the air to watch the doomed craft plummet, and then flickering and disappearing just as it exploded on the road in front of the SUV. Maria Luis whipped it onto the shoulder and drove blindly through the smoke of the wreckage as pieces of metal pinged on the roof and sides of the car. One cracked the windshield. Tonho moaned as they bumped over bits of debris. She gunned the vehicle as they cleared the other side.

Moments later, they saw the mid-rise buildings of Washington South clustered around the train station and the Silth swarming above it like angry bees defending their hive. They headed for the hospital, and Tiny let Joss know they'd made it.

They pulled up at the hospital emergency room, and Tiny rushed in. It took him a few moments to flag someone down, who breathlessly explained that they were preparing for a flood of wounded from the battle underway at the military base. Though he rarely did so, he pulled out his UN credentials and demanded immediate attention for Tonho. The Triage Manager directed a gurney out to the car, and the orderlies loaded an unconscious Tonho onto it. Maria Luis followed them back into the hospital, waving goodbye to Tiny and Fetu over her shoulder.

As they pulled away from the hospital, a voice on the walkie talkie said, "Fort AP Hill has stopped answering. We think it has fallen."

Tiny hoped that Bien was all right.

# *Scene 2*

CASIUS (SILTH)

Casius slumped in the chair on the balcony high in the trees above the square. Although the current council chair had offered to vacate his former offices here in the old colony, Casius declined and took over this residence instead. The occupants said it honored them to provide it.

At the moment, he had the place to himself. He had a glass of the locally brewed rum on the table beside him, not his first. Though nothing in the Newfie creed forbid it, he rarely drank and was never drunk, preferring to stay in control. He was dreaming of a new religion—outlining it in his mind. Despite the Trow's best efforts, they would not wipe out the Silth. It was too easy for them to blip away from danger. Eventually, Thest would grow tired of chasing the remaining ones. Disheartened and confused, the Silth refugees would need leadership.

That would be the time for Casius to step forward. Did he even need to cloak himself in religion? He might step forward with a powerful vision. The advantage to leading through religion is that even when you have no bread, you can feed your flock with faith. He was sure he could provide an equally filling vision of a Silth-led Earth, shared with the Trow, but run by the Silth. They would hunt down any remaining Humans and help the Trow eliminate them.

Casius heard shouting from the square and looked down, trying to identify the source. A crowd was gathering around a tall, lanky Trow, his dreadlocks pulled back off his shoulders so that his officer insignia was clear. More Silth came into the square. Casius leaned forward, his hands tight on the railing. Why were the Silth coming out to greet him? They should hide in the trees. It was because of Casius, he realized. They were sure the Trow were coming to reward them for supporting him, the Trow champion. Because of the square's design, he heard the excited murmur of the crowd from his balcony. The Trow—Casius supposed from the insignia he was a lieutenant—spoke in soothing tones, saying how much the Trow appreciated their support. He told them of the rewards that awaited them.

Casius thought about screaming "Run!" but he didn't do it. He could transport down behind the Trow and kill him. But he didn't do that either. The Trow was telling the mob that had gathered around him he had a gift for them today. *Run!* Casius screamed in his mind.

The brown mounds appeared throughout the crowd. The Silth clustered around them, speculating on their purpose. Casius was on his feet now, thinking, *Run! Get away from those!*

Simultaneously, the tops of the mounds broke open, and a brown mist covered the crowd. He heard the Trow still calmly explaining over the crowd's screams, "These are spore bombs. When they enter your lungs, they rapidly grow." Silth were lying on the ground, clutching their chests before their ribs burst and a cloud of spores emerged. Unaffected Silth were fleeing the square.

The Trow Lieutenant waited until they were out of sight before continuing, "And one of the amazing things about this gift is that it just keeps giving. About 10% of those infected do not die immediately. They gather with their families and friends, and then they explode, infecting them and continuing the cycle." The Trow looked up directly at Casius. "You are welcome!" He disappeared.

Casius heard the screams echoing in the surrounding jungle. He released his death grip on the balcony rail, wiped the tears from his face, and whispered, "I'm sorry," before flickering and disappearing.

# *Scene 3*

NADARA (SILTH)

*War causes things to rise quicker. Like some kind of yeast causing the perfect loaf of bread to transform quickly from the paste of dough,* Nadara thought as she watched the ceremony.

The fourth wedding or commitment ceremony she had attended in three weeks, this one had one interesting twist. She was here not only as a former member of the Tiki Crew, but also as Jules' plus one. She glanced at Jules sitting next to her, the red of the hather at his temples a pop of color against his black hather and dark skin. For once, his daily clothing of top hat and tails fit in with the surrounding attire.

The Silth music ensemble played an old Australian Silth tune based on the story of Tanton and Galslip. Like most Silth music, it echoed the sound of nature in their daily habitat. This part, where Galslip would become the beach and Tanton the waves, was a favorite for these sorts of ceremonies. The whistles mimicked the gull cries and the drums the lapping waves.

Slatt flew in from the north with slow, deep beats of his dark gray wings. He wheeled and landed in front of the assembled friends, the gadgets attached to the loops of his canvas shirt clicking and tinging as they knocked against one another. He removed his pith helmet, and the wispy red topknot on his red hathered head popped up. Thane, Slatt's significant other, flew in from the south, with a rapid flap, flap, glide cadence of his birth mother. Most Silth fledglings learned to fly before the Silth separated them from their parrot colonies. He touched lightly down next to Slatt, almost a head taller and dressed in a white suit and hat that put Jules to shame.

There was no officiant for Silth weddings other than the audience itself. Thane read his vows, fairly conventional commitments of care and love. *I know Slatt can't speak, so how's this going to work?* Nadara wondered. Slatt gave his innocent smile and handed Thane a piece of paper. Nadara couldn't read it, but she could tell it had writing on it that looked like English. The Silth had no written language, and although they read other languages, without years of study, they couldn't write them. Slatt must have found someone to write this for him.

With a couple of creaks and a soft growl, he urged Thane to read it.

"Thane, I promise to treat you as one of my crew, so I won't kill you or cheat you out of your share. I promise to share adventures with you and squeeze as much out of our shared life as we can. I have a dangerous job in dangerous times, but I promise to try to stay alive so I can wrap you in love for all the rest of our days." Thane's voice broke on the last few words, and he swept Slatt into his embrace as their friends clapped and whistled their approval.

The music began again, and everyone moved toward the reception.

"I love the brevity of Silth ceremonies," Nadara told Jules, looking at a tiny watch she had pulled from her pocket. They were standing in a small garden next to the reception tent. "Have you been to a Human wedding yet? The one I attended yesterday lasted for hours. It was beautiful, with flowers and costumes, and a band and exquisite food at the reception. I'm sure that it cost enough to feed a village for two years." She tucked the watch back into her pocket. "But a Silth wedding finishes in the space of a work break, essentially what I'm on. One side benefit of being able to pop around the world in an instant."

"But it's something like midnight back in Washington," Jules said, not hiding the disappointment in his voice. He leaned closer. "Stay, it's just sleep you'd be missing."

"It's already tomorrow here." She smoothed the red hather on his face. "This whole *date line* thing is very confusing. You know there's a war going on, right?"

"All the more reason. Who knows what tomorrow brings?"

She laughed. "I heard that line in a Human movie the other day."

He kissed her upturned lips. "Wisdom is often repeated."

"So are old pickup lines."

"Stay awhile. We'll enjoy the party. Go have some dinner, and then I'll show you one of my favorite spots nearby." His smooth voice was low and coaxing. "You can still be at work on time tomorrow."

Nadara watched Thane and Slatt working their way through the crowd together. Slatt, whom she knew was a stone-cold, remorseless killer, always stayed within touch distance of Thane, frequently reaching out just to brush his arm or put a hand on his back.

Later, as she and Jules combed the beach looking for the clothes they had dropped from high in the moonlit sky, she thought about the challenge of making love in the air. Getting the rhythm of wing flaps right, timing the gliding falls so that you didn't hit the ground, while simultaneously going through the movements of lovemaking. Turned out she and Jules were great at it.

She smiled to herself as she bent down to pick up a shoe.

# Scene 4

Aran (Silth)

Fortunately, Aran had fought alongside the man's father, perhaps all that stopped General Cogbill from killing Aran for kidnapping him.

Aran had appeared in the air beside Cogbill as he was about to walk into the briefing room, put his hand on his shoulder, and both flickered and disappeared. They reappeared on the beach above the Neirad home with Aran rushing to explain what he was attempting over the General's profanity laced shouts. When Cogbill calmed enough to hear that Aran needed to introduce him to a secret asset, one that promised to help change the course of the fighting, he relented in his oath to have Aran's head on his wall. But as Aran helped him onto the manta ray and blindfolded him, the General reminded him he had a world war to fight and that the meeting he'd just diverted him from was one with the leadership of the world's Human armies.

"Time is our most precious commodity, and we seem to have little of it. I don't have time for games."

"No games. This will just take a moment. I would simply transport in, but they won't allow it. And I have to keep their location secret."

Surrounded by dozens of stingrays, they rode the mantas into the underwater harbor of the Neirads. When Aran removed the blindfold, Cogbill saw the Trow guarding the passageway from the harbor and looked at Aran with raised brows. Krackle flew in and landed beside them.

"Hello, General. G'day, Aran." She eyed Aran's expression. "That's right, isn't it? I'm in the right part of the world?"

"I think *Maeva* may be more appropriate. Or even *Bienvenu*."

"You guys want to do your language lesson some other time?" Cogbill grumbled.

Aran, Cogbill, and Krackle sat on the rocks in the arrival grotto. As the guards stood motionless and small waves lapped at the sand, Aran explained to Cogbill who the Neirad were.

"You think that these former courtesans can help win this war? What happened to your Sohi? They seemed like fighters. I like them."

"First, I don't think that's quite the right word."

"What word?"

"*Courtesans.* It means aristocratic prostitutes. Not the best way to make the introduction to new allies."

"If I get one more freakin' language lesson from you guys—"

"Second, the Sohi are engaged. In a big way. But they will only fight defensive battles. And before you ask, I can't tell you what they're doing yet."

"You and your damn secrets."

"Nothing constrains the Neirads except their inexperience."

"Well, we need help. We're getting our butts kicked. The Trow have already killed thousands of people, torn up the cities, and destroyed infrastructure. They've stolen countless weapons from military bases around the world. We couldn't stop them. We couldn't lay a finger on them. And then they just stopped. Presumably, to regroup and learn how to use our weapons. It's not good."

Cogbill shook his head. "Are you sure that we can trust these

Trow? Trust seems to be your default mode with these guys."

Krackle laughed. "Tell that to the Trow enclave in Tokyo. Oh wait, no one left to tell it to since he killed them all."

Cogbill stared at Aran, who said, "Another day. Today, I'll say that they've earned our trust so far by not killing us when we discovered them, by considering and agreeing to help when they might have just stayed hidden, and by agreeing to allow Krackle to stay here and observe them. She's been here several days. What do you think, Krackle?"

"I like them. A lot. I've seen how they deal with their children. With each other. They are kind and open. They tell me it's a reaction to how they were when they first arrived. They were from the Queen's court, and their primary occupation was gossip and intrigue. It almost tore them apart before they came up with a fresh way. Mostly Tethra's doing. They don't want to go to war. They are thriving here and hesitate to risk it, but they've decided it's the right thing to do. I trust them." She paused and cocked her head slightly as though listening to something. "Other than that Lir. Lir is one sneaky coati."

"I do not know what a coati is, but I assume it is an awesome, magnificent beast, worshiped by Humans and Silth alike," Lir said, walking into the grotto.

"Oh yes, walk into any bar and shout, *I'm a coati,* and you'll get free drinks the rest of the night," Krackle shot back.

As Cogbill scowled, Aran tried to placate him. "Future of the world. Many dying. You remember," he said to Krackle.

Krackle said, "I asked Lir to come here first so that General Cogbill could talk with a real individual before he met with the Council. I've found that it's easier to begin this way.

"Lir, this is General John Cogbill. He leads the Human coalition of armies working with the World Silth Council to stop the attack on Earth. I don't know him from Adam's house cat." She paused and looked at Cogbill, "Did I say that right?" Then she continued without waiting for an answer, "But his father is very famous for defending a Silth enclave from Human attack. So, he comes from good people."

She went on. "General Cogbill, Lir is my friend, and is one of the three council members who lead the Neirads. Lir understands Human affairs, at least as TV and the internet portray them."

Lir bowed deeply, holding out a small package. "It is my great honor to meet you, General Cogbill."

"The honor is mine," he said, taking the package and returning the bow. "I would have some proper gift to return, if I hadn't been kidnapped and brought here with no clue what was happening."

Lir sat on a rock next to them. "Tell me how you think the Neirads—that is who we are—can help you in the battle with Thest?"

"I have no idea." He outlined the attacks so far on the cities and the suffering left behind. He talked of the armories being pillaged, further reducing their defenses, and presumably arming the invading force. He told Lir of the difficulty of defending against the ability of Thest's warriors to pop into the Human planes and tanks, and the failure of the Humans and Silth to shut the portals.

Cogbill talked for several minutes, becoming more dejected sounding as he cataloged the many ways they were losing.

"I know we can help you hide your sensitive weapons," Lir said. "We can go places that Humans would have difficulty reaching. We are very good at hiding. But I don't know what else we can do. My colleagues on the council are wise. Let us sit with them and see what plans we can devise. Also, I do not know whether it will be of any use, but there is a reason we called this place *Magh Meall*."

"I wondered about that," Krackle said.

"Well, that would have to be the one question that wandered through your mind that you did not blurt out." Lir gave an eye roll. "It means *plain of joy,* and for the early Irish was a realm achieved through death or glorious acts. They sometimes thought it was an island to Ireland's west or perhaps a kingdom under the ocean, inhabited by gods, which mortals got to visit. The Trow who arrived by the portal in Ireland tried to create a new portal, hoping it would lead to lands even more beautiful than the Earth. The portal failed in that intent, but connected nearby here, in the Pacific. Most Trow forgot the connection as a failed construction project. But when Xafar rose and killed the Queen, we escaped by using that forgotten passage to come here from Ireland. I don't know if it matters, but it will also take you back to the portal in Ireland."

While Aran didn't react to the information, the plans in his mind grew another dimension. Cogbill had him send word to the General's team that he was safe, merely the subject of a *friendly kidnapping,* and would return that afternoon. They spent the rest of the day with the council, discussing ways the Neirad might help change the war's inevitable outcome.

# CHAPTER SEVEN

## *Scene 1*

THEST (TROW)

A soldier escorted the messenger from the zone into which he had transported. The escort turned around at the door, and in a violation of protocol, the messenger entered the room where Thest sat without invitation. Thest looked up, about to chastise him, but stopped when he got a good look at him. Blood and sweat matted his hair, an eye was black and swollen, and one arm hung limp beside him. Waving him over to his table, Thest motioned him to sit and pushed a large glass of water toward him. Thest drank his wine while the messenger drank and caught his breath.

"Everything was under control. We had routed the Human and Paerrie defenders of the Irish portal at Newgrange and weathered their attacks with planes and other technology. We had removed their dust trap and allowed all your warriors through with no material disruption. As ordered, we sent them on to the staging camp."

Thest had already received this report, so he waited for the rest. Pushing a serving tray of food forward, he tried to be patient while the messenger stuffed a few bites into his mouth, barely chewing them before swallowing. He choked and grabbed some more water before continuing.

"Most of the troops guarding the portal were inside the stone passages or on the roof of the primary Newgrange structure since the Humans were being careful not to harm the stone structure itself with their bombardment. Of course, under protocol, there were guards all around the perimeter as well. Mostly, we were watching for Paerries, because the land is so open there you can see a Human army miles away."

"Get to it." Thest shifted irritably in his chair.

"They arrived all at once, hundreds of them. And they began firing as soon as they appeared."

"Who appeared? Silth?"

"No, Humans. Humans wearing suits that neutralized our bolts. They just came up out of the ground next to the portal. And they fired beams of light similar to our bolts but cutting through rock. They did not penetrate our shields but cut anyone without a shield in half.

"No one had time to react. They incapacitated the entire outside force within moments. The attackers anticipated where our guards would be and took them out as well. The only ones left were the few of us inside. We made ready to make our stand—to fight to the end to guard the portal—but then it was as though a sickness spread amongst us, everyone doubled over clutching their stomachs, writhing, and screaming. They just walked in."

"The Humans walked in and took the portal?"

"No, Trow. Trow took the portal. No one fired a shot. The pain was too great to function. And when we could get a break in the waves of pain to challenge them, they simply swatted us aside."

"Who were they?"

"The Sohi. The Sohi took the portal."

"The Humans wiped out the guarding force and the Sohi

control the Newgrange portal now?"

"No. That is what was so strange. Once they controlled it, they passed through the portal. All of them. They left no guards behind. And all our forces not killed by the Humans were only temporarily sickened. All are fine now."

Thest sat thinking for a moment.

"And then you came straight here? You did not stop to speak with anyone?"

The messenger shook his head. Thest looked around, turned to him, and shot a bolt through his head. Not in anger. Instead, he regretted a good soldier had to die, but he could not allow this story to go any further. He would have to isolate all the warriors who had seen what had happened. He would leave them there guarding the portal, with no contact with the rest of the forces. They would accept that they were being punished for their poor performance.

He stood at the glassless window hole, rubbing the back of his neck, and watching the camp lights through the rain. He thought about his children and realized he would never see them again. Then he thought about Demest, his wife, and her death at the hands of the Paerries. He sucked in a long breath through his clenched teeth and let it out in an extended, lung-emptying whoosh. Finally, he thought of Faelen, who had given them the secrets to Trow magic.

He swept the lamp off the table. The bioluminescence broke apart and splattered the body lying on the floor. He did not care he might never see the Land again. He did not care he would no longer be King. He only wanted to destroy the Humans, the Paerries, and Faelen.

He must not fail. If he returned the Earth to them, he would be a Trow hero. If he failed... Well, if he failed, it was because he was dead.

# Scene 2

Aran (Silth)

*It's hard to find some time for yourself in a war,* Aran thought. *Harder still for those who are responsible for others.* And that was to find time with just yourself.

To find it with another in a similar role...

Tomorrow morning, he and Merit were to meet with the Steamtiki, Storng, Nadara, and perhaps even Krackle and Temkaa here at the Iguazu Falls in Argentina. This was Aran's council. His small group of friends and advisors upon whom he relied, not just for their advice, but because each of them was better at implementing than he was.

He pondered that phrase *responsible for others.* Who was he responsible for?

He hadn't been to a WSC meeting in months. No longer having any formal title, he wasn't officially responsible for anyone. But the Sohi were risking everything because of him. So were the Neirad. Cogbill was taking risks that Aran had set in motion. The Steamtiki had risked their lives many times now because of him.

He felt responsible for everyone. All the Humans, the Silth, and even the Trow.

But tonight was about him, not the world. Finding time alone with Merit was almost impossible, but he'd arranged for her to come this evening, hoping to steal a few hours together before the others arrived.

It was the lull before the storm, and he sensed the hurricane not far away. He would be foolish to waste this time, spending it in frantic motion. Mostly, what could be done had been done. There were a few more arrangements to make tomorrow morning, but win or lose...

The Humans had a saying he'd inquired about: *the die is cast.* It turned out few of them knew where it had come from. *Alea iacta est* had been around at least since the early Greeks and Romans and meant that in this game of chance we call life, the dice have been thrown and we are waiting to see our fate. The point of no return has passed.

He sat in the treetop, the sun setting above the magnificent falls. As far as he could see were steps of waterfalls, crowded by green jungle. It was as if the Earth had declared a council of waterfalls, and they gathered in this remote place to judge the world. The roar deafened, and the churning water ionized the air with a special crispness. There were no Humans. No Trow. No other Silth as best he could see.

They were all hunkered down before the storm.

Merit appeared in the sky above the falls and approached him in the canopy. Despite the spells protecting them from being found by the Trow, they'd worked out how to find one another.

"A surprisingly romantic meeting place, Aran Shaman."

He grinned. "I have no idea what you mean, Dawn Defender. It was simply convenient for a group spread out around the world."

She squatted on the limb next to him. "Gorgeous sunset."

They stayed and watched as the sun set and darkness settled around them. Then they flew lower in the tree, where its big limbs branched out to create a natural platform. Aran spread a blanket, and an oil lamp provided lighting for their dinner of nuts, fruit, and some bread that he had brought. Merit contributed wine, a white fruity blend that she liked, and some lemon tarts that he loved. They talked about everything except the war.

He shared with her why he thought it hadn't worked out with Nadara, but how impressed he was with the work she was doing. She talked about her long years with no one steady in her life, and how she wondered whether that was her nature, avoiding the complications of romance.

"But for the last year," she said, "I've entertained thoughts like I've never had before. What would life be like not having a battle or some kind of confrontation on the immediate horizon? The idea Silth can have babies has been on my mind a lot lately."

"Is that something you want?"

"I don't know. I think so. But then I worry I don't have the skills to be a mother. And nothing about being *pregnant* itself seems that appealing. What about you? Do you want to be a father?"

"Yes. I do. I guess. I don't think that I would be unfulfilled if I'm not a father, but it interests me. Mostly, my mother raised me, so I'm not sure I've got the role figured out. The closest thing to a father I have is Storng."

"I'm sure having him as your role model disqualifies you," she said with a laugh.

"I think I want to have children. I know I want to settle in a colony where they don't think of me as anything other than Aran. And they don't make me go to any meetings or be on any committees."

"That's a big dream," she said, rolling her eyes. "And what do you want to do in this colony besides not go to meetings?"

"Still working on that. I know I still want to travel and visit other parts of the world. I enjoy seeing unknown places. I would want my children growing up knowing it's a big world, with so many ways of living. So many wonders."

He lay back on the blanket and listened to the roar of the falls. "Tell me a story."

He pulled away from her, his mouth open. "You've never asked for a story before."

"Things change."

He thought about it while she stretched out on the blanket beside him. Her perfume, an orchid scent, clouded his brain for a moment. Instead of her usual leather battle gear, she had on a silky cream blouse and white shorts.

"The first Silth was a female. She lived beneath a great waterfall." He gestured at the falls surrounding them. "Maybe one of these. Because she was alone, she could not defend herself against the many beasts in the world. Back then, there were tigers with sabers for teeth, bears which ran like wolves, and enormous eagles, many times the size of those today. Not that she was helpless. She would forage around the mouth of the cave in the safety of the early morning and care for herself in her cave just fine. She had no magic, but more importantly, a single Silth, no matter what their skills, could not stand against a hostile world. So she hid. Back then, the Earth watched her creatures closely and spoke to each of them.

'Why do you hide?' she asked the Silth.

'When I go out, I have no one to come with me. No one to watch my back. No one to watch for the saber-tooth while I harvest berries. No one to talk to. No one to care about. I don't even have a name because there's no one to call it.'

'Of course you have a name. Each of my children has a name.'

'What's my name?'

'I cannot say it aloud, because if anyone heard it, a bird, an ant, even the morning breeze, they would have power over you. I will whisper it to you.' And she did. 'This is your secret name. But I will call you Urthela.'

"Still, Urthela didn't come from behind the waterfall except to snatch some food from the surrounding jungle. Her existence was sad. She survived. But she didn't fly above the jungle trees or listen to the morning birds. She told no stories because there was no one to tell, and made no art because she had never felt the touch of another nor experienced anything but fear.

"The Earth made other Silth. Because they were born in the nests of parrots and no one removed them, these Silth were feral and wild-natured. Urthela would catch glimpses of them as they moved through the trees when she came out to forage. She was curious, but when she approached, they flew away. She spent more time in the jungle trying to get close to them.

"One night, she built a large platform in the big strangler fig near her waterfall, placed stones in its center, and built a fire. She heard the wild Silth in the surrounding trees. She talked out loud while sitting in front of the fire, and she spoke of her conversations with the Earth and her lonely life. She heard the wild Silth move closer. She talked of how she dreamed of having others to talk with, go into the jungle to hunt seeds and berries with, and perhaps build a house with.

"After three nights of the same ritual, one of the male Silth came and sat on the edge of the platform. Each subsequent night he would come closer to the fire, and other Silth would come to the edge of the platform. Urthela expanded her stories to talk of the explorations they might undertake, things they might build, and the village they could make together.

"She told them about the different nuts and which berries were safe to eat. This was knowledge the Earth had given her, but for which she had little use since she rarely ventured out. She told them the names of the jungle animals and which ones would hurt them. After a while, she built a roof over the platform and stayed there instead of behind the falls. She fixed meals and shared them with the wild Silth, but the meals were small because she couldn't gather enough in the time she would spend in the jungle. The wild Silth brought her food. Lots of food.

"She fixed it into fresh meals, making drinks and cooked foods they'd never experienced. And she gave them names. One night, the one she had named Evet approached her gently and shared an experience common among the wild Silth, but new and magical to her. She looked forward to Evet's presence, and as she taught the wild Silth language, they stayed longer and lounged at her platform. She and Evet built more platforms around them, and before long, the wild Silth were staying there all the time. They used the language she gave them to tell her stories about the surrounding world and the many experiences it held. They told her about flying above the trees in the moonlight or watching lightning bolts strike the big waters.

"They told her of the excitement of exploring unknown places. She loved the stories, but she still feared going out further into the world.

'You should come with me to watch the sunset,' Evet said to her one day.

'I've watched the sun drop below the trees many times,' she

replied.

'There's a large lake nearby, and to sit in the canopy and watch the sun drop below the horizon and the clouds light up in colors is a joy.'

"She reluctantly agreed to go. Despite her terror, she was excited as she flew with Evet up above the trees for the first time. Her fear gave way to wonder at the sights below her.

"He flew close to her, making her feel safer. This was a world with which he was familiar and in which he felt comfortable. They settled into the canopy and watched the sunset over the lake, the colors spreading out like the juice of enormous berries on the sky. She had never had such a magical experience.

"They were flying back to her home, the jungle below beautiful in the moonlight, when an eagle grabbed her, its talons so tight around her she couldn't even scream. The eagle pulled her away, but Evet wouldn't let go. Though the eagle struck at him, its sharp beak opening large wounds, still he would not release his hold. He gave a great shout and the trees below erupted in the sound of wings as the wild Silth poured out from the canopy, rushing up at the bird.

"They overwhelmed it so it began falling from the sky. The eagle let go of its hold on Urthela and flew away, the taunts of the wild Silth following it.

"That night, as they lay in each other's arms, Evet whispered *Urthela* over and over as he stroked her hather. Then, under her breath, so soft a moth sitting next to her face would not hear it, she whispered her secret name. His hand stopped in mid-stroke, and he took a sharp breath in.

"She too held her breath. They lay still for a few moments and as he finally breathed out again, he too whispered his secret name so only she would hear."

Aran finished, but Merit said nothing. He thought maybe he caught the glint of a tear in the lantern light. Since he knew she'd be embarrassed if she had to acknowledge it, he said, "Why don't I set up our hammocks?"

He got them out of the bag and was just finishing tying them up on the branches when he felt her arms wrapping around him from behind. She leaned her head against his back and said nothing.

They spent the night in their hammocks, able to see the stars peeking through the sparse branches above them and with the roar of the falls beside them. They slept little as they talked of their hopes and fears. They were honest about the low probability that either of them, much less both, would survive the war. They agreed it was a stupid time for hearts to be shared.

Yet hearts were shared.

# Scene 3

ARAN (SILTH)

Normally, Human tourists would be around, but there were none today. Like the songbirds in the forest when there's a falcon gliding beneath the canopy, the Humans had all hidden away. They felt the weight of the predator's shadow. Whether it was because he was used to being hunted by the Trow or just because he was confident the spells they erected would shield them, Aran didn't feel the burden of the impending war today. In some ways, it felt like how he imagined a family reunion must feel.

They were at the base of the falls now, their entire world framed by the spectacular energy of the falling water. He watched as Nadara and Merit spoke, a small distance away from the others. They were both laughing, and it left him unsettled, but in an oddly pleasant way. Storng was catching up with the remaining Tiki Crew and meeting the Steamers. Even 3 of 5 seemed respectful as Storng thanked them all again for saving his life. Next to the river's edge, Temkaa, Krackle, and Jules were laughing at some story Krackle told.

Aran led them to a tourist station with tables, far enough from the falls for them to speak as a group. The meeting's purpose wasn't completely clear—he had simply sensed there should be one. Whether it was his desire to see friends, his belief each of them had a major role in the unfolding events, or the feeling that no matter how the war went, this might be the last time they would all assemble. As they flew up to the building, a pack of coati scrambled away from the trash cans in front but skulked just close enough to see if there might be food to steal.

Nadara picked the door lock, and they set up on the tables, spreading out the food and drink they'd brought. While they settled down, Storng said, "I cannot believe that Aran, Hater of Meetings, has called a meeting."

Aran listened to the good-natured ribbing for a few moments before he spoke. And as always when he spoke in front of a group, he was immediately aware of how rough his magic-damaged voice was, even when he tried to speak softly.

"Thank you." He grinned at Storng. "I think. Thanks for coming today. I know all of you are busy, and the times are dire. But I appreciate you taking this morning to come together."

"I heard there was free food," Nick mumbled, his mouth full of nuts.

Ignoring him, Aran continued, "What I thought we'd do is open by going around the room so each of us can update the others on what they are doing and any problems they're facing. We'll spend a little time discussing and then at the end, we can come back to anything that needs more work. We have all bound ourselves to secrecy about what we hear, and if you feel you need to share something outside the meeting, you can request the one who shared the information to release you. Let's start this way." He nodded toward Storng.

"I've been working to integrate Silth and Human societies. This is complex, in part because the Silth are finding out they are a collection of disparate groups, not just one group. We have to organize ourselves before we can talk about what *we* want. The Humans have made a place for us at the UN, and part of my job is to figure out what to fill it with. At first, they tried to group us with the Indigenous Peoples, which wasn't a bad idea as we have much in common, but that wasn't really a good fit. We've now created our own organization, sort of like the European Union."

He watched as several of the Steamtiki Crew stifled yawns.

"Alright, never mind," he continued. "In the big picture, relations are all across the spectrum. The international institutions and the tops of governments welcome us. The Humans know they have no chance in this war without us. But at the individual level, there is still a great deal of prejudice and rising animosity as we insist they honor their deal on technology and relations with wildlife. If we win the war as things are right now, we can reasonably expect some long period of struggle to achieve our goals. The closest analogy is the alliance of the US with the Soviet Union to fight in World War II, followed by decades of an ideological cold war."

This time, the yawns were very evident.

"You should read more," Storng said as he leaned back.

Temkaa picked up the discussion. "We see these tensions around us in my colony. We reached out to work with the local Human tribes to protect the wildlife from poachers, but they don't want to talk to us about moving farmers off some refuges where they illegally squat.

"And then someone comes along and offers them a sizeable amount of money for a trophy or to put an industry on a migration route, and they take it and offer to share it with us. They are trying to plug us into the existing system rather than accept fundamental change.

"I have been off on adventures with Aran, which he can tell you about. Otherwise, my principal job is to help preserve the Human and

Silth leadership structures in Africa through the Trow invasion. We helped construct a leadership refuge, but none of the Humans will use it. The Silth do, but the Humans in North Africa have built their own facilities, and the ones in the rest of Africa prefer to remain mobile and be able to hide in the bush. I'm not sure they are wrong."

"The Trow can find them easily," Aran said.

"Yes, but no one carries a beacon announcing their leadership role, so they have armed all the people and pushed them into the bush. The Trow will have to kill every one of them to be sure they got the leadership. These Humans think this strategy is better than going to the center and painting a target on their backs."

Several Steamtiki Crew spoke, and all followed the same theme—*we go where we're told and do what we're asked.* Like Temkaa, they made a vague reference to Aran's adventures.

Nadara joined in with a "Me too," drawing raised eyebrows. "I'm working with the World Silth Council because Aran told me to. And I live in the Human city of Washington South because he made me work with the Humans." She took in a big breath. "And I'm loving it. I'm not sure how much impact I'm having, but each day, groups of Silth and Humans get closer, working together on art, history, approaches to habitat loss, use of chemicals, location of technology, and countless other things. Yes, there are huge disagreements over the approaches, but these groups are patiently working through them. I'm hopeful. We're not on different sides, we just have different thoughts on how to reach the desired ends.

"But much of that work has stopped for now. Much of Human society was already fragile because so many people were lost in the impact of the volcano eruptions. Pessimism has crept in that the invasion makes the work meaningless. Having experienced an attack, I feel it too. If we can't win this war, what's the use of planning?"

"As best I can see," Merit added, "we can't win this war. Our hope was we might stop them from coming into the world." She paused, looking defeated. "We weren't able to stop them. They are here, presumably training for their push to destroy us all."

She let the whispers among the groups finish before speaking again.

"We have trained every Silth to use the shield and the bolt, and to transport. They also have non-magical weapons. Every Human has one or more guns and other weapons. It will not be enough. If we found the Trow, perhaps we could attack them, but we can't even find them. When they attack, it may take them longer than they think, but they will win."

Aran felt the energy bleed from the group. In the otherwise silent room, they heard the constant thunder of the distant falls.

"Perhaps it's time for a break," Aran said. They practically bolted from the room, as if they might escape the news by going outside. They broke into several groups, and Aran tried to decode the meanings. Merit stood talking to her long-time frenemy Storng. From their talk last night, Aran knew Merit felt she was not up to leading in this war. She'd fought with jaguars, and she had led in battles with Humans and Silth. But to fight the Trow was too much.

She questioned her ability to strategize with Human technology and worried the more the Humans created mechanisms to deal with the Trow's bolt, shield, and transport, the more they gained the power to fight the Silth as well. Storng seemed to be comforting her. Before long, Krackle joined their conversation.

Other groupings were easier to decipher. Don and Kristn, Nick and Loana, remnants of the Tiki Crew and long associated couples, were in one area, while Slatt, Ada, Vander, and Valente were in another. The former Steamers and former Tiki Crew worked well together but socialized little.

While the Tiki Crew members had become romantically involved many years ago, the Steamers found their partners outside the group. Even as he was thinking this, Aran saw the two groups merge and begin talking. Slightly more of a surprise was Temkaa, who stood talking with the 5's—Tara, Abney, and Blay. Their heads were together in an almost conspiratorial way.

The biggest surprise was Jules and Nadara, heads also close together, and their *conspiracy* was easy to discern. Aran mused for a moment before deciding they made a wonderful couple.

After a few more minutes, he called everyone back into the room. They drifted back into their seats.

"Krackle, what have you been up to?" Aran asked.

"Oh my, I've just been sittin' around knitting and tending to my chickens. Storng 4 and Storng 15 were feeling poorly, so I had to do some doctoring before I left the village a month ago." Storng had his one black eye fixed on her. "It's gotten very confusing there now that everyone has named their chickens Storng." She let the laughter die back down.

"I've been on a mission, as most of you know. Living with a group of Trow who've agreed to help us in the war. They've been preparing and are almost ready. Our fear has been they would *committee* their path so long they would never join the fight, but I think they'll be there."

"I suspect they're afraid of you if they aren't."

"They should be afraid, be *very* afraid." She looked as though disappointed no one got it.

Aran was about to skip the 5's, who never talked in these gatherings, when Tara—3 of 5—spoke up. "I have something to share with you." He nodded for her to go on.

"A group of us are fighting to hold the Humans to their word. We're the ones who have been pursuing the poachers and trophy hunters. We do not believe the Humans will do what is necessary to stop them, so we will. We will use the fog of this war to eliminate all the known groups. We always give the Humans the first opportunity to fix the problem, but if we survive this war, things will be different. One way or the other."

He was certain he had just heard more words from Tara than ever. He knew why she was telling them now. The group had bound themselves to silence, so they could not talk about Tara's revelation to anyone. There would have been no such limitation if they had figured it out themselves.

Nadara spoke first. "This isn't the way of the Silth. We don't kill for crimes."

"We don't kill Silth for crimes. But we kill cougars who develop a taste for Silth." She slid a look at Merit, who said nothing. "Besides, it is the Human way. When a tiger kills Humans, they kill it even though they are trying to preserve tigers. When a wolf kills their sheep, they kill it. We are simply culling the Humans with undesirable traits."

"It is much more complex than that," Storng said. "Humans and Silth are working through how we share distinct sets of laws. Humans have more experience with this than we do, having tried to integrate the laws of indigenous people with the laws of the surrounding colonialists. And trying to integrate the codes of various religions with the secular laws. It is still very difficult, and they have rarely gotten it right. But Humans believe vigilantism never works. Innocent people get killed. Prejudice overrides facts."

Storng and Aran both went through the arguments against what Tara and the others were doing, while Tara countered. Finally, she said, "I understand your arguments. It is one reason we'll act in the next few weeks. When the war ends, there will be no more poachers left to divide us from the Humans."

"More will take their place," Storng said. "Until the Humans eliminate the market, more poachers will step forward to supply the desire."

"Our definition of poachers includes those who employ them and those who pay that employer," Tara replied.

Storng shook his head. "Those will be very high-profile deaths, sure to invite attention and response."

With her chin thrust forward and her arms across her chest, Tara looked at the floor.

"I am not asking your permission. I'm telling you what will happen so you can do your best to mitigate the harm. I will not be stopped, and I am not alone."

The room was quiet except for the roar of the waterfalls. Aran finally spoke. "We can return to this later if there are any more questions or suggestions." He saw the anxiety in the room.

Krackle looked around it. "Tenser than a mouse in the middle of a pack of javelinas." The nervous laughter gave some relief.

Aran rolled his shoulders to loosen them before he stood to

speak. "I agree we can't win this battle with the Trow." Despite having heard a similar statement moments before from Merit, several of the assembled group looked crushed. "But it is possible that we can still win the war. One book Storng made me read was *The Art of War*. Mostly, the book is about winning without direct battle. *Supreme excellence consists of breaking the enemy's resistance without fighting.*

"Yesterday, an elite force of Humans attacked the Newgrange portal, clearing the way for the Sohi. They had the element of surprise because they used a secret passageway from the Pacific Ocean—a portal that exited beside the Newgrange portal."

"So far, just sounds like more war to end war," Kirsten said.

"The Sohi left Earth and returned to the Land," Aran said. "They went to assert Faelen's claim to the throne. They hope the Trow are tired of the madness of kings and can take over the Land with little resistance. Several of the Sohi are old names among the Trow and highly respected. If they simply took the Land and cut it off, that would only make those who are here fight harder. But if they are successful, families will begin calling their members home—to return unarmed, to leave the fight. A few will not. Thest won't. Casius won't."

"Have you heard from the Sohi?" Merit asked.

She'd grown used to these sorts of reveals from Aran and appeared unfazed.

"No, which is of great concern. The Trow may have killed them instead."

"Why would you trust these Trow?" This from Temkaa. "I've never heard of a trustworthy Trow."

Aran was silent for a moment. He put his hand on the apparatus around his head and dropped his glamour, so all saw how he really looked.

"I do not trust easily. My Silth brother, not a Trow in a battle, took my sight. Faelen, my Trow teacher and friend, gave me the weapons and defenses you use. He saved my life. He saved Merit's life. It was he who identified the antidote that saved Storng. Lornix, one of the Sohi, gave me the sight I enjoy. And the difference that enabled us to suppress the volcanoes came from the Sohi. I trust them with my life and the lives of all I care about."

"So, we wait?"

"No, Jules, we assume they will be successful. We also assume Thest may already know of their success and will quickly grow desperate. There is no going home for him. Same with Casius. And there will be others who follow each of them. We prepare for some desperate attacks, not the major war."

"And if we are wrong? If the Sohi lose, or do not reach back to stop the war?" Jules asked.

"Then we lose a war we would have lost anyway. We just lose it faster."

They spoke for another couple of hours on all subjects. When they broke up the meeting in the early afternoon, they were no more certain they would ever see one another again, but a new sense of resolve had settled in each of them.

Merit and Aran flew up to the top of the falls again. Their next stop involved meetings with the Humans at Washington South. But they took time, in the trees above the thunder of the falls, to make love with the desperation of those not sure they would live to see tomorrow.

# Scene 4

ARAN (SILTH)

"I'm going to meet with General Cogbill," Merit said as she and Aran appeared in the transport zone of Washington South. Autonomous vehicles filled the street and the surrounding air. The security personnel checked their identification before allowing them entry.

"He may not be around."

"Not that General Cogbill. The other one, his son."

"I know. He may not be around," he repeated.

She looked suspicious. "Why would you know the comings and goings of the Human general in charge of this war?"

He avoided her eyes. "He might, or might not, have been involved in the Sohi plan. His part is complete, but he may not be back yet." At her frown, he quickly added, "I'd be happy to tell you all about it."

She sighed. "Not now. And I'm not mad. It's like being angry at a coati for being a coati. Is there anything we need to do differently given what is going on with the Sohi?"

"We need to buy time. Otherwise, it's out of our hands now. If you have any ideas on how to do that, put them into motion. I'm on my way to meet with Storng and Penfield."

He reached out to touch her hand, but she'd already turned and was flying.

He headed on toward Penfield's office. As he moved along the sidewalk, bustling with activity, he was pensive. He saw all the Humans and Silth around him and imagined the many lives connected to them. They might all be gone in a second. When the Trow began in earnest, places like this would be among the first targets. There would be no prisoners, no siege, no terms, and no negotiation. The Trow would eliminate the leadership quickly, and no one would be alive to organize resistance to their extermination of the remaining population.

Most of the world of Humans and Silth was using a *hedgehog* defense. Prickly, difficult to swallow, but the hawk and the badger would still eat hedgehogs. That was Cogbill's explanation, at least. Aran had seen porcupines, but never a hedgehog.

An assistant showed him into Penfield's office, and Aran found him and Storng in full *old guy* mode, telling stories and drinking iced tea with lime.

"Aran! So good to see you." Penfield stood and gestured to the coffee table and empty Silth seat beside Storng.

"And you," Aran said as he sat, noticing his iced tea was already there. While Storng and Penfield might normally have shifted to some form of liquor this late in the day, for meetings with Aran, everyone stuck to tea. They made small talk for a few minutes and Aran asked, "Are you ready? Are *we* ready?"

"Humans and Silth are used to fighting enemies they can see on the horizon and keep to the perimeter," Penfield said. "Centuries of fighting focused on the arrival of an enemy force. Drones, long-range artillery, and even nukes changed some of that for Humans, but still it was at least something you could see coming."

"Merit says the tactics for fighting an enemy who can spring up in the middle of your troops are completely different."

"Yes, and preparedness for their appearance among a civilian population is almost impossible. We used all the strategies we can think of. In some places, we've concentrated populations and laid in place every militia, national guard, and troop defense we can. Other places, we've spread everyone out, armed them all, laid booby traps, anything we can. But we don't think it will be enough. It might delay things, but we have no reason to believe Thest is under any time pressure, so eventually he will win."

Aran and Storng looked grim but didn't disagree.

"We have another option, but it has risks, risks that may be unacceptable."

At the press of a button, Penfield's laptop caused the lights to dim and the wall painting behind them to turn into a monitor. The screen showed many warnings regarding the secrecy of the presentation's contents. The slides were mostly words and formulas and statistics. The last slide was a Trow, strapped into a cot. Blue blood ran from his nose and he appeared dead.

"The summary of all of this is we have developed a virus. We used one we found in the Flower Fairies as the base, and modified it. The good news is… it'll kill the Trow." Penfield looked away from the Silth. "There are several pieces of bad news, however. It will kill *all* the Trow. Our friends as well as our enemies. It will remain in this world forever. The Trow could never return. If it gets into their world, it will kill them there. There is no vaccine, and nor, because of the way we made it, is there likely to be one. And—" Penfield turned off the presentation, "It may kill the Silth as well, we don't know yet. The military has already distributed it around the world. Still within US control."

Storng said nothing as Aran sat stunned. Finally, Aran said, "I think you call this genocide."

"Yes. But in response to an effort to wipe out humanity, I think it's justified."

"I'm not buying it," Storng said.

"I assure you it's real."

"Oh, that I may believe. But something doesn't add up. Why tell us? We can't do more than we are doing to stop the Trow. You risk us deciding to side with the Trow or fight you both. It's an unnecessary risk and one you're too smart for." Penfield said nothing.

"Here's what I think. Yes, you have such a virus. But it isn't useful offensively because it spreads too slowly. It is more like a death curse than a weapon. If the Trow crush Humanity, its last act will be to release the virus. Not particularly useful in winning a war, but perhaps useful in negotiating survival. It's not useful offensively because the dying race will have time to destroy the Earth before succumbing."

Storng's ability to chart these waters amazed Aran. "But why would he tell us this lie if you would figure it out so quickly?"

"It wasn't a lie. It was a bluff. One someone required Penfield to tell to create the impression this is an offensive weapon. But he knows the consequence of this bluff would be a permanent separation of the Silth from Humans. He has told it in this way so it would arouse my suspicions, and he will have complied with his order, but not have done any harm."

Aran frowned at Penfield. "Is this true?"

"I can neither confirm nor deny that I rely on Storng being one of the smartest beings I know."

"I can't believe I survived for a moment as the ambassador to

Humans. Diplomacy is too coati-crazy for me."

"Irvin, any more games to play before we share actual information?" Storng asked.

"No. We're scared. We have great navies, but no navy to fight, no shore to assault or defend. The Trow can appear inside our planes and kill the pilots, rendering our air force useless. We make that more expensive by filling the cockpit with dust so the Trow die with the plane, but it's not a winning strategy. I don't think we *have* a winning strategy. What about you?"

"Maybe." Aran told Penfield about the Sohi invasion of the Land.

"Brilliant! I assume you trust Faelen and the Sohi to stop the invasion." Penfield's face lit up, and he sipped his tea.

"Not directly. They won't be able to stop Thest, but they'll be able to take much of his power from him. They can call home his troops if they've been successful in the Land. We've heard nothing for days. In the meantime, we should assume Thest knows we've cut off his avenue of retreat and his strength may ebb away soon. As you might imagine, he'll become desperate. It's possible for us to win, but we're now in the most dangerous time. The cougar may realize it's cornered."

# Scene 5

Thest (Trow)

Thest stood by the window of the room, small backpacks and little toys strewn around him. The walls had scenes of dancing bears and friendly lions, and a giraffe in a clown costume. With no lights, the room would have been dark in the settling night except that orange light from the flames outside flickered within.

The animals seem to move in the stuttering light, animated by carnage.

He did not know what country he was in, but he knew that this was the last of the Human *governance centers* not protected by the Silth. It, like the other centers, had been easy to attack, and they were almost finished.

He had used spore bombs on two of the ten Silth-protected centers. Those were excellent because they not only killed all the Humans and Silth there, but when the Silth transported away, they infected new locations. Unfortunately, when the Trow tried to set off the third and last of his supply, one of the Silth had immediately grabbed it and transported away, presumably to a remote location where it would be the only victim.

The willingness of the Silth to die to save Humans still surprised him. And he had seen Humans die saving Silth. It amazed him. He had not believed such altruism was in the character of either race.

They used Human created *nerve gas* on the rescued center. It was so fast acting that it killed the Trow who dropped his shield to turn the canister valve. At least no Silth could get near it to transport it away. It killed everything—Humans, Silth, dogs, birds, and bugs. Thest, who had watched from the sky over the center, was relieved when the gas finally began dissipating beyond the edge of the center.

*What a barbaric creation,* he had thought. *There is an evil in these creatures that goes beyond Xafar.*

Unfortunately, this was the only container they had found. The soldiers they tortured told them where others were stored, but by the time his warriors went there, they had moved the nerve gas, as had all the attending personnel.

But they had not needed to resort to such weapons in today's attack. With no Silth to guard it and no dust traps, it had been a straightforward military operation. Once the buildings were ablaze, fire had done much of their work for them.

This building, however, had been constructed to resist fire. It housed the country's prime minister and the royal family. They were all dead now. The last communication center, occupying most of the basement, had been destroyed too.

Thest surveyed the large room on the fourth floor. This must have been a nursery and school for the younger children of the government officials gathered in this center. As he surveyed the walls, he saw drawings and handwritten papers affixed to boards. There were four windows, two doors, and a mirror. He almost felt bad about killing young Humans; they were innocent and even amusing, and he enjoyed their creativity in play. But Human children grew up to be Human adults, and that was the problem. That, and the fact that Humans made so many of them. Before Humans began breeding on their own, back when they had to be handmade by Trow artisans, they were easy to manage. Now, there were too many to sustain.

He could see the corridor through the upper part of the one door. But the other door was opaque, an entrance to some kind of closet. He walked over to the adjacent mirror and saw the gaunt, armored figure, orange on the side facing the windows and black on the other. He would not have recognized himself in a picture.

Thest could smell them in the room behind the mirror, accessed by the adjoining door. Standing this close, he could hear the whimpering and the shushed warnings to be quiet. The mirror would be some sort of impact-resistant material that allowed the occupants to observe him, and the door would be metal, secured with deep bolts into the frame. The very best security the Humans could imagine for their most precious possessions.

He transported into the room. The screaming quickly stopped.

# CHAPTER EIGHT

## *Scene 1*

MERIT (SILTH)

Merit noticed she missed Aran, who'd departed Washington South two days earlier. Over the past several months, he'd often crossed her mind as she tried to decide where they stood, or he vexed her with some particular decision. This was the first time she had caught herself wishing for his presence. *Maybe I'm unstable from lack of sleep.*

She'd been busy. The Humans called the fight they were expecting *living room to living room* because there would be no massed armies, not even the *door-to-door* fighting typical of urban warfare. The enemy could just appear in your living room and kill you.

She was teaching the Humans there were some limitations. The Trow could not use magic infinitely. They would exhaust themselves and have to recover. The more you forced them to use their magic, the faster they would resort to conventional weapons.

She was flying through the town center of Washington South. Many business owners had boarded their stores shut, the air was heavy, and few people walked the normally busy street.

*How many deaths does it take to exhaust a Trow?*

Unfortunately, a similar limitation existed for the Silth. They would exhaust their magic as well. In fact, the average Silth had only a third of the sheer magic power of an average Trow. Their bolts were not as powerful, so it took more of them, and their reserves of magic were not as extensive. With their magic spent, the Silth warriors had to rely on the small guns they now carried. These had been Jules's idea, and she had to admit, not too bad.

Human guns were either too big for the Silth and took two Silth working together to operate them, or too small to make any difference in a fight. Most small guns only held one or two bullets, and shooting Trow with a derringer just irritated them. Jules had suggested they combine their knowledge of fast-acting poisons with Human gun technology. Each Silth now carried a gun firing twenty darts. The guns were small since they no longer had to propel a bullet with enough velocity to make a difference.

They just had to blow a dart for up to twenty yards. The various Silth tribes had developed different poisons based on their regions and resources. Merit's clan derived hers from the poison dart frogs the Silth had been cultivating over the past year. They developed a way to harvest poison from the frogs without roasting them over a fire, the traditional production approach.

The siren wailed through the empty streets, bouncing off the mid-rise buildings around her. She didn't know where the attack was happening. She scrambled for her phone, ripping it from her backpack, and saw the auto text: "Everywhere. Blue." She traded the phone for her gun and headed for her team's rally point. The *blue* reference meant there were so many Trow that Martha had suspended the prohibitions of blipping within the ring fence of the town.

Merit flickered and disappeared, reappearing on the edge of the sizable park extending down to the river. Her team began appearing around her. She'd decided this strategy was better for her than the war room the Humans used. Her team would move when threatened. As her communications support appeared, they updated her.

A large force of Trow had appeared next to the executive compound, their arrival triggering the dust, which had neutralized the transport abilities of all fifty Trow. They were battling the guards and security measures there, trying to get to the ambassadors, cabinet members, and senators of the five countries sheltered here.

"Do we join the battle?"

Merit listened to her communications team as they summarized the information received on their phones. "No, it's a feint. Let's go to the President's compound." The President's compound sheltered the chief executives of all five countries.

The communications officer quickly typed in the code warning the guards of their arrival. They arrived seconds before the Trow attack on that section began. This time, all the incoming Trow appeared outside the dust ceiling. The ceilings triggered automatically if someone transported beneath them but otherwise required manual activation. Now, there were so many Silth inside the ceiling area that Martha could not release the dust without grounding several dozen Silth as well.

A separate system was in the room holding President Percrow and the other leaders.

More Trow arrived, around one hundred massing outside the compound. In the distance, Merit saw the first smoke of fires, and the radio confirmed the Trow were appearing throughout the city, killing anyone they found and torching the buildings. Three enormous explosions occurred in quick succession, and lights flickered when the buildings lost power from the grid and shifted to their battery power.

As the Trow outside advanced on foot toward the building, several stepped on the mines. The others lifted off the ground and advanced on the building. Machine gun fire ripped into the group from the sides, but several Trow immediately transported away and in moments, there were explosions.

The gunfire ceased.

The Trow reappeared in front of the compound. This time, a fleet of fast drones mixed in with airborne Silth attacked both flanks, again forcing the Trow back. When the Trow changed tactics and engaged the attack from above, the surrounding Humans fired on them from the building.

Merit thought of Stalbon, her harpy eagle, and of how quickly he would have perished this fight. One of her communications officers tapped her shoulder and told her things were becoming dire at the other compound.

"Have you gotten through to Aran?"

"No answer."

"Keep trying."

Leaving one of her best captains in charge of the Silth part of the President's compound defense, she took five elite squad members and transported to the VIP compound. They appeared behind the Trow, who'd made significant progress inside even though they were a smaller force than was attacking the President. The Trow had their shields down and their backs to them. If the Silth fired bolts, they might wound the Trow, but the Trow would likely just raise their shields. The Silth warriors pulled out their dart guns. Each of them carried two.

They mowed through the Trow, never spending over one dart on each one.

Merit was trying to make sense of the fighting in front of her. The Trow had broken through the outer defenses and were among the residents. These must have come through the dust because none of them were transporting, and now they fought forward, some in the air and some on the ground, alternating between their shields and bolts.

Most Human and Silth fighters were dead, their bodies and those of many Trow lying around her. The civilians were doing their best to defend themselves but their guns were ineffective because the Trow merely raised their shields and advanced into the gunfire until close enough to use their swords. They killed everyone, man, woman, adult, or child standing in front of them.

Merit saw a flicker as a Silth appeared in the air above the fight. For a moment, it looked like Aran, but then she realized it was Casius. He flew deeper into the compound, ignoring the fight immediately around him. She gave a quick order to her squad to continue fighting and took off after him. He was apparently looking for something or someone, but she kept losing him as he wound through the maze of paths separating the compound's residences. When he saw any unprotected Human, he fired, and they crumpled. At first, she thought he was just very accurate in his shots, but then she suspected his bolts were more powerful than those of a normal Silth.

Around them, a few of the Trow had made it into the section and were breaking down doors.

She saw Casius veer toward a group of Humans who'd gathered in a circle beneath a shed roof, normally used for vehicle storage. They were facing outward, protecting the children in the center, a defense used by fish and other animals around the world. Several Trow were advancing on the perimeter. On the crowd's edge, Merit recognized

Joss, with Tiny standing between her and the advancing Trow. Just as the Trow stepped forward, a bear of a man holding a sword launched himself at him, sending him sprawling.

As the man stood up, Casius killed him.

"Luis!" Joss screamed and looked up at Casius. "You!" she spat into the air.

"Hello again," Casius smirked as he dropped his shield and raised his arm to fire at her.

Tiny stepped in front of Joss. Just as Merit shot at Casius from behind, he raised his shield as though he had sensed the attack. He whirled and dropped his shield again, firing on her so fast she barely got her shield back up in time. The bolts hit her shield, not with the force of a Silth, but with that of a Trow. He kept firing, pounding her backwards.

She heard him shout, "This is what I was hoping for, a worthwhile hostage."

He hammered her back into the wall of a building, and as she felt herself losing consciousness, she flickered and disappeared.

She reappeared next to Joss and Tiny, flickered and disappeared again, taking them with her.

They emerged in the train station forming the heart of Washington South. Bodies littered the station here, but there were no Trow.

Merit heard a loud hiss as an autonomous train pulled in, and dozens of people rushed out of hiding to board it. She pushed Tiny and Joss into the fleeing group and flickered and disappeared, reappearing this time on the outer edge of the Presidential compound. She didn't believe the other compound would survive the attack so she'd fight here, where it might still make a difference.

The Humans and Silth still held the Trow at the edge, but the Trow numbers had grown significantly. Maybe those who'd been marauding the city had joined this group.

Merit dropped from the air and hid behind a car, watching the assemblage and catching her breath, getting ready to rejoin the fight. As she watched, hundreds more Trow began popping into sight, and among the last was the biggest she'd ever seen. He was massive, a head and a half taller than even the tallest around him, with dreadlocks almost to his waist. As soon as he appeared, he tipped his head back and gave a mighty roar, and the other Trow cheered.

*Nake nula waun. I am ready for whatever comes,* Merit thought as she flew from behind the car.

# Scene 2

FAELEN (TROW)

"Hail Faelen!" came the meager cheer.

"Stop that," growled Faelen. The assembled court looked confused. Faelen appreciated the throne room much more than the last time guards had dragged him inside to face his father. While it still held terrible memories for him, at least it no longer smelled of the dead.

He was tired, having not slept for three days. He eyed the two Sohi standing quietly beside him, as unobtrusively as their bright red robes allowed. He was proud of them and of how they had taken the Kingdom. Or perhaps not *taken the Kingdom*.

That was still his to do. So… he was proud of how they had gotten him to this point.

Silth shuttled them to Newgrange, the Irish portal, in the middle of the night. By the time they arrived, the Trow had cleared away the Human and Silth defenders, and a steady stream of Trow continued to arrive through the portal.

The Sohi assembled out of view in the large courtyard of a sheep farm. They were beside the River Boyne, a little more than half a mile away. There was no talking among the Sohi, no signs of fear or excitement, just alert attention to the world around them.

They heard the Human attack on the Trow perimeter. They had come through an old portal the Neirads had shown Aran, attacking using sophisticated technology developed specifically to fight the Trow. Apparently, it was effective, but they didn't have much of it. Before long, the Humans sent word to the assembled Sohi to advance. The entire Sohi enclave traveled together, with the very young and the ancient at the back of the column.

At 4:00 in the morning, they assembled and walked to the portal, armed with small swords, throwing knives and naginatas, ancient Human weapons with blades on the ends of long wooden shafts. As they approached the prehistoric Human structure, they surrounded themselves with the blue shields and continued through the bolts of hidden snipers. The Humans saturated the area with fire whenever snipers showed themselves, forcing them to erect their shields and become visible or kill them. When any Trow tried to approach the Sohi assemblage, the naginatas poked through the blue shields like porcupine quills and stabbed the defender.

The Sohi reached the portal with only a few remaining Trow warriors clustered around it. Lornix moved her hands in a complex pattern and the defenders doubled over, clutching their stomachs. They fell to the ground, writhing while the Sohi walked up to the portal threshold.

As the Sohi poured into the Land, they encountered guards, but Thest had never imagined anyone attacking there, so the defense was minimal and designed to capture spies, not armies. Because no magic existed in the Land, the Sohi's advantage increased through their knowledge of martial arts, and they easily incapacitated the guards, despite their bioweaponry.

Where possible, the Sohi spared the lives of those they encountered.

They split into three groups, one staying at the Newgrange portal, another marching to secure the portal entrance from Angkor

Wat. And the last, with Lornix and Faelen in the lead, marched to the palace. Trow came out of their houses to watch, but no one took up arms against them.

They just stood in silence and watched them pass.

Word spread before them, and they arrived at an undefended palace. There, they found the advisers still working in the throne room and Thest's children and their families in the private ones. They called them all together, summoned Xafar's former court, and Faelen and Lornix prepared to speak with the stunned assemblage. Faelen faced them in the red robe of the Sohi, his head and his face shaven. He felt calm, ready for whatever direction the day took, but pacing, nonetheless.

"I am Faelen, son of Xafar, and I am asserting my right to the throne. Do any deny me that right?" No sound came from the group as he stopped and looked around, his gaze landing on his mother. "Mother, step forward."

She was holding a small boy and nervously took a step.

"Historically, this would be the point where I killed my younger brother to make sure he did not grow up to challenge me."

She said nothing, but clutched the small boy closer.

"Do you, here in front of these Trow, renounce all claim your son may have on the throne and commit to raising him without desire to become King?"

"Yes. Oh yes, please. Please show us a mercy we would not expect from your father."

Faelen said nothing and stared at them, weighing the risks. He knew his mother had long ago lost her sanity. He had little affection for her as she had not tried to save him from his father, instead replacing him with this brother. But as he looked at her holding the small child, he thought about what her life must have been with the mad King.

"There are not enough Trow children to waste any. Meet your vow of today and raise him to never lift a hand against me or my family, and you will both prosper."

Looks of surprise spread around the room.

"Children of Thest?" As a female and two males stepped reluctantly from the gathering, their heads hanging low, Faelen stared at them and said, "You are the children of General Thest. The General who betrayed his oath to my father and killed him. Your father is still alive, fighting a campaign on Earth. Before these Trow, do you recognize me as your King?"

"Yes, Your Highness."

"We are yet again at the point in Trow tradition where I would kill you to prevent you from taking up arms against me." As the crowd involuntarily drew back from the three forlorn figures, Faelen said, "Your father has tried to kill me many times and has killed others about whom I cared. He killed my father." He paused, then, "But he was not the one I cared about. I suspect he killed him to protect you. And…," he looked over at his mother and little brother, "Thest has already broken tradition by leaving my mother and brother alive, a worthy act by an unworthy Trow that still deserves a worthy response. Therefore, if you swear before these Trow not to take up arms or foment insurrection against me or my family, you will live and prosper."

"We so swear," Thest's daughter and younger son said with enthusiasm and stepped back into the crowd.

Thest's oldest son, about Faelen's age, stared darkly at him.

Faelen moved to stand a few feet in front of him.

"Perhaps you had dreams of succeeding your father and being King. This will not happen. Perhaps you have heard your father's rants that I am responsible for your mother's death, and you fear submitting would be a betrayal of her. Your mother died not by my hand, but by the hand of those I empowered, just as others empowered your mother. She was a fierce warrior and chose to go to battle. She died with honor, as she would have wished. Do not dishonor her by questioning the merit of her death or making her the reason for your decision. Make your own decision."

Faelen turned his back on Thest's son and walked a few steps away before facing him again. "Perhaps you feel it would be disloyal to your father who still fights on Earth to complete his commitment to genocide. To extinguish the races of Humans and Silth our people created there.

"I understand and respect such loyalty, but your father's quest is as mad as that of my father. We have already shown we can live in peace with these races. There is no need for the precious sons and daughters of the Land to die. I will give your father a chance to stand down if he is willing. You do not need to die on the altar of his madness."

He paused again.

"You may see my father in me. Someone who most likely threatened you or your brother or sister to control your father. I am not my father. I hated my father and I join you in that hatred. Perhaps we can build a place where no one like my father rules again.

"But do not mistake my mercy as weakness. I will not live looking over my shoulder for you to attack me or the ones I love."

Faelen raised his right hand. "Make the oath and choose life." He raised the other hand, which now held a dagger. He said nothing, waiting for the son's decision.

The son's eyes softened, and he nodded as though answering a question to himself. He bowed his head slightly and said, "I so swear." Then he stepped back next to his brother and sister as the court murmured. Faelen returned to the front of the room.

"The last time the Land had an extended time of peace and prosperity was under our Queen. Xafar brought us madness, and Thest wages a war to exterminate our own creations, our own children—the Humans and the Silth. Your new era will be different. I will rule together with my Queen." He held his hand out and Lornix approached from the side.

She took his hand for a moment as she faced the group.

She was taller than Faelen, but otherwise wore an identical red robe, and her head was also shaved, the same as the Sohi standing unobtrusively around the room.

"I am Lornix, Speaker of the Sohi Will. We too are Trow. But the Trow of the Land have hunted us for centuries. We come to defend ourselves and to defend the Humans and Silth. We have no wish to impose our beliefs on you. We will re-establish an enclave like that from which Thest drove us, and we will return to our work of making ourselves better to more fully understand the Earth, this Land, and ourselves.

"We, the Sohi, make decisions differently than you do. We use consensus building for which you are not yet ready. Nonetheless, we believe it is time to change the Land's governance process. We will do six things. We will establish a set of rights for individuals that even the King or Queen cannot violate. We will establish a set of rights for the community that no individual or group may violate."

She let them absorb the words, then continued.

"We will establish rights for the Land and the Earth and their living creatures. We will work with the Humans and the Silth to change the way they live on the Earth so we can join them there. We will welcome the Humans and the Silth here, where they can help us refresh the Land and perhaps help create a world we are not so eager to leave. Finally, we will create a *senate* where the citizens of the Land will elect representatives. First to advise us, and later to manage and govern the day-to-day life in the Land."

Faelen stepped back up beside her.

"But now we must end the war on Earth," he said. "Send word to your sons and daughters, to your fathers and mothers. Call them home to the Land. Tell them to leave their arms on the other side of the portal and come back. We will welcome them into a new day. If they try to bring their weapons through the portals, we will kill them as soon as they appear. If they raise a hand against us, they will die. If they fight on, we will never allow them to return here. Eventually, I will come to find them, and I will kill them. Tell them to come through the portal to live and prosper."

"Long live King Faelen! Long live Queen Lornix!" someone shouted.

Faelen started to object, but Lornix put her hand on his. The crowd took up the shout, continuing until they were too hoarse to speak.

# Scene 3

### Merit (Silth)

As Merit hurried behind the attacking Trow, she caught a movement in her peripheral vision. Turning, she saw the sky full of flower fairies—hundreds of them—following a truck speeding toward the other compound. She recognized one of the two large men in the back of the truck waving the flower fairies on. *No, that can't be. I put them on a train out of here.*

When she neared the Trow, she realized something was wrong. Instead of the massive wave of Trow breaking over the last of the Human and Silth defenders, the Trow appeared to be fighting among themselves in front of the compound barriers. Krackle was flying among the Silth, and neither Humans nor Silth were firing into the group unless a Trow began rushing toward the barriers. Then she knew what was going on.

The late-arriving Trow were the Neirads, the undersea Trow.

*But they aren't really fighters. Once they've lost the element of surprise, Thest's warriors will slaughter them.* Even as she had the thought, she saw some Trow on the battlefield changing their glamours so that suddenly, they wore enormous hats with shaggy red feathers sticking high above them. This had to be one of Aran's plans!

Merit transported to Krackle, who said, "Just in time."

The Silth shouted and surged out past the barriers to join the fight, as did the Humans. The Trow in hats dropped back, leaving the ground littered with the Trow attackers they had taken by surprise.

They grouped into a ball and marched ahead again, engaging the experienced warriors with a more defensible formation. Before the attacking Trow realized what was happening, the Silth and Humans were upon them.

Merit noticed a few Humans wore the new and very expensive suits developed by a collection of world engineers. These absorbed the powerful Trow bolt when it hit the Humans' head or chest, spreading its impact in the suit. While it still hurt, and even incapacitated for a few seconds, the wearer survived. Furthermore, they had powerful lasers built into the arms. Human magic at work.

Merit and Krackle fought alongside the others, and things were close for a while. But with the relentless march of the Neirads' mass, Silth using practiced tactics of assembled transport—a squadron would appear, feint or attack, and quickly move to another part of the battlefield—and the advanced Human training and weaponry, the battle turned against Thest's warriors.

At some signal from the Trow field leader, the Trow transported out of the battle, leaving dead or unconscious Trow still strewn around the parking lot in front of the barriers.

Merit noticed the big Trow lying among the unconscious bodies. He perplexed her. She had assumed he was with the Neirads because he had arrived at about the same time, but as they tended to their wounded, they ignored him. A mystery, but one she didn't have time to unravel.

She gathered the Silth and they flew to the other compound, leaving the Humans on watch in case Thest's army returned. Merit dreaded what she would find; there was no way the Humans in the other compound could have survived. Perhaps the Silth transported a few away, as she had Joss and Tiny. But even they had returned. *Why?* It had been hopeless. As she and the Silth materialized, though, there were no sounds of battle. There were, however, many bodies—Silth, Trow, and Human.

Cautiously, they moved through the compound.

Still no sounds until they heard voices talking. Just talking. No screaming or shouting. They cleared the corner to find many survivors, some wounded, but far more than Merit expected.

She saw Tiny and Joss bending over. Well, Tiny was actually bending while Joss sat on a chair, helping a woman with serious bolt burns. Around the plaza, on every surface on which something could roost, sat or lay a flower fairy. They looked exhausted. Some were removing things from their hands, but Merit couldn't tell what they were. Kimper, Aran's familiar, swooped in front of her face, growled, and held her hands out like *claws.* Merit saw needles of all sorts lashed onto her fingers with what looked like duct tape. Kimper burst into giggles at Merit's expression and flew away.

Merit waited until Tiny finished and landed between him and Joss.

"When I rescue people from the fire, I don't expect them to turn around and rush back in."

Looking abashed, Tiny stammered, "We… we… we couldn't just leave. These people are our friends."

Joss just laughed. "There was this passing mob of flower fairies. Kimper had gathered a bunch of them, armed them with their claws, and brought them to Washington South. But she didn't know where to go from there."

"My friend Fetu," Tiny said, gesturing at a bloody but smiling man sitting nearby, "commandeered a truck, and we led them here. They were fierce. Anytime one of the Trow dropped their shield, two or three of these guys were trying to stab their eyes. If they put up their shields, they couldn't shoot. When they dropped their shields to shoot at the flower fairies, the Humans would shoot them."

"Can I help here?" said a young woman in fatigues.

Tiny stood up and smiled. "Bian, you made it out of AP Hill!"

Bian returned the smile and bent down to help the injured woman. She and Tiny continued talking.

"Even when they started blipping around, they couldn't get away from the flower fairies," Joss went on, looking around at the roosting flower fairies with affection.

Merit saw Humans carefully gathering the broken, dead fairy bodies and grouping them together on tables beside bodies of slain Silth and Humans. On the other side of the courtyard, Trow bodies were being dragged to a pile with far less care.

Merit flew over to the Silth bodies and quickly returned. "Where is Casius?"

"I don't know. I lost track of him when we returned," Joss said.

Merit did a quick tour of the bodies still lying in the courtyard. "He's not here. I have to go. You need to get these people moving to the other compound. When the next wave comes, we don't have enough warriors, Human, Silth, or Trow, to defend two compounds."

"Trow?"

"A long story about a coati-scat Aran plan," Merit said, adding, "Which worked pretty well."

She blipped away and reappeared in the middle of the cleanup operations at the President's compound. She tried to reach Aran again.

No answer. She was worried. For all his toucan behavior, it wasn't like him to not come when someone needed him. She dove into helping with the cleanup, organizing Silth teams to reset the defenses and remove the bodies. Lots of bodies. The cost of the defense had been high. They'd won this battle, but only by exposing their reserves.

It was plain on the face of every officer among the Humans and Silth. They knew. They had won a battle, but they would not be victors in the war.

Krackle and the Trow, wearing the ridiculous hats, were gathering Thest's still living warriors. After sprinkling them with the dust, removing their ability to blip away, they secured their hands behind them with heavy metal cuffs and chained these to the chains binding their feet. Finally, they put a collar on each. Merit knew the collar would explode if tampered with, or on command. Even with all that, the medics approached the prisoners warily as they finally stepped in to tend their wounds. One was the big Trow who had arrived with the Neirads.

Merit flew over to Krackle.

"Howdy Dawn Defender! How was that for an entrance?" Krackle laughed as Merit gave the big, feathered hat Krackle wore the hairy eyeball. "Hey, this is a group with style."

Merit studied the unconscious giant. "This one arrived with you. But he isn't one of yours?"

"Well, he's kind of memorable, big javelina that he is, and I don't remember him. And he didn't pull out a hat with the others. So no, he isn't one of mine. Mine have great hats. And I can't tell what's wrong with him. Don't see any bumps or cuts." The team clipped the collar on him.

"Watch out for Casius. He was around here earlier with some of his Newfies."

"Aiee, that's a snake in the house."

Merit nodded and flew on. She kept working as night fell and the stars emerged.

***

Casius was furious. He had no awe left for the Trow. How could Thest fail so massively in this simple attack? It should have been just a milestone along the way to controlling the world. He really was an awful general.

Casius also had to admit he no longer believed the Silth would survive the war. Sometimes, he questioned whether that was ever a possibility, but mostly he blamed this result on Aran. Without him, they might have negotiated some peace with the Trow instead of expending their energy defending the Humans. Perhaps the Trow weren't the saviors Casius had once worshiped, but until Aran's interference, they had no reason to exterminate the Silth.

He felt the side of his head, where the hather had grown back patchy and oddly textured through the burns. He wanted nothing other in this world than to kill Aran, and he knew he was running out of time. Either this war would be over in a few days, despite Thest's incompetence, and the Trow would kill Aran, or if by some miracle the Humans and Silth won, it would be all the harder for Casius to get near Aran. Now was the time to strike—here in the middle of chaos.

But he could not find Aran.

Casius had captured and tortured several Silth, to no avail. No one knew where he was hiding. Did Aran know he was hunting him? Casius smiled to think of him locked away somewhere in fear.

He needed to find someone who would either lead him to Aran or flush him out. He might not be in such a target-rich environment again, so he stayed behind, even after Thest's warriors left Washington South. He was resting among the solar arrays on the roof of the data center. He'd lost his Newfie assistants, but he wasn't worried.

Whatever his competence as a general, at least Thest had armed him well. He might take Merit, or perhaps the President. He knew the President from the videos he had seen. He'd had Penfield before, and that only brought him Storng. Merit was too dangerous unless an easy opportunity presented itself. His target would be the President. It was time. The first thing he needed was a distraction, and he had a pretty good idea what that might be.

He transported to the darkness above the captured Trow. The Silth and Humans weren't even bothering to guard them, and in the starlight, he saw why. Several captives had tried to remove their collars and now lay headless in the row of chained figures. He just needed two or three to cause enough mayhem to create the opportunity for him to get close to the President.

All he had to do was touch her.

Once he had her, he would demand Aran come. Then he would kill them both. At least that last move might soften the Trow's animosity, so that if the Trow won, they would not hunt for him so hard in their quest to finish the Humans and Silth. Maybe he would even gather a few followers. He focused on his surroundings and dropped to the level of the captive Trow. Several were still unconscious, but a huge Trow and two next to him were stirring.

Casius approached them. "I work with Thest. I'm here to free you." The three looked fearfully at the nearest headless body. "Don't worry. I can do things few others can."

Flying to the closest of the Trow, with the big one eying him warily, he put his hands gently on the collar and it disappeared. He knew it was exploding somewhere in the empty area of the Land. While it wasn't as good as the spell that had sent him and his bomb there, since he had to touch whatever he sent, it still was a solution. And he was able to separate out what he sent rather than sending everything attached to it. He quickly freed the other two.

The first one he released stood watching for a moment, then flickered and disappeared.

"Son of a toucan!" Casius turned to the remaining two. "Any more cowards?" They just stared back at him. He considered moving down the line and finding another Trow but decided two would do.

"We're going to finish your mission. We're going to take the President. But I need her alive so I can use her for something else. Then you can have her." He outlined his plan, and they nodded agreement.

Casius went first. He flew to the top of the building containing the President of the United States and the other important leaders and removed a portion of the roof, sending it into the Land as well. Below him, he saw the mechanism of the dust machine. As he sent that to the Land, he chuckled at the notion of the junk heap building there. The process made no noise and there was no sign of alert below.

He waited.

In a few moments, the alarms blared. Casius had instructed the smaller Trow to blip in and out of the building in multiple places to create a distraction and draw the bulk of the President's Human defenders away. Because the larger one couldn't transport, having been covered with dust earlier, Casius told him to fight his way through the defenders. Those would only be Humans because of the dust.

Casius blipped into the President's section. Since he had no clue where the President would be, he went where their spy had shown the main living area. The guards immediately fired at him, and he dropped the three flashbangs he was carrying on the floor as he raised his shield and made it go solid. This was one trick the Trow had taught him, and the first time he'd been able to use it since he'd returned to the Earth with its magic.

The solid sphere protected him from the sound and light occurring within seconds. He dropped the shield and shot the guards as they clutched at their ears and eyes.

Right on time, the two Trow appeared at the door.

The big one threw a handful of dust at Casius and put a bolt through the head of the Trow beside him. Casius wiped at his eyes and spit dirt out of his mouth. He had already raised his shield as soon as the dust hit him.

With a sinking feeling, he tried to transport.

Nothing.

As he now recovered his ability to see, he looked in vain for the large Trow. He also searched for a window, but of course, none existed in this part of the building.

"You have this one chance to give up. Please don't take it," a familiar voice said.

Casius dropped behind a sofa. "Great trick, brother. Where did you learn that?" Casius used the moment to catch his breath.

"After seeing how the bolt and other Trow magic spread, I

decided it best not to share everything Faelen taught me."

"Didn't you have to kill some Humans to get here?"

"What makes you think I can only appear as a Trow?"

Casius dropped his shield and fired a couple of bolts in the voice's direction.

Aran went on calmly, "I notice they've shown you how to amplify your bolt. Must use up a lot of energy though."

"Why don't you show yourself and find out?" Casius replied.

He'd need to attack soon, while he still had enough power to overcome Aran. He stood from behind the sofa, surrounded by his shield, but no shots came. He reached around and made certain he could grab the dagger behind his back.

"I'm not who I was, brother," he insisted, hopefully convincingly. "I've had the veils lifted from my eyes. I know the Trow for what they are now, but I don't think the Humans are any better. Join with me. Let's play them off against each other and lead the Silth to a new age of glory with the magic of Humans and Trow at our service."

Aran appeared in his normal form, partially protected by a bookcase and shield still up. If Casius could get him to drop his shield, he would throw the knife. He'd practiced with it a lot in his exile in the Land.

"I have no love for Humans, and don't trust them," Aran said. "But why would I trust the Trow?"

Casius believed a show of vulnerability would work. He knew Aran would never take advantage of someone trusting him.

He lowered his shield.

Aran  brought his arm from behind the case, raising the dart gun, and fired. The dart struck Casius in the throat.

"And once I knew what a treacherous snake the fer de lance was, why would I ever trust one again?"

# Scene 4

Thest (Trow)

Thest sat in the darkness of the fishing shack porch, built on stilts five hundred yards from the Lake Maracaibo shore. This was his favorite place on Earth. He watched the lightning as it punished the surrounding hills and forests and the throat of the lake itself. It backlit the massive clouds in white, orange, and yellow. The thunder shook the ground. Boats dotted the horizon between him and the lightning.

The war was proceeding on schedule and the results were inevitable, but the costs were higher than he expected. They'd taken all the leadership centers except for the US and China, but casualties had been extensive. Still, he had hobbled any leadership most of the world had and cut off the communications from what was left. He would switch now to exterminating Humans and Silth wherever they hid. They would sweep through the lands, leveling all like locust.

The remains of the Human and Silth fighting forces would come to him.

He rocked in the chair, a relaxing motion in the charged, humid air.

When a messenger appeared beside him, Thest ignored him, unwilling to let go of the lake's spell just yet. The messenger remained still. Thest knew it would be bad news—his order was not to disturb him except in an extreme emergency. He closed his eyes and listened to the rumble in the distance. So much power. So much violence.

"Report."

"Word has reached your troops that Faelen has taken the throne. The Sohi occupy the Land and control both portals."

"So? We can always take them back and drive the traitors from the Land."

"Their families have allied themselves with Faelen. He and his Queen, Lornix, speaker for the Sohi, have announced a truce with the Humans, the Silth, and the Neirads to create a period to negotiate a lasting peace. They have called for your troops to lay down their arms and return to the Land."

"Surely our warriors will not fall for this foolishness. And what are Neirads?"

The messenger took a step back and looked around as though searching for cover.

"The Neirads are exiles, members of the Queen's court who have hidden on Earth for centuries." The warrior's chin trembled, and the tendons stood out in his neck. He tried to take a deep breath, but it shuddered as he drew it in.

"Many of the troops have already left their posts and are going through the portals as fast as they can."

As Thest vaulted to his feet with a roar of outrage, the messenger flickered and disappeared from the porch. Thest gave one last look at the lightning branches strobing the horizon, then he too disappeared.

He reappeared next to the portal in Newgrange. A mob of warriors surrounded the portal entrance, which would only accept a few at a time. Some disappeared as soon as they saw him, and Thest lifted his arms toward a group of twenty talking, not noticing him. An orange glow surrounded them, quickly intensifying before it strobed white. They collapsed, writhing and screaming, their clothes and skin completely gone.

Like a wave sweeping through the mob, the remaining warriors all flickered and disappeared.

He watched as the twenty's convulsions slowed to twitches. If he were Xafar, he would keep them alive. Perhaps pin them above the entrance to the portal. He was not Xafar. But as he watched them grow still, he thought, *I am only two steps away from being him.*

He transported again, this time to the Angkor Wat portal. A few of the troops who had witnessed his punishment in Ireland had come here, either to slip through or to warn the others. Many of them flickered and disappeared as he arrived. Again, he raised his arms and enveloped ten warriors in a black roiling cloud, but two were quick enough to raise their shields, and they came running out of it. In a few moments, the cloud cleared, and eight bodies lay on the ground, still living but their bones extracted and lying around them.

They struggled to breathe with lungs unprotected by ribs. The last of the warriors were disappearing from the surrounding fields.

Thest walked over and eyed the struggling heaps of unattached muscles and organs; both spells he had learned from Xafar's advisers. It turned out Xafar performed many of his more macabre stunts by bringing his victims to Earth and then hauling the terrifying results back to the Land.

*Now I am Xafar.*

# CHAPTER NINE

## *Scene 1*

THEST (TROW)

Thest returned to Lake Maracaibo. While he might stem the flood of warriors back into the Land, he knew it would be impossible to find them all and make them fight. He sent word for all the troops still loyal to him to come to the lake, and in due course, almost two thousand showed up.

Between the battle losses and desertions, he felt fortunate to have these. But they were a small fraction of the expeditionary force with which he had begun. He sent a hundred to each of the portals to block further efforts to leave, but also to guard against incursions from the Land.

As the balance regrouped, rested, and searched their ranks for spies, he walked along the edge of the water thinking about his children and his wife. He knew his children would formally mourn him, but he doubted they would truly miss him. He had not been that kind of father but he had kept them alive and away from Xafar's torture.

How they would fare with Faelen and the Sohi he had no idea.

The lightning had started up again in the afternoon darkness brought by heavy cloud cover. As Thest walked, he noticed the thick black tar of an oil spill covering the lake's shore and continuing farther out into the water, capturing debris and endless garbage. None of the sea birds would even land in it. His mouth tightened and his fists clenched as he tried to see its edge.

He imagined Demest flying through the lightning and across the lake into battle, her beauty belying the carnage that would accompany her. Was he responsible for her death? He had let her go into her last battle. But that was both her desire and her job.

No, that was not where his responsibility lay. It was on his watch that the Paerries had changed from cowed primitives to deadly adversaries. He should have killed Storng when he had first broken their rules. He should have immediately killed Aran. Most of all, he should have quietly killed Faelen, the one who caused all of this, when his father sent him to exile on the Earth.

Now, Faelen sat on the throne of the Land. Thest imagined his smirking face.

He sent an enormous bolt of energy into the congealed mass of oil, garbage, dead fish, and birds lining the lake. It exploded beside him and all along the water's edge. He barely had time to get his shield up before the fireball engulfed him, the ensuing explosion running along the side of the lake, finally dying out on the horizon. Boats and shacks also burned along the shore. He turned his back on the scene and returned to his base of operations. He summoned the three advisers and the last of his generals he had brought into the field with him.

"Can we take the Humans' nuclear devices and detonate them?"

"We have already taken several," a wrinkled and elderly Trow female adviser said. "But we cannot get them to explode. And because we cannot remotely detonate them, it would be suicide for the Trow who detonated them."

Another adviser added, "And even the Trow could not occupy

the Earth left behind if we use these devices to kill the Humans."

"I need solutions, not excuses," Thest shouted. He almost added that he did not care about the consequences, but he realized his hold on the group was tenuous. "What about the nerve gas?"

"We have located two more canisters. But the radius of effect is limited. Even if we could disperse it from the air, it would still only go so far."

"Why are we not able to disperse from the air?"

"It is a contact agent, so as soon as the one releasing it gets it on their skin, they drop the canister. We actually located four canisters but lost two trying to overcome this problem."

The third adviser said, "Biologicals."

"What?" Thest rounded on him.

"Biologicals. The Humans have extensive weaponry for delivering biological agents causing mass death. We have tried to release these subtly in the past, but it never resulted in much damage. The delivery mechanisms are simple, however. We understand biological weapons better than technological. As long as we pick one specific to Humans, there should be no risk to the Trow. And it will leave the Earth undamaged."

"While it will not solve the Paerrie problem, it would solve the Human problem," added one of the other advisors. "It would surprise me if the Humans have not already created some sort of biological agent that kills the Paerries. They probably began figuring out how to do that as soon as they discovered them. We have a small container of one of their biological weapons and have already captured some of their scientists, so we can find out."

Thest stood with head bowed as he listened. After a few

moments, he said, "I like this plan. Where we have such biologicals, release them immediately after you have ensured they do not harm the Trow. Get more. Take their scientists so we know how to release them with maximum impact. Determine whether they have developed anything to kill the Paerries. If they have, get it. If they have not, put them to work developing such a thing."

Thest told the general, "Prepare to defend this place. They will try to finish us here."

"There are better places to defend, my King."

"I know. But this is where I feel we have the power to end this."

# Scene 2

**ARAN (SILTH)**

Aran watched Merit making the last preparations. Her lieutenants organized the Humans so ten of them were with each Silth warrior and would join them in the jump. There were barely enough Silth. Even after all the able-bodied had been trained, there had never been that many of them working as warriors. Now those that had survived were spread out in the world. Some of those who were fighting today had no magic, so they couldn't transport Humans or even speak their languages, but they could carry a gun and fight.

The Neirads' fighters had transported to where the Humans were marshaling their heavy equipment, and they would help the Humans protect their machinery as they joined the attack. They would shield themselves, the plane pilots, and the others who operated the Human technology, protecting them all from the Trow warriors' bolts. They would not be able to stop them from transporting into the equipment, but they would fight them there if needed.

This would be their biggest assault and biggest gamble yet. But it was also their chance to end the war. There was so much at stake. The Humans reported Thest had stolen three canisters of their biological weapons, including one of the agents that if unleashed might kill both the Trow and the Silth. The scientists managing these agents of death were missing as well.

*Did Thest know that what he held would kill not just Silth but potentially all the Trow?* Aran wondered. Thest had already used one of the canisters in a population center in Poland.

According to the Silth reporting to Aran, the effect was horrible. The virus moved quickly through the population and within two days of contact, the individuals had died a messy death, infecting anyone around them or who came near the bodies. The Polish army isolated the city and was forced to kill anyone trying to escape. There had been dozens of suicides in the army ranks.

He rested on one of the portable towers brought to the enormous field in southern Florida where they were marshaling, and spread all around him were troops and the mechanisms of war. The ground shook as the sounds of heavy trucks, tanks, helicopters, and jets almost drowned out the shouts of orders and clank of packs and weapons surrounding him. All he smelled was diesel fumes. This was not how he had expected to return to Florida, and his earlier trip seemed a lifetime ago; never in his wildest dreams had he imagined this would be his life.

He'd been a peaceful being. A storyteller. A shaman. A thief.

But he'd spent the last couple of years as something else. While he wasn't even sure what to call it, he was tired of this role, deeply tired—soul weary. He saw flashes of faces he recognized—the Steamtiki Crew, Krackle, Jabtar, and Temkaa. Suddenly, Storng was beside him.

"Thinking about life after this?" Storng asked.

"I can't seem to get that far. I can only think about how much I don't want to do this anymore. I never want another day where those I care about may not see the end of it."

"No days are promised to us except this one."

"I know, but…" Aran stretched. "I cannot imagine a life beyond now. If you asked me, *what will you be doing in a year?* I'd have no answer. I wonder if it's a portent. Have you seen any portents?"

"Many."

"And? What do they show?"

"You know, I never was very good at reading those." Storng looked up at the jets racing across the sky. "A year from now, I would like to be teaching. Penfield and I have decided to create the first college for training Silth, Human, and Trow together. We have so much to learn from each other, and we've so many challenges to overcome together. So many opportunities."

"That sounds perfect. A chance to think."

Storng laughed. "And an excuse to read. We want you to teach there as well.

"There's a Human, from a University called Harvard, who teaches storytelling as advocacy. He has helped many Humans understand their role in noble causes.

"We want the two of you to develop a program for storytelling in the new world. You'd be working with the International Storytelling Institute as well. In this age of competing media and distrust of experts, Penfield and I think people will follow the stories they believe in. With the blip, you can live wherever you want and simply show up to conduct classes, though Humans are increasingly doing much of their training virtually.

"How all this gets balanced is a question for those working on managing technologies. You already have experience with that too, being the only Silth to have appeared with Oprah."

"I am truly honored, and I'll think about it," Aran said. "But let's see if we can make it through this day first."

A voice over a loudspeaker boomed, "Operation Porcupine

launches in ten minutes."

Aran pulled out his watch and noted that would have them beginning at 6:30 a.m. Sunrise at Lake Maracaibo. The defectors had told them Thest's remaining army had gathered there.

"I remember giving you that watch."

"As do I. So there would be no misunderstandings."

"You've come a long way since then. We all have."

Planes took off with the roar of a waking dragon.

"It begins." Storng flickered and disappeared.

The planes would arrive at the Lake encampment in about forty minutes, dropping anti-personnel bombs and releasing Fairy Dust into the air above the camp. The engineers had calculated how long it would take before that dust settled and the Silth could join the battle without losing the ability to blip. Then they would begin strafing the encampment. They would use napalm as well, but only in the area just outside the camp, to reduce the likelihood of Thest trying to retreat.

The Silth and the Human military leaders fought over this tactic because of the wildlife that would die from the napalm. As a compromise, Silth agents had been warning the animals out of the area for the last twelve hours. Those not too slow or too obstinate had left.

Because of their shields, the Trow wouldn't suffer many casualties, but the aim was to confuse, disorient, and disrupt the enemy. Learning they could not easily disable the jets would magnify the effect. The Humans couldn't use their big bombs for fear of releasing the biological agents. A special Silth and Human team would seek those weapons, trying to find and secure them quickly.

No one really expected Thest to retreat. He had nowhere to go and no reinforcements to call upon. At the same time, the remaining warriors were some of his best and most loyal. They would probably fight to the death as long as Thest was alive.

The Silth and Humans gathered in the field were mostly silent.

As Aran stood, Merit appeared in front of him. She said nothing, but embraced him, pulling him hard into her body. As she leaned back, he kissed her, and they held the kiss for several moments before she flickered and disappeared.

"Troop launch in five minutes," came the voice over the speaker.

Aran flew to the ten Human soldiers waiting for him. He noted how young these men and women from around the world were and thought again about the different life he wanted, not just for himself but for them as well.

"You ready to ride?"

"We're honored to be jumping with you, sir," a young man said, the others nodding in agreement.

"The honor is mine. Stay alive."

As the voice over the speaker said, "Launch troops, Good luck," Aran told them, "Grab hold."

They reappeared in bedlam. Thick smoke washed over the field, one of the jets screaming as it spiraled down, and the ground shook as it exploded. As bolts and lasers quietly sliced through the smoke, the chatter of automatic rifles and quickly set-up machine guns was unrelenting.

A building exploded after the bio-team cleared it for biological weapons and rushed to the next one. The Humans who arrived with Aran quickly moved to execute their orders.

"Aran!" Jules called as he appeared a short distance away.

The rest of the Steamtiki Crew coalesced around them, with

the Tiki members close by and the Steamers on the periphery engaging with any Trow they encountered. Aran and the group had a mission—to find Thest. Nick was listening on a radio, and when he pointed inland from the lake's edge, they moved that way. Around them, both Silth and Trow would suddenly appear and then disappear. They'd known their dust wouldn't reach all of Thest's troops. The planes had done a close overflight to draw the warriors out of the buildings and then set off their dust bombs. But the troops remaining in the buildings would have been unaffected.

The air filled with screams of rage and cries of pain.

With Nick by his side, Aran led the core of the team through the chaos. The Tiki Crew members—Don, Kirstn, and Loana—fired their dart guns at Trow when they appeared but continued to huddle behind Aran and Nick. The Steamers were a blur of motion around them. Jules and Slatt moved on point for the group, clearing away any Trow that appeared there. The 5's—Tara, Abney, and Blay—along with Ada, Vander, and Valente, covered their flanks. The mercenaries made no sound. But periodically, there would be a whoosh and brightness as Ada's flame engulfed a Trow, or they would hear the moan of Valente's magnet quickly followed by the shriek of Trow as the bits of metal in their armor pulled through their body. Jules checked in with Nick and Aran for direction, but the others simply followed the sense of flow of the team.

Aran couldn't tell how it was going. Their progress was slow.

Time seemed to stop, though the sun moved across the sky above them. They adjusted directions, took sips of water when able, and kept moving, adjusting as new reports of Thest's presence came in. They didn't want to keep jumping around after him, because they would use too much of their magic energy, and they would need as much as they could keep. The Steamers were using their deep arsenal of weapons instead of bolts, so this too conserved energy.

By late morning, the sound of the battle had changed as the noise of guns increased and the frenetic blipping had almost ceased. Lasers and darts still flew quietly across the field and there was still smoke, but it was mostly gray, not the early morning's black. The radio informed them the Humans and Silth had established a zone of control, a beachhead along the Lake's shore, and were rearming and re-provisioning from there. They were staging medevacs from that zone and protecting for transport the two canisters of nerve gas they'd found so far. They believed they'd recovered all the engineers for the biological agents.

"But Aran," Nick said as he lowered the earpiece, "the canister that will kill the Trow and the Silth is still missing as is one more that will kill Humans."

"Coati-scat," Aran swore, looking at the exhausted Steamtiki Crew.

Nick continued, repeating the words being fed into his ear. "The one that will kill Humans is in a small red container inside a larger silver protective vessel. The one that will kill Trow, and maybe Silth, is in a green container in an identical protective vessel."

They still could not identify where Thest was, and black clouds gathered overhead. Out over the lake, the lightning was already punishing the water.

Because both sides had spent almost all their magical energy, there was almost no transport occurring and no sign of bolts. The Trow and Silth were using whatever energy they had to maintain shields, and each had retreated mostly to a separate part of the open areas with a rough battle line between them. They made their way back to the area maintained by the Humans and Silth.

Aran searched the chaos of the beach head for Merit and Jabtar, finally finding them huddled with other leaders of the attack. "I need two minutes of your time."

"You can have one," was Merit's reply.

"I need help. We can't find Thest, and we need to before he releases the biological weapons or escapes."

"Why would he release them? They'll kill him and his troops. And how would he escape?" Jabtar asked, shaking his head, his eyes wide.

"He has two different weapons. One will kill Humans, and the other Trow and maybe Silth. He hates us, the Silth, and particularly the Silth here today. If he believes he is going to lose, I think he'll take us all with him. But then again, he's likely to still be able to transport or have held someone in reserve who can. He might go anywhere in the world and release them from there. At least we need to get those weapons. But I'd rather stop him here as well."

"Ok," Merit said. "I think that's what we're working on."

"I have a plan."

"We don't have time for one of your toucan-brained plans," she said, but with little real conviction.

"All I need are three healthy shamans who still have some magic and a few warriors to guard them and Jules." Aran looked at Merit as she guessed what he was doing.

"He'll need to know what these biological weapons look like."

"They're silver canisters about the size of a Human," Aran said.

"He won't be able to pick them up. But he'll see them and maybe clear some room around them for someone else to either take them or kill Thest. The Steamtiki Crew have saved most of their power and with some space, can get the canisters."

Merit thought for a moment. "Ok, not your worst plan. Jabtar, do we have any shamans who aren't exhausted?

"Only youngsters we've held back from the fight."

"Get them. I'll surround them with warriors," she told Aran, "And Jules as well. Then we will go after Thest." She looked at him hard, daring him to protest. He knew better.

Almost half an hour later, a giant Jules rose into the lightning flashes of the early evening.

For a few moments, gunfire stopped as everyone stared at the enormous figure. Then the Trow fired furiously, using Human weapons and draining their last power into bolts. Someone among them—Aran thought it would be one of Thest's advisors—decided to attack the source and Trow appeared in ones and twos to try to disable Jules and the young shamans. Merit's warriors dealt with them as they appeared.

Jules's projection moved across the battle lines in a few steps, and the Trow stopped firing as they realized the feet of the apparition were not crushing anything they stepped on.

Jules bent down, peering at something Aran couldn't see. They didn't have speakers for him this time, so Aran, who was standing next to the real Jules, heard him say, "There you are."

"Let's go!" Aran, Merit, Temkaa, and the now rearmed Steamtiki Crew blipped to where they estimated Jules was looking. They found themselves in the middle of a mass of Trow.

And there was Thest, next to a large silver canister.

The fight was immediate and furious. While the crew members worked to hold off the Trow, Merit and Aran surged toward Thest. Aran looked back to see Ada be overwhelmed and go down, igniting her backpack to take as many Trow with her as she could.

Valente disappeared beneath a crush of Trow. In front of Aran, Temkaa winnowed through the Trow, shield up and club swinging. But Thest's last line of warriors had saved their magic. Temkaa's shield absorbed bolt after bolt until he staggered. He fell to his knees, still swinging. As his shield flickered out, a shotgun blast knocked him back several feet where he lay unmoving. Aran couldn't find Merit and didn't see any of the other Silth through the surrounding Trow.

Aran's heart sank—this wasn't going to work. There were too many of them.

Suddenly, an explosion occurred in the ranks of Trow trying to reach them. Trow, whole and in parts, went flying. Another explosion, and another. Aran looked up at a furious Jules firing enormous bolts into the Trow ranks, and he saw Merit ahead of him. She ignored everything else and pushed toward Thest, breaking out of the crowd of attackers as a well-placed bolt from Jules cleared the area ahead.

Thest stood close to the canister so Jules wouldn't fire at him. When he spotted Merit, he stepped around the canister and placed it between them.

Jules fired one last time into the Trow mob before the giant apparition collapsed, either exhausted or injured. Thest fired at Merit with such ferocity that, despite her shield, he drove her backward, tripping two retreating Trow. As their fallen bodies protected her for a moment, Aran took the opportunity and fired at the shieldless Thest.

But Thest restored his shield before Aran's shot struck.

As Merit flew from the tangle of Trow and attacked Thest from above, Aran moved forward at ground level. Thest had obviously conserved his energy, and now he reduced his shield to a three-quarters circle and rotated the opening to alternate firing at Merit and Aran.

They had to raise their own shields to block the powerful bolts. Because he was on the ground, Aran dug in his feet and avoided being bowled backwards. But in the air, each time a bolt hit Merit, she rolled for several yards and had to fly back to attack again.

Thest used the canister and the fact neither of them would fire close to it to guard his flank.

Thest fired four times, knocking Merit farther away. Then he turned back to Aran and fired bolt after bolt. It took everything Aran had to hold his shield up, and it was flickering as his power ran out. He remembered when Angel had used this tactic against him. This time, there was no tree for him to turn to. Aran began to lose consciousness.

But Thest paused. Aran shook his head groggily as he saw Thest point toward the canister and blast the valve. Mist spewed from the device. Thest used his magic to fling the canister out onto the battlefield and then turned to face Aran.

Over Thest's shoulder, Aran saw Merit speeding to help him, shield down, hands raised to fire. Thest whipped around and fired a bolt that hit Merit in the chest. Her eyes opened wide, her jaw dropped, and her hands brushed ineffectually at her chest before she dropped from the air.

"No," Aran shouted as he pointed to the ground below Thest's feet and quickly muttered the words.

Thest was turning back to finish him as Aran shouted the last of the words.

The ground disappeared beneath Thest, and he dropped into the hole Aran had created by transporting a cargo container-sized amount of dirt to the Land. Aran brought it back again to drop on top of Thest with a thud that shook the surrounding ground.

Aran rushed over and lifted Merit's head. He tried to transport her to the beach where the medical teams were, but he didn't have enough energy. Kirstn appeared beside them, tears running down her dirt-covered face. She put a hand on each, and they were back at the beachhead.

Aran lay Merit's head on the ground. Her wings stuck out at odd angles, broken from the fall, and she had burn marks across the front of her leather armor. She wasn't moving.

He put his hands on her chest and tried to force energy into her, but he had little left. In fact, he realized as the adrenalin left his system, he was in danger of passing out himself. It didn't matter—he couldn't lose her. He pushed his energy into her body and was losing consciousness when he was roughly shoved away. Storng crouched over Merit now, putting his hands where Aran's had been and pushing energy into her broken body.

When Merit moved and opened her eyes, Storng stood and stumbled back, color drained from his face and panting. He looked over at Aran, still conscious but unable to move, and dropped to his side. He put his hand on Aran's heart.

"Ah, too much, Fledgling." He leaned down to listen to Aran's breathing. "You are leaving us."

Aran tried to speak, to tell him it was alright, but nothing came out. He felt his glamour slip away, leaving him to die ugly, with this stupid device on his head. He felt cold, bone-chattering cold, and he blinked inside the device, his eyes too heavy to keep open. He closed them and sighed in relief. He wasn't cold any longer, and he wasn't scared.

He felt as though he was floating on the water in a small boat among gentle waves. He didn't need to row. He didn't need to steer. The boat knew the way. The sun was warm on his face, and he heard the gulls and other shorebirds in the distance. He was flooded with gratitude for the life he'd led and those around him. And he was at peace.

*So, this is what it feels like.*

The sun grew warmer, and then hot. His chest burned, and he heard his voice cry out from some distance away. The boat disappeared, and he felt hands on his chest, pushing down, driving energy into him. Aran pushed Storng away as soon as he had strength.

The old shaman fell backward and lay still.

Aran crawled over to him and shouted as loud as his broken voice allowed, "Help! Someone help." Others took up the cry, searching for a shaman who still had magic.

Kirstn dropped to her knees beside them. "They're all dead. They used the last of their energy so Jules could fire the bolts," she sobbed.

Storng's eyes fluttered open, and he smiled at Aran.

"It was a grand day. A grand life. I'm glad I was here…. To the next adventure." As Aran held him, the one black eye closed and then the one white eye.

And Storng died.

\*\*\*

Kirstn struggled to her feet and reached over to pull Aran away from Storng. "Where's the canister?"

"I don't know!" Aran tried to pull back to Storng's side.

"What color was the container inside?"

"I don't know! Let go of me," he said as he tried to push past her.

"Aran, it could kill us all!"

Aran struggled to focus on her. He turned and flew into the dwindling battle. The Trow who could transport away were doing so, taking any of their fellow warriors they could reach. The ones who couldn't transport or get to someone who could were working their way to the edge of the fighting so that they could dash into the forest.

"Where is it? I don't see it?" Aran shouted.

Nick appeared next to him. "It's gone. Tara and Don got to it almost immediately when it hit the ground and transported away with it."

"Where?"

"I don't know."

Both turned as shouts and screams pierced the sounds of the battle. Near one of the few remaining buildings, Humans, Trow and Silth were on the ground writhing. More fell in a slowly expanding semicircle around the building's entrance. Someone in a full bunny suit, helmet and all, came running from the building waving their arms.

Aran heard several of the Human soldiers shouting, "Nerve gas! Nerve gas! Gear Up!"

Human soldiers were quickly putting on respirators and suits. Others, without suits, were rushing toward the Silth who were collecting them and then transporting away. Aran knew he did not have the magic left to transport himself or anyone else.

"Go get Merit." Aran pointed to where she was on the beach, "Blip her away and make sure the others are leaving as well." Nick flickered and disappeared.

The wind had picked up the gas and was moving it quicker through the remaining troops. Aran watched as a Silth who had returned to transport Humans misjudged the timing and fell to the ground, screaming in pain with the Humans he'd tried to transport out.

The Trow, at first confused by what was happening, now seemed to understand, and were running as fast as they could. Some were escaping into the forest, but others weren't fast enough. As the wave moved toward the forest on one side of the battlefield, the Silth began shouting to the animals to fly or run. But then the breeze shifted back toward the other side.

Aran flew lower and waved his arms, shouting to them all, "This way!"

He waved them toward the beach. At least the Silth could evacuate them from there, and helicopters were taking off from there as well.

One of the Trow warriors ran up to Aran, his eyes wide. Aran waved him toward the beach and kept shouting and waving until the instructions had been taken up by the crowd of soldiers—Human, Trow, and Silth. Then he flew toward the beach. He arrived just as the Human who had run from the building was reporting to one of the field commanders.

"We came into the building just in time to see one of the Trow take a sledgehammer and drive a steel wedge into the side of the large canister. He knocked it in twice and then hit it on the side, so it fell out. The gas started roaring out."

Around them, Silth were shuttling Humans and Trow who couldn't transport any more away from the beach and then returning for more. Helicopters also swooped in for more.

*Where are Don and Tara?*

*What is happening with the biological agent? Which one was it? Was it the one that would kill Humans or the one that would kill Trow and Silth?*

*Were any of the Humans, Trow, or Silth on the battlefield infected? As the soldiers of all races scattered through evacuation or into the jungle, were some of them carrying the death of their race? What could they do?*

Behind him, he heard the field command say, "Oh, alright." The commander turned to his communications crew and said, "We've got one of the biological canisters. It's the Human virus."

"So that means the missing one is the Trow virus?" an aide asked.

"Yep, thank God."

Aran grabbed one of the Silth warriors as he headed to help a group evacuate.

"Send warriors to both portals. None of the Trow who were on the field when the biological was released can go through the portals. Isolate them. They may carry the virus and infect the Land."

"So?" the warrior said, his eyebrows raised.

"Our friends are in the Land." He didn't try to explain that these warriors might also carry the death of the Silth in their infected bodies.

# Scene 3

**THEST (TROW)**

Thest arrived at the Angkor Wat portal half an hour after leaving the battlefield. Only two of his guards remained, preparing to go back to the Land.

"Your Highness," one said as they both bowed. "We thought you were dead."

The other stammered, "That's what we were told by those who came from your camp. They saw you die under a mountain of dirt."

"No, they saw me fall in a hole while still shielded. They didn't see me transport away before the hole refilled."

"What are your orders, sire?"

"Continue to get ready. We will go through the portal together." His answer caused their eyebrows to rise.

"When we get through, you can go on with your life. Do what you want." He started stripping away anything not on the common warrior's uniform. He unhooked his cloak and it fell to the ground. He then took a plain cloak from one of the soldiers.

"I have one more thing to do, but I suspect it is best done by myself."

After removing the several weapons hidden in his clothes and boots, he piled them in the enormous stack next to the portal building's doorway. They passed through single file, with bowed heads, one warrior in front of Thest and the other behind. The Sohi waiting at the other side were alert but did not appear to recognize Thest. They had each of them fill out information on who they were and where they lived. Thest made his up, but the Sohi had no reference so they could not tell. And then they were through, released into the Land to return to their homes.

Thest waved off the two warriors, and even though they offered to go on with him, he saw their relief. He walked toward his home without them, the rough woolen cloak pulled around his face.

When he arrived at the ruins of his house, he found them untouched. He rummaged through the contents of his closet, some relatively free of char, though everything smelled of smoke. He changed his clothes, putting on the finest royal courtier outfit he could assemble from the unburnt bits and pieces. *Ha, good fortune! An unburnt cloak.* After replacing the rough cloak with a fine, soft one, he moved to another part of the former house. Here, the fire had reduced everything wooden to ashes, but fortunately it had not rained since. He located a stick and poked around, having kept a store of weapons in this part of the house.

After almost an hour's search, he had assembled a knife with its wooden handle gone, but it was still serviceable, a short sword in fine condition, and five throwing stars. He hid these in the pockets of the cloak. Poking the stick into the ashes again, he finally heard the thud of it striking metal. He knelt and clawed through the charred pieces of wood, uncovering a metal box blackened by the fire. Because the fire had caused it to warp, it did not open easily. Finally, the lid popped back and revealed a Human gun with an undamaged box of ammunition.

As he was preparing to leave, he saw a burned photo frame with a picture of his wife and his children, young then. Angel had taken the picture when Thest brought his family to Earth many years ago. Pictures were rare in the Land; back when this was taken, you had to know a Trow on Earth with a phone, or a camera back when this was taken. They had to know how to take them and have the means to print or develop them. In this picture, they were all smiling, taken on a day of adventures and whimsy.

He pulled the badly damaged fragment of a picture from its frame. But before he could put it in his pocket, it fell apart, and the wind scattered the pieces through the ruins.

He sighed as he stepped carefully through the debris of his life, making his way back to the road. He was not sad, however. His step was light as he walked toward the palace, looking forward to his task. Only one thing left to do. One task and then he would rest.

When he saw the palace, he picked up his pace and joined the entering Trow procession. Two Sohi guards stood at the entrance, watching the crowd, but not challenging or questioning anyone. The palace design placed little security before the ballroom and the first courtyard where the King and Queen's courts gathered and interacted. There was art on the walls of these spaces, and once there had been performances, but Xafar had done away with those. The heralds announced proclamations here, so messengers were always hanging around, ready to dash off to summon those they served. The courtyard, packed with Trow, had none of the usual Silth or Human slaves that served as messengers.

Moving from the courtyard into the main palace was trickier. Thest found one of the servant entrances and ducked into it. If, as he suspected, the Sohi had immediately done away with slavery and freed the palace servants, these would be empty. But they were not. He slipped into a room when he heard Human voices down the corridor.

"How about you, what are you going to do?"

"I don't know. I've been here so long, I'm not sure I can function back on Earth."

"Well, it's not been such a long time for them on Earth."

"I may take the Sohi up on their offer to stay in the Land and work for wages."

"Me, I'm out of here. I had children I'd like to see again. I don't know how I'm going to explain to them what happened to me."

"From what I hear, their eyes are open to the two worlds now, so it won't be so strange."

"I just hope they are alright."

The voices moved away, and Thest slinked down the corridor, past the kitchens and laundry. It appeared most of the former slaves, if they were still here, were in their quarters. As he passed the corridor leading to their rooms, he heard several voices. Normally, there were guards on these corridors, but apparently the Sohi had thought they were to control the slaves rather than protect the King and Queen. Thest came to the servant entrance to the throne room. Two doorways faced one another across a section dropped back about four feet from the main wall. The walls of the room extended past the edges of the doorways, the effect blending the doorway into the wall, making it unnoticeable except from a nearby angle.

"Thest, do come in. Skulking in the doorway is unbecoming for royalty, past or present."

In the acoustics of the room, Faelen's voice was eerily similar to his father's, the mad King Xafar. As Thest stepped inside, he pulled the short sword from its sheath against his back and the dagger from his cloak.

"The Sohi saw you come into the palace, and I pulled the guards out of the passage—there was no use in them getting killed. We both know their bio-guns will not fire on anyone when they become King, whether or not they lose that position. Have you come to take back the throne?" Faelen gestured to the seat he occupied, wearing the red robes of the Sohi.

"I do not care about thrones. I have come for you."

Thest glanced around the room, confirming they were alone.

"Not to protect your children, who by the way, are well. How typical of you." Faelen leaned forward as though trying to see inside Thest.

"Then your child may survive your death," Thest said, inching closer to the throne. His spies had told him that Faelen had a wife who was pregnant now.

"I promised your son I would give you a chance to forfeit, lay down your arms, give up your war, and live the rest of your days in peace. This is that chance."

"I can have all those things following your death."

"Hmm, I do not think you will defeat the Sohi, and at my death, my Queen and co-leader will end you. So you have nothing to gain."

"Your death is the only gain I seek."

"You know," Faelen said, as he reached down to the hidden side of the throne, pulled out a sword, and stood, "conversation with you has grown no more interesting with passing time. Death, death, death. I know your tricks. You are trying to bore me to death."

Thest sprang forward in attack, which Faelen blocked. They fought back and forth across the room. Thest had many more years' experience with this type of fighting, and while Faelen had gained a high level of competence in fighting with magic on Earth, Thest had the edge in skill here. Mostly, Faelen was on defense and was soon bleeding from multiple small wounds.

But fueled only by adrenalin, Thest began to tire. A mistake left an opening in which Faelen cut a deep gash in Thest's arm. Thest dropped the dagger and reached into the pocket he had filled with sand, which he threw in Faelen's face. As Faelen stepped back, trying to wipe the sand from his eyes, Thest knocked the sword from his hand. He moved forward to thrust the short sword through Faelen's throat but stopped with the point barely touching the skin. He pushed hard to drive it home but couldn't move it—something restrained him. Thest stepped back and looked around to see another red-robed figure standing nearby, hands raised.

She lowered her hands. "I am Lornix, Speaker of the Sohi Will and Queen of the Land."

"No magic exists in the Land," Thest spat out, his brow furrowed in confusion.

"So you say. The Land says otherwise. In its shriveled, neglected heart, the Land is connected to the Earth, and has magic. Like overused and untended soil, it has been fallow, uncultivated for a long time. Worse, it has received no nutrition, nothing to re-nourish it for years, so it is dust-like, meager, but not dead. Just waiting for reawakening."

Thest held up his hand and tried to fire a bolt at her, but nothing happened.

Lornix did not flinch. "Not enough magic for that," she said.

Thest spun a pointed star at her with his left hand and rushed forward with his sword held high. She brushed the star from the air with a wave of her hand and pulled a short, thick metal rod from the arm of her robe. It had a point on one end and a ball weighting the other. Holding the rod parallel with her arm between wrist and elbow, she blocked the downward stroke of Thest's sword and then quickly swung the end with the ball, smashing it into the wrist holding the sword.

Thest bellowed in rage and pain as he dropped the weapon.

His other hand reached into the cloak and extracted the gun, pointing it at Lornix's face.

Her hands flew up defensively. Thest pivoted to turn the gun on Faelen, who had rushed forward to assist his wife. Before Thest could pull the trigger, Lornix drove the point of her weapon into the side of his neck, through his throat, and out the other side.

As Thest lay gasping for breath, his hands clenching and releasing, Faelen stood over him.

But instead of the taunt Thest expected, Faelen whispered, "May your heart find peace wherever it journeys next. Rest knowing your children are safe, and we allowed them to give you a general's funeral."

Thest relaxed and let the darkness seep in.

# Scene 4

Aran (Silth)

*Where would they go?* If he could get close enough, he could do a finding spell. Whichever of them reached the canister first would have transported them. Was it Tara or Don? Would they have picked different locations? Neither had a *home* currently. They would have picked some place with few Trow or Silth to contract the virus. A desert? The Artic? For two days, he and the others searched for them. It was now morning on the third day.

Aran decided to look at the falls where the team had last met.

Penfield told him that if they were exposed to the virus, they would have died within two days if the Silth were susceptible to it. None of the Silth from the battlefield had died, but no one knew whether that was because none had been exposed, thanks to the quick thinking of Tara and Don, or whether the virus didn't work on Silth.

None of the Trow had died either, as far as they knew. They had stopped those in the battle, other than Thest, from going through the portals. Today, they were being allowed to return home. While the Silth were all accounted for, there could be dead Trow lying in the jungle or wherever they transported. Aran imagined a bloated corpse with flies landing on it before carrying the virus far and wide. He tried not to imagine the bodies of Tara or Don in the same condition.

Aran stood at the top of the falls as he cast the finding spell.

It wouldn't work if they were dead, and their bodies had disappeared. And he didn't know if it would work if they were dead but the bodies still here. No one understood Human magic well enough to know whether the virus resulted from Human magic or was just diabolically clever.

They were here, down at the base of the falls. He flickered and reappeared outside of the building where they had met before. He had a bag with all the gear he was supposed to wear if there was a body, but he wanted to stay positive as long as possible.

"Tara! Don!" The sound of the falls swallowed his shout.

He kept calling as he walked around the building. Then he thought he heard Don's voice coming from the patio, so he hurried forward. Don had his back to Aran and was waving his arms like someone fending off bees.

"Son of a toucan. These mosquitos are going to carry me off into the jungle. Where was I? Oh, right. So, we were in this Dollar store, and Aran was supposed to be on guard duty outside."

"Supposed to be?" Aran said as he walked up behind him. "I was the best guard you ever had. None of you would have figured out how to make a police car go."

"Aran Shaman!" Don started forward, but then stopped. "You should stay back. We both got covered in the virus trying to shut off the valve."

"And you would be dead if it worked on Silth, but it doesn't. If it doesn't find a host, the virus dies in two days."

Tara put her head in her hands. "Then please just kill me now. Put me out of my misery. I cannot listen to any more of his incessant chattering. I have thought of 100 ways to kill him. I must leave now. Can I go?" Don looked down at the ground, frowning.

"First, let me thank you both. What you did was very brave.

Other than Don fatigue, are you feeling okay?"

"Perfect." She flickered and disappeared.

Aran turned to the sheepish-looking Don. "You?"

"I feel great. I've spent the last two days waiting to die and wondering how long it would be before we knew. So, it's a relief not to have to worry about it. I take it we won?"

"I'll tell you all about it while we move the canister to storage." Aran stepped forward and folded the big Silth into an embrace.

"I'm very glad you are alive."

"There's not much food around here. Can we get something to eat first?"

# CHAPTER TEN

## *Scene 1*

Aran (Silth)

The sun rose with its orange light flowing into the blue and green of the morning sky, reflecting off the calm waters of the Caribbean. In the distance were the clouds of a thunderstorm that wouldn't make it here today.

Four days earlier, word had come from the Land that the war was over. Given the proximity of the date to the end of October, the UN and WSC declared this an International Day of the Dead. Many were using it not just to remember their ancestors, but also to bury their dead or to say goodbye.

No longer uncomfortable on the ocean, Aran particularly relished being on the water in the early morning. A pod of dolphins cavorted beside the boat, and a squadron of pelicans floated in a huge V overhead in the cool and salty air.

Today was a day around the world for endless parades, huge celebrations, and dancing until you dropped, as Humans, Silth, and Trow rejoiced at being alive and remembered those who were not. It was a day for quiet tears and knowing embraces as too many empty tables reminded families of their losses. This was the first shared holiday, and for many, the first time they learned the customs of those with whom they now knew they shared a planet.

Aran was on a large, single-story ferry used to move vehicles and people among the islands. They were here, off the coast of a national park in Costa Rica, to celebrate the dead of the last battle, the one that had saved them all. All the many dead were being celebrated, but four in particular were being honored. Ada had died of gunshot wounds. The technology of guns grew from Human magic, but their bullets were not magical, and so her body had disappeared upon her death. In the Silth tradition, a small doll hung from the corner of the boat's cabin. It was white with a bright yellow crest and had a small leather apron and black goggles. All the Steamtiki Crew members were there, joined by Nadara, who stood holding Jules' arm, and Ada's son, whom Aran had never met. He always thought of the Steamers as completely untethered, but Ada had apparently wanted to raise a family in the new world of Silth.

Temkaa had died similarly, and while his colony, several hours ahead of them, had already honored him today, two of its shamans had joined them on the boat for the morning's celebration.

Lir and Manan attended to honor Tethra, who had died protecting a Human pilot as Thest's warriors tried to take down her plane. Aran assumed Tethra must have died by the bolt, but the fire of the plane crash was so intense the Neirads had not located a body. They knew a little of the story behind the crash.

An Ecuadorian major named Pruna had been flying the plane, leading one squadron attacking the Trow on the lake. Tethra occupied the second seat in her fighter. The first of Thest's warriors had transported into her cockpit and Tethra blasted him before he harmed the major, but Tethra had to get the large Trow body out of the plane so that Pruna could operate. Tethra transported out quickly with the body and dropped it from the air.

However, before the Neirad could get back in the jet, a second warrior transported into the plane. When Tethra returned, there was a fight, with the struggling Trow firing multiple bolts into the plane's console, setting it on fire. Pruna ejected, but the two Trow continued to fight as the plane crashed into the jungle.

The only body they had to address was Storng's, who'd left instructions that if he died leaving a body, something the Silth didn't have customs for since few Silth had ever died from magic, he wanted it buried at sea. He found the whole idea of a sea burial beautiful. No one had known whether Storng's death would leave a body or not. He had died by his own magic, saving Merit and Aran, but his body remained.

So, besides the others, Merit, Penfield, Joss, Tiny, and Krackle were on the boat to say goodbye to Storng. Jabtar, the only shaman besides Aran who had survived the battle at the beach, was there as well. He'd been knocked unconscious at the time the energy was sucked from the other shamans. What was left of the Shaman Council would have another ceremony later in the day to honor Storng and the other shamans, and another was occurring at the UN. There, the US President and other world leaders would honor all the fallen.

Jules said that Ada had died the warrior's death she desired. He spoke of how she had risen above her harsh upbringing, and of what it had meant to her to fight for a cause she believed in. Ada's son spoke of his mother's gentle love. The young Silth trembled and his voice broke as he too acknowledged that she died the way she would have wanted, only far too early.

One of Temkaa's shamans spoke of his colony's pride that Temkaa had joined *the big fight* and been a key part of the world victory.

She also spoke of how they would miss his wisdom and guidance.

To the surprise of all who knew her, 3 of 5 stepped forward, her eyes red and raw. She spoke of how Temkaa wanted to make sure that the Humans honored their commitment to wildlife following the war. Hand shaking, she tapped the Temkaa doll hanging from the cabin rafter tail, so it swung back and forth. She talked of how he wanted to help bring the Silth into this new age of Human contact, but how important it was not to lose their connection to their brothers and sisters in the wild.

A somber Lir said that while the Neirads did not fear death, they did not rush toward it either. Lir spoke of Tethra's desire for the Neirads to make a difference in the war and regain the honor they had lost by going into hiding. Manan talked of how the Neirads would miss Tethra's leadership and counsel, but also of their pride in the place of honor Tethra had given them in the world.

The group quietly moved to stand around the body of Storng, hidden beneath a blanket of flowers. The boat rocked, with the water periodically slapping the side while they lowered their heads.

Krackle began. "You all know that I thought Storng was a bit of a *knucklehead*. Is that the right word? What with his crazy schemes and silly names for things. He and I were in shaman school together and became... good friends. It didn't go past school, but I will always have a special place in my heart for him." She turned away before adding, "And the chickens will miss their namesake."

"Storng was perhaps the perfect *first encounter* a Human might have," Penfield said, sharp in his black suit and black tie, but face pale and lips tight. "He was well-read and already knew the good and bad of who we each are. He was curious and had a great sense of humor, and he became my friend and confidant, so I will miss him very much."

He pulled a case out of his pocket and opened it, showing the medal inside to the group. "Later today, the President will present this, our country's highest honor, on behalf of Storng. I understand there will be similar honors from around the world."

They all stood quietly for a moment, and then Joss said, "I first met Storng long before any of us had heard of Silth or Trow or any of that. He saved my life. First, he rescued me physically, breaking a lot of Silth rules in doing so. But he also showed me there was magic in the world, which rescued me in other ways. He could be the wise elder, but he could also be the trickster or the fool, whichever one accomplished what he wanted. But he was always the friend and the protector." She teared up and couldn't say more, so she stepped back into Tiny's great arms.

When no one else spoke, Aran stepped forward and began as softly as his broken voice would allow. "Storng was these things. And more. For me, he was teacher, tormentor, mentor, and the closest thing I had to a father." Aran's shoulders slumped and his voice cracked.

He paused for a moment, collected himself, and continued.

"He saved my life too, but he was also reckless and most of the trouble in my life came from him. He was vain and manipulative, but he manipulated for the benefit of others, not himself. He leaves behind a hole in the world so big I can't imagine how it will be filled."

Aran moved to stand at the head of the flower-covered figure, staggering when a rogue wave struck and the boat gave a little lurch.

"Only Storng could get a bunch of Silth out on a boat, a place wholly unnatural to us."

The group chuckled. He continued more formally. "We are

here today to say goodbye to fallen friends, old and new. The Silth believe when we die, our bodies return to the Earth to form into the trees, the eggshells, and the rain. Death releases our energy, which carries our consciousness into the world. For a while, it remains a coherent personality and nearby.

"For us, therefore, Storng is still nearby, riding this breeze and feeling our emotions and thoughts. So, we try not to weigh him down by feeling too sad. We know he will stay to comfort us as long as we require, but he needs to become part of the newborn gull. He needs to join the energies of those who have gone before and become the moonlight and the lightning as it strikes the water. He needs to ride the storms he so enjoyed. We know the energies of those who have loved us surround us, and this is part of what makes the world a joy to us. And we look forward to blending and moving with those energies, which is why we do not fear death. It is also why this fine Human notion of a *day of the dead* is natural for us. In this tradition, this is the day the dead, if we remember them, can move amongst us, and join us in celebration. For Silth, this is every day.

"But Storng went beyond this belief. He believed we could blend with those energies while still in life. This is how he became *Storm Rider*. He believed we did not have to wait until death to experience the energy of our ancestors. He believed he could look for it, experience it in the surrounding storms. And once he had practiced that, he believed he might tap into the living energy of those around him and become closer to them. He also believed there was some relationship between magic and this energy.

"Our loss, the world's loss, today is huge." Aran stopped and stared down at the deck before blinking a few times and continuing.

"But these individuals, Trow, Silth, and Human, paid a price for us to shape a better future. That duty falls to us now. To honor them, we must build that better future."

He gave a nod, and several Silth stepped forward to pick up the four corners of the pallet holding Storng's light, Silth body. They carried it over to the side where a platform, held by a winch, lay on the deck. Tiny turned on the winch motor, raising the platform and shoving it over the side, before lowering it into the water. The pallet floated off, and as the bamboo tubes beneath it filled with water, it sank. According to Storng, its designer, the concept was that the pallet and body would sink beneath the water, leaving the blanket of flowers floating on the surface.

Some of the group gasped, however, when a pod of dolphins suddenly appeared, swimming around the sinking pallet, one jumping over the veil of flowers.

The sky darkened as black clouds rolled in on a brisk wind, but no rain fell. Then from all directions at once, what seemed to be dozens of blue and yellow parrots and a score of green flower fairies silently settled on the floating apparatus. A moment later, eight huge butterflies made from light floated down and landed on the pallet. They lifted it from the clear green water and as they held it aloft for a few seconds, the group on the boat stared at the bottom, water cascading back out of the bamboo floats. Then it dropped, slamming down on the surface of the water.

But it was empty, both body and flowers gone. The parrots, butterflies, and flower fairies scattered, and the clouds evaporated, leaving the sun shining on the boat.

Krackle let out a gleeful shout. "Excellent!"

# *Scene 2*

ARAN (SILTH)

The agenda for the day was straightforward. The group had returned from the water, freshened up, and gathered for lunch at the Almonds and Corals Hotel where most were staying. They would spend the afternoon in play, reflection, meetings with old and new friends, and attending some other ceremonies around the world. That evening, they would gather for a wake on the beach.

The restaurant was beautiful, with dense green vegetation to the edge of the glassless window, dark tropical woods, and a thatched roof. The ocean waves provided the background music, and the fragrance of Caribbean spices filled the air.

"How did he do that?" Penfield asked when Aran joined him, Tiny and Joss at a table. "Did you know he could do it?"

"Why would you assume someone has taught you everything they know?" Aran echoed a phrase repeated to him by both of his mentors, Faelen and Storng.

"No ill effects from the baby's first battle?" Aran asked Joss.

Tiny, his arm resting on the back of Joss's chair, answered, "The docs say baby and Mom are fine. Some babies have moms who take bubble baths and soothe them with the sound of Mozart and language class…"

"This little boy led flower fairies into battle and grew accustomed to the sounds of guns, bombs, and bolts," Joss continued.

"Little boy?"

"Yep. We're naming him *Fetu Storng Palepoi,* but we'll call him *Jake.*"

They talked of Tiny's decision to leave volcano work for a while because he didn't want to be away so much. Because they expected Joss to be pretty busy for several years, he would take the lead in keeping Jake and managing the physical grounds of her Directorate.

Then they talked of Penfield's plans for a university.

"It will be in Virginia, near Washington South. We already have a gift of the land, and between Silth and Human benefactors, we have one of the world's largest endowments. We'll have colleges focusing on the many aspects of a shared world we need to develop, as well as sharing the strengths and learning of three races over the centuries."

Penfield rubbed his hands together in gleeful anticipation.

"You're going to be around this afternoon, right?" Aran asked, and Penfield nodded. "I'd like to talk to you some more about this plan." He turned to Joss. "There's someone I need you to meet. Can you excuse us for just one moment?" he said to Tiny and Penfield.

Joss followed him, and they walked over to the table with the Steamtiki Crew.

"Aran!" came the shout as he approached. "Join us," Nick said.

"I will this afternoon. Would you mind if I borrowed Tara for a moment?"

They all made non-committal noises, none wanting to speak for her, and most surprised she was taking part in such a social moment to begin with.

Aran led them to a quiet terrace nearby.

"Joss, this is Tara. Tara, Joss."

Joss gave a slight bow. "It's a pleasure to meet the famous 3 of

5. All the males on my staff are fanboys, and most of the women follow your social media."

Tara rolled her eyes but still seemed pleased.

"We share a deep concern about wildlife in the post-war period," voiced Aran.

He paused to choose his words carefully. "But we have different approaches. Joss is managing the worldwide program, trying to deal with all the distinct threats. But Tara, you're focused on a persistent and rebounding threat of poaching."

Joss stared at Tara for a moment and then seemed to realize what Aran was hinting at. "Ahh," she said, and Tara's eyes narrowed. "You know, my office is only now up and running again, and we realize that among the many Human casualties of this war, it appears the ranks of poachers around the world have been decimated. They are just gone."

Tara crossed her arms and stared.

"While we believe that any unnatural loss of life is tragic, we won't be mourning these casualties of the Trow aggression. But their disappearance is a lot like when you've just finished weeding a flower bed."

Lifting her chin, Tara said nothing.

"You've pulled all the weeds," Joss went on, "but the soil is the same, the seeds of future weeds are already there, and you know they'll just come back. You can't get rid of them until you change the soil and crowd them out with the flowers you want. I hate the poachers. The trophy hunters, particularly those who seek endangered and rare animals, are almost as bad. Their murders, however, besides being morally wrong, would do more harm than good.

"Did you know in the last fifteen years, over fifteen hundred conservationists have been killed? That's right, over a hundred people a year killed because they stood up for nature.

"Some believe execution of the poachers justifies this kind of violence. Because the people who want to exploit nature use these kinds of tactics to smear all environmental work, the violence keeps us from being able to stop the pesticides, deforestation, pollution, and development that kills so much more wildlife."

"I cannot control what stupidities Humans believe, and we can't sit idle while Humans murder our brothers and sisters," Tara said through clenched teeth. "We've done it for too long. Silence is the gateway for evil." Her hand sliced the air as though attacking. "The harpy eagle and the jaguar, major symbols for the Silth here in Costa Rica, are extinct."

"I agree," Joss said, speaking even softer than before and not moving her hands from her lap. "But let's change the soil. Let's work with the local communities to help them love their brothers and sisters like you do. Let's send the poachers to jail for a long time, like they deserve.

"Help me have eyes where I don't have eyes and proof where proof is hard to find, and I promise I can stop them. And I need big-time help in another way. It's plain the next revolution we will face is communicating with the animals around us and understanding them better. They are becoming more coordinated and clearer in their expectations. We need experts who can talk with them and guide them into ways we can live together and thrive.

"My organization is working to build E. O. Wilson's dream of fifty percent of the Earth set aside for wildlife, but we need cooperation and communication for this to work. I think the Silth are the key. I need Silth to lead this effort. Let me introduce you to Dimba Tsago.

"He is leading our worldwide efforts to deal with poachers. You'll like him. He shares your passion for wildlife. He needs the information you can give him on the operations when they reappear. I can promise you he will respond."

Joss turned to Aran, saying, "Dimba is just coming out of the hospital. He was shot twice in the raids we conducted over the summer. I'm trying to get him to spend more time in the office setting up the prosecution, and less in the field. I think that he's used the last of his *nine lives.*" She spent a few minutes explaining where the term *nine lives* came from and why Humans would believe that cats had more than one life.

"You know Africa has been devastated by the impact of the volcanos, the Silth attack, and the loss of leaders because of the poachers' violation of the Human promise. The Africans are banding together to build a new path forward. It will center on a new city they have planned. They're calling it *Wacanda,* after the country described in the Black Panther movies. They need someone to lead the Silth side of the continent-wide wildlife response. We hope that their approach will be a model we can use in other continental organizations."

Tara showed no emotion as she stared off into another corner of the room.

Joss leaned back in her chair. "Temkaa was going to lead this group. You and Dimba can eliminate the culture of poachers in Africa, and I can present the model to the rest of the world. We'll kill two birds with one stone." She looked at Aran and rolled her eyes. "Though PETA says we should say *feed two birds with one scone.* This confuses me, since feeding scones to birds is bad and probably kills them at a higher rate than stones."

Aran laughed, "So they've accidentally said, *kill two birds with one scone?*"

Joss rocked forward laughing, and then stood. "Tara, it's a pleasure to meet you. Come see me. I think we could make a difference."

As Joss walked away, Aran told Tara, "Joss is my oldest Human friend. She saved my life before she knew anything about me or what a Silth was."

Tara looked after her, then asked Aran, "What's a *scone?*"

On the terrace, Aran sat next to Nadara as she, Penfield, and Lir talked in the shade of a thatched umbrella. Nadara and Lir had drinks with small umbrellas in them while Penfield had a beer. Aran sipped on a club soda with lime.

"Lir was telling us about the Land," Nadara said. "Apparently, a large part of it, the Faraway, is wasteland where only toxic flowers grow. The flower fairies come from there, which is why they have had no trouble eating toxic stuff here on Earth. Speaking of flower fairies, Aran, where is Kimper?"

"When I saw her last, she was so proud of leading the flower fairies into battle she was trying to convince them they needed her to be Queen. I don't think her campaign was going well."

Penfield's eyes were alight with excitement. "We were discussing the proposition that terraforming is something Humans do pretty well. Lir was also pointing out how empty much of the ocean floor is. So, we were playing with the notion of restoring deserts, sending Humans into the Land to restore it, setting aside half the Earth for wildlife and non-tech play..."

"Because the water mutes the effects of technology, moving industry onto the bottom of the ocean deserts, and maybe some into the badlands of the Land," Lir said.

"Although Lir tells us the Sohi say the Land has magic, it was just used up years ago, so the Sohi have begun cultivating its rebirth. Oh, and then we got to talking about the Trow expertise in bio-morphing and how it fits with Human biomimicry and whether these would be the skills of the future." Nadara, like Penfield, was buzzing with the energy of the conversation.

"And don't forget the speculation by one group of Human scientists. It is the nature of our electricity that is causing the Trow problem, and we may mitigate it by switching to DC current," Penfield added. "An acquaintance of mine used to shout *My hair's on fire. My hair's on fire.* I feel like that right now."

The others looked quizzically at Penfield's lack of hair, causing him to laugh.

"I feel like I stepped into one of the most advanced classrooms ever," Aran said, shaking his head. He spent the next couple of hours talking with them, and when he left the table, he found himself hoping a new set of leaders might emerge to take these ideas and knit the worlds together.

He realized he hadn't seen Merit all afternoon. She had disappeared after they'd returned from the boat. After searching the eco-resort in vain, he did a finding spell and located her in the jungle not far away. She had lost weight in this last recovery and looked gaunt to Aran.

She looked up as he approached, her eyes red and wet.

"Why are you here by yourself?"

"Just needed some time to think about things." She gazed off into the jungle.

Aran looked down and poked a stone with his toe. A scorpion dashed from beneath it to take cover under a larger stone.

"The doctors took the splints off my wings yesterday and told me I wouldn't be able to fly anymore."

"I'm sorry. That's terrible."

"It's everything. It's banishment." Her voice grew fainter, as though she was speaking to herself. "I can't be a warrior. I can't be a Silth. I can't be me."

"I don't understand. It's not like banishment. Now that we can transport, it's not like you'll have to walk—"

"I don't want to talk about it right now. That's why I'm out here. I just finished setting Stalbon free."

"What?"

"It's not fair to him," she said, her voice catching. "I'll never fly again. I'll never fight again. And he can't fight bolts or guns. So, I let him go. And now I'm sad. There's nothing for you to do but let me be sad."

He was quiet for a moment, moving some debris on the ground around with his toes. Then he said, "It's getting dark. How about you come back with me, and we go to Storng's wake? Then I have to leave for a couple of days. We'll get together again on the morning of the third day."

She was still for a few seconds before wiping her eyes roughly with the back of her hand and walking back with him toward the resort. Though the sky was still a light blue, it was dark beneath the trees. The pathway lights were on, as were those in the high-ceilinged thatched bungalows.

Voices floated out from them as people got ready for their dinners or put little children to bed after a day of adventure. Life was going on again.

They headed down a wooden walkway ending at the edge of the trees where the beach began. As they stepped into the sand, he sighed. He stopped and scrunched his toes in the squeaky moistness. He noticed how different the Silth footprints, with their three toes in front and one at the heel, were from the Human prints. He savored the moist, salty, seaweed-scented air.

Down the beach, a bonfire roared, and blankets had been spread among glowing round lanterns, all underneath a full moon. They got food at the buffet and stayed on the edge of the gathering. They spoke little, and he let her lead to whatever she wanted to talk about. Mostly, he watched the bonfire, listened to the voices, and thought about the time in Florida with Storng as he came to know the Tiki Crew. Similar bonfires and voices, many of them missing now. Around midnight, he kissed her goodbye.

# Scene 3

ARAN (SILTH)

Transporting from Almonds and Coral at midnight put Aran in New Zealand around six a.m. He found a quiet tree and slept for three hours before his meeting with Jules.

They had arranged to meet at Dolomite Point, a dramatic landscape on the western coast of the South Island with soaring cliffs and pancake rocks. While back in the northern hemisphere fall was lapsing into winter, here spring was giving way to summer. It wasn't far from Jules's new home in Paparoa National Park.

As Aran sat waiting, the ocean entertained him with a pod of dolphins swimming parallel to the beach, a whale breaching in the distance and a couple of sea lions flopping on the sand. Jules quietly appeared, and they watched the scene for a few minutes before he spoke.

"The Steamtiki Crew is mostly sleeping in today, the ones that aren't still on the beach in Costa Rica. It was a good wake."

"A lot of folks to remember." Aran continued weaving a couple of grass blades together and tied off their tops. "When do you start your new duties?"

"Already started. I am officially Head of Council for the New Zealand and Australia colonies."

"Any bad feelings left from Rangi?"

"Not really. Australia is so disorganized, they appreciate help restoring their world, and New Zealand... Well, they're just happy I'm not Rangi. Then there's lots of work to negotiate a world of equality for

Humans and wildlife. There are ingrained farming practices here that are very hostile to wildlife, but there're also a lot of good people who care about these things."

Aran smiled. "What? Did I just hear you say something nice about Humans?"

"I'm learning that new diplomacy thing and all. But it isn't easy. As the wildlife finds its voice, a lot of anger and grieving exists over what's lost. The Steamtiki Crew is great, though. They're helping interpret the wildlife to the Humans and the Humans to the wildlife. It helps that the Humans now know what it's like to face someone who wants you eliminated for their own convenience."

"All the crew are living here now?"

"Well, not quite all," he said, picking up a rock as though he needed something to do with his hands.

"I'm not sure she counts as crew anymore."

"The pleasant thing is that the commute between here and Washington South is about ten seconds by blip. But I've never had to deal with a serious phone bill before."

"How about Tara?"

Jules said nothing, just stared out at the water.

"I introduced her to Joss, with the hope they might work together."

"It might work. It's hard to tell. And where she goes, the rest of the 5's follow. During the war, Benfica, a large bush meat market, opened in Angola, and the President of the Republic of Congo died. His death happened because the violation of the binding occurred in Congo. Two days later, the market closed because no one could find any of the hunters who had killed the animals or the brokers who'd arranged the sale to the shopkeepers. Or the wardens who looked the other way, the shopkeepers who sold it, or the police who the brokers bribed not to stop the sale of the meat. All who ate anything purchased on the last day got very sick too."

"Tara?"

"Presumably, though she was never missing from any of the fighting. The 5's and Temkaa led others, I think. I have no idea how they did it. As you know, it doesn't violate any Silth law for them to do this. We could banish them. They wouldn't care. No one's foolish enough to try to clip their wings. It also seems strange since until a few months ago, one of our biggest crimes was communicating with Humans, which we all do daily now.

"The Humans in the region are investigating halfheartedly. They are in danger of new wars as potential leaders emerge. They barely have their government re-established from the volcano chaos, and then, like everywhere else, the cities suffered large casualties from the Trow attacks. The Silth there did not suffer as many losses."

"Another sore point with the Humans."

"We can't help that the Silth could blip into hiding, and it was easier to find Humans. A lot of Silth died saving Humans. And yesterday seemed to remind everyone how close to disappearing we all came.

"But wildlife also loses when the Humans go to war. The Africa Silth are trying to help feed everyone and avoid another round of famine. There are similar challenges all around the world. The war is over, but the world is one of the wounded."

"Well, congratulations on your new role as council chair. I'm sure you'll have all this fixed in no time."

"Ha! Well, today you get to help. You are what the Humans tell me is the *keynote* speaker for our first big meeting with Humans. It's called *Conference on the Future of Silth and Humans in New Zealand.*"

"What's a keynote speaker supposed to do? Besides telling you your conference has a very boring title?"

"Apparently, you're supposed to inspire us for the impossible task we face. Send us into the day with hope, great ideas, and confidence we are up to the task." Aran gave him a side-eye.

"Shall we go?" Jules flickered and disappeared.

Aran sat a moment more, watching the waves as they rushed in among the rocks stacked like pancakes, blowing fountains of spray out of blowholes. Then he transported.

He reappeared in the Sir Owen G. Glenn Building at the University of Auckland Business School, according to the sign on the door. He listened as the first speaker, a Human, told the room of five hundred that hundreds of thousands more around the world were watching them on the livestream. Aran really didn't pay attention until he heard him introducing a Maori storyteller.

He was interested in Maori stories because, like the Silth, the Maori had no written language before colonization. They seemed to use tone of voice and facial expressions in their telling more than the Silth did. The storyteller told the audience of the breadth of Maori stories and how they were used to help the young understand society's expectations and to heal.

She also talked about how many Maori had grown up with few of their own stories and instead read stories from the Greeks and popular writers. She said that as the tribes in New Zealand and Australia had lost their stories, they had also lost their culture and their way. According to her, as the Humans, the Trow, and the Silth came together, it would be important to preserve their old stories even as they created new ones with the blended beings of the Earth.

She introduced Jules, who talked about the various committees and conferences underway to create a shared future. He wore his usual attire and looked exotic even to Aran as he stood on the lectern. Aran wondered if the audience had any idea how deadly the creature that stood before them was. Although he sounded like any good bureaucrat, even after having shed all obvious weaponry, he could probably kill half the people there if given a reason. Yet here he was, building a new world. Aran wished he could stay until the afternoon when Lir from the Neirads spoke, but he would leave right after speaking. He needed to visit Penfield and make one more stop before meeting with Merit. He returned his attention to the room when he heard Jules say his name.

When Aran landed on the lectern, the audience jumped up, clapping and whistling.

He looked over his shoulder at the two large screens, showing two more twenty-foot-tall versions of himself. He waved at himself, wearing his shaman cloak and glamoured so the apparatus around his eyes was unseen, and then laughed.

He turned to the audience and spoke as gently as he could, giving them time to quiet down and get used to his voice. "I'm told I'm supposed to inspire you. Tell you some of my exploits of the last couple of years. But I am inspired by *you*. I look around this room at the Silth and the Humans here, your excitement, the way you are talking to one another."

He spread his arms as though embracing them all.

"I want to read you a little from a letter the head of the UN World Interspecies Directorate shared with me." He took a letter from a pocket in his cloak and held it close to his eyes so he could see it in the dim light of the auditorium. He read:

*'I've given a lot of thought to what you said when we last met. This helped to distract me from the fear I experienced as the Trow hunted my grandchildren. I appreciated that you spoke about the honor and tradition that I hold dear in hunting. But I agree with you and the Silth that Humans must change our relationship with wildlife. I would like to help you find a way forward.'*

"This letter is remarkable because it was written to the Director by a man who held a gun on her in an assassination attempt.

"It makes me believe there is hope. I'm also inspired by the speaker who preceded me. She said our stories might *serve as our guardrails* to help us remember who we were, even as we become something different. So, I want to tell you a story today."

The lights faded and big screen became a video of a burning, crackling bonfire. Many in the audience leaned forward to hear him better.

"Costa Rica, where I grew up, is a land of many blessings, among those being that it is home to both coatis and raccoons. The closest thing you have in New Zealand are stoats and possums, and they are close only in the sense they are also mammals. There is nothing on Earth like a coati. Except perhaps a raccoon. They both love to root through Human garbage, are exceptionally clever, and can be brazen in their encounters with Humans or Silth. One will distract you while his brother steals the food right from your hands. But one major difference exists between them. Coatis are sociable, traveling in packs to protect themselves, and raccoons are pretty solitary, sometimes living in family groups but eventually even fighting with them over food. When coatis and raccoons meet, they act like brother and sister, fighting over the cat food left on the porch.

"Back in the old days, each of the animals had a tribe, and that tribe a ruler or a leader. The raccoons called theirs a king, and the coatis called theirs a queen. Another blessing of Costa Rica is it has many tribes of monkeys. One was the squirrel monkeys, let by a toucan. She was a beautiful yellow-eared toucan, with a green, orange, and blue beak, purple, yellow, and black feathers, and blue feet. Her name was Selena.

"Selena hated the raccoons because they stole her eggs and ate them. But she also admired the way they would solve puzzles, avoid the traps set by the Humans, and elude the jaguars. They would even sneak into places with guards. Although the monkeys voluntarily followed her, she enslaved the raccoons by capturing their King. The monkeys tied up the Raccoon King when he was sleeping and carried him off to Selena's prison.

"Clever as he was, he couldn't escape the tree hollow where she held him, guarded by monkeys with sharp sticks. She made the raccoons serve her and the monkeys.

"The raccoons worked all the time, gathering food for the monkeys and Selena. The monkeys grew fat and lazy, and the raccoons became sad. At first, the coatis were happy; the raccoons spent so much time gathering the type of food the monkeys liked, and they didn't have time to compete with the coatis for the foods they both enjoyed.

The coatis didn't get in fights with the raccoons much anymore, and when they did, the raccoons were so thin and weak they always lost.

"But after a while, the coatis grew sorry for their old rivals. They didn't enjoy seeing them taken advantage of by the monkeys, imagining that one day, it would be them serving Salena.

"The Coati Queen called them together and said, 'I know these foolish raccoons are like our irritating little brothers, always pestering us, but they are still our brothers. They don't know how to do things as a group, so they can never break free from Salena. Would you like to help them?'

"The coatis decided they would. They assembled four of the sneakiest coatis, all magnificent fighters, sort of like ninja coatis."

When Aran held his hands claw-like up close to his face, he drew light laughter.

"In the jungle, there is a saying—'The trees have ears'. I think Humans say something similar about walls. Well, at least three monkeys had been listening to the Coati Queen, and they reported the conversation to the Toucan Queen.

"'Well, I'll be ready for those silly coatis when they come', she said. She organized the monkeys to attack the coatis when they tried to rescue the Raccoon King.

"But a raccoon also overheard the discussion and reported it to the other raccoons. It embarrassed them the coatis needed to step in and fight for them, even though they were appreciative they would do so. The raccoons knew they were so weak the monkeys would easily defeat them in a battle. The acting leader was a big, elderly, raccoon named Tebbie. He was still obese, despite the low rations of the raccoons.

"He sent a raccoon to negotiate with the Toucan Queen, but

the Queen didn't even listen, just locked her up with the Racoon King. He then sent three more negotiators, each of which got locked up with the others. Before long, Tebbie himself went to speak with the Queen. He lumbered up the gigantic tree and stood on a limb before her.

"'Toucan Queen, I want to talk with you.' She called for the monkeys and they dragged him off to the tree with the hollow. But no room was left in the hollow, and he was too big, so they brought him back.

"'Toucan Queen, I want to talk with you,' he said again. She decided she had to listen because she had no place to put him.

"'Toucan Queen, if we stop eating your eggs, will you let our King go?'

"The Toucan Queen thought and preened her feathers, before saying, 'No, I don't want you eating the eggs of my daughters either.'

"'Then, if we don't eat the eggs of your daughters either, will you let our King go?'

"The Queen preened some more before replying, 'No. I don't want you eating the eggs of my cousin birds, the parrots, crows, or flamingos either.'

"Tebbie thought for a moment. 'We have to have food. What if we limited the total number of eggs we ate and never emptied a nest?'

"The Toucan Queen cocked her head. 'That would work, but everyone knows the raccoons can't organize anything without breaking into fights. I don't believe that you can get the other raccoons to live by this rule. They will say it's unnatural.'

"Tebbie's fat, masked face was inscrutable. Then he said, 'We will get our cousins the coatis to help us organize and tell everyone. We'll ask them to teach us how to work together like they do. We need to learn to work together, anyway.' He looked around at the monkeys, thought to be among the smartest of the jungle animals, but now ruled by a toucan. 'Otherwise, we're destined to be ruled by something even worse than a toucan.'

"'What?' the Toucan Queen said.

"'Nothing,' Tebbie quickly answered."

The crowd laughed, and Aran continued.

"Selena released the Racoon King, the coatis taught the raccoons cooperation, and peace was the result. The raccoons prospered without harming the toucans."

Behind Aran, the bonfire in the video flared into blue flame before settling back into its normal colors. The crowd stood again, clapping and whistling their appreciation.

Jules returned to the stage with a couple of local Human leaders, and with Aran, they discussed the challenges of the shared future. As soon as they finished, Aran said goodbye to Jules. His early evening arrival at Washington South would allow him to have dinner with Penfield. The next morning, he would complete his last stop before seeing Merit.

# CHAPTER ELEVEN

## *Scene 1*

ARAN (SILTH)

Aran hummed an old Silth song about traveling to the Land. He hadn't been able to sleep the night before, but despite that and yesterday's double load of activity, he wasn't tired. Still, as he passed through the portal into the Land, he checked to make sure he knew how to make a quick exit.

All his life he'd been told stories about the dangers of going to the Land. How time worked differently there. How hard it was to come back from there.

Don't accept gifts. Don't eat the food. Don't go to sleep.

A new, rudimentary visa process was in place, mostly to keep track of who was there and warnings that an hour of Earth time would be three hours in the Land. Exactly the opposite of the old tales of how someone would go to the Land and come back to Earth young while all their loved ones had aged.

He walked from the portal with Kimper, who was returning to the Land to visit family, he supposed. It appeared she had failed to persuade the flower fairies they needed a queen. As he listened to her tinkle excitedly, he realized she'd never done this either. She'd transported involuntarily to Earth with a load of his swag.

Movement across the portal was anticlimactic, however. One

moment you were on Earth, then you stepped into what seemed to be a dark closet and out into what looked like a partially sketched version of Earth someone had colored in with oddly inappropriate crayons.

On the portal's other side, Sohi guards waited. They recognized Aran and waved him on. Kimper stood, looking confused. She jumped into the air as though trying to fly, but simply dropped back to the ground.

"Apparently, flower fairies can't fly in the Land, only on Earth. It's magic."

She frowned, and her little shoulders slumped.

"Will you be okay? Can you walk to where you want to go?"

She shook her head and kicked at the grass.

Aran reached down and held out his hands. She stepped forward, and he picked her up.

"Which way?"

Kimper sniffed the air, looked at the sky and pointed to the distance.

Aran flew for about ten minutes across the oddly colored fields and sparse houses of the Land. He passed several villages, clusters of smaller houses, landing as he came to the edge of a vast, purple grassland, stretching out with no discernable end.

"Is this okay?"

Kimper nodded a vigorous *yes,* jumping from one foot to the other.

"I'll return here in about nine hours local time. If you are here, I'll take you back to Earth. You are welcome to come back with me or stay longer and come back on your own."

Kimper looked up at where the sun was, then back at Aran,

and nodded. She dashed into the tall grass and disappeared. Aran saw no movement showing her passage.

Aran paused for a moment, wondering about their conversation. He had always assumed that the ability of the Silth to communicate with other creatures was magical. Not all Silth had it, but someone unevenly distributed magical abilities among the Silth. Did that mean the ability to communicate was one inherited from parrots? But as far as he knew, parrots couldn't read. Maybe he wouldn't be able to read here in the Land.

Aran flew under a gray sky with no evidence of sun other than the pale light leaking from the grayness. He passed the strange fields and the manor houses toward the palace in the distance. Little moved in the landscape, no traffic of any sort traveling on the road except for one Trow on foot. When he saw Aran, his mouth dropped open.

Otherwise, Aran saw no birds, wildlife, or even domestic animals.

Aran landed in front of what he assumed was the palace. It was not the spired castle of the sort that came to his mind when someone said the word *palace,* but an enormous blocky building made of a marble-like stone. The little niches for statues along the top were empty.

Trow were coming and going with brisk purpose. They mostly ignored him, though he caught several sideways glances. He passed three Trow wearing the distinctive patterns of the Neirads, and they stared at him openly. He felt small in the massive entry among the towering figures.

Once the guards allowed him through the enormous doors, the scale of the rooms became more manageable, still not to Silth proportions, but at least the ceilings were only sixteen feet high. Again,

Sohi guards let him pass without challenge, and before long he was in front of the doorway to the throne room. A red-robed Sohi guide explained he was about to pass through a mind-reading portal into the public chambers of the King and Queen.

As Aran carefully composed his thoughts, the guide escorted him through. On the other side, Faelen and a no longer pregnant Lornix were bent over plans spread on a sprawling table.

"What does *smelly old croc bait* mean?" she asked without looking up.

Faelen grinned. "It means Aran thought the portal would transmit his thoughts to me. Welcome, august hero of the Earth and the Land."

"I'm not sure I'm a hero anywhere, so why would I be a hero in the Land?"

"You were the one who talked the Sohi into this adventure, and mostly, both the Sohi and the Trow seem to like it. And you found the Neirads, reconnecting them with their people. The Trow are experiencing..." He paused as he thought about the word. "...calm. They are experiencing calm for the first time in many ages. And in this, you saved the Earth."

Aran laughed. "Well, few on Earth know it was my suggestion, so I don't think there is much likelihood of stories told of my great heroism."

"Everyone knows. And I did not say you were a hero to me. I am stuck with this pain-in-the-ass job of being King, and you have set former courtiers on me as well."

"You'll like the Neirads. They were very brave, going into battle with few skills. Their leaders fought in the front lines, not behind the scenes. And they have a great sense of humor."

"Well, that will be a change of pace." Faelen frowned at the Sohi advisers huddled over a separate table.

"The Sohi have an excellent sense of humor," Lornix insisted. "We played one of the biggest jokes on the Trow the Land has ever seen—getting them to accept you as their King."

"Ouch," Aran said.

"And this complaining about *your* job," she went on. "You have made it very clear to me and everyone else it is *my* job to run things."

"Delegation is the mark of a genuine leader. Aran, come over and look at these papers, we have much to discuss."

"And I need to meet your daughter."

"That you do."

They discussed the plans to allow Humans in the Land. Businesspeople were excited about *time mining,* as they called the utilization of the difference in rates of time between the Land and the Earth. Restoration ecologists who'd been studying Mars were seeking permission to apply their skills to the Faraway, while others were exuberant over the possibility of Land's magic awakening. The opportunity to take part in re-energization called many. It was also a cautionary tale for them all because it suggested something had cost the Land its magic at some early, unremembered time. If it could happen to the Land, it could happen to the Earth as well.

They ate lunch on top of the palace, with Tegras cooing in her cradle nearby.

"Lornix and I wanted to name her after Tegrat, who was Lornix's mentor and allowed me to stay in the village when my real rescue occurred."

"We were sad to hear you lost your mentor. Storng I think was his name," Lornix said, as Faelen handed around food from a basket waiting for them when they reached the roof.

Aran looked around at the Land spreading to the horizon with its odd colors and stunted vegetation. "He would have enjoyed this moment so much. He was always interested in the Land. He would also have so many questions about what you're changing here. What is the consequence of freeing the slaves? What's it like to come back? Do you worry about allowing Humans here?"

"Humans are alright, but not Silth. They ask too many questions."

"For me, it is not coming back," Lornix told him. "I was born on Earth. I am as much a foreigner as you."

"It is not back for me either," Faelen said. "Things are so very different without Xafar here. The older Trow remember the time before him, a time when the Trow reveled in their love of beauty, their fondness for nature and its adaptability into tools. The way they have welcomed us amazes me. It has been... better than I expected."

He smiled at Lornix.

"Of course, it helps I am King only in name. She is managing everything, and they love her. She assigns only the grumpy to deal with me as their punishment. When we freed the slaves, there could have been a revolt. Most of the Trow had either Silth or Human slaves. Even some Trow slaves. Few Trow have done a proper job outside the military in centuries. But there was no drama, and no hostility. In many cases, they begged former slaves to stay and work for wages.

"Most slaves, however, couldn't get out of the Land fast enough, returning to homes where they appear to have aged three times as fast as their peers. The Sohi have offered them counseling, as have the Silth and Humans. It is hard for many Trow to understand the emotional part of it.

"They do understand that there are Humans clamoring to come and work here in the Land, including as paid servants. But first, the Trow have to learn the difference between *employees* and *slaves*."

"Humans are finding out some of that now," Aran said, "as wild animals are freed from zoos, circuses, and private ownership. Of course, it is different when the slave doesn't have the fears, hopes, and dreams of a Human or a Silth. Or at least can't communicate such things. The animals around Earth are now sharing with people their feelings, their hopes for their children, their fears. It's much easier to tolerate someone harpooning a whale when you don't know it has dreams. Or to eat a lamb chop when you don't have to acknowledge that the lamb experienced bliss."

Lornix said, "Some former slaves plan to return as guides in the efforts to develop the Faraway. These efforts make us nervous. We have seen what the Humans did to their world, and we now learn the Trow did something similar to the Land in the time before memory. We cannot let the development of the Faraway introduce new types of pollution into this world. We must not let the Silth and Humans become an invasive species problem."

"Which is why I have a favor to ask of you," Faelen told Aran. "I want you to be a part of a university we are creating to study these issues, the changes we are implementing and their consequences. It would also integrate the arts beloved by the Trow. The music and stories of Silth and Humans fascinate them. It would train the Trow who want to go to Earth to lead Humans on transport adventures—to appear at the North Pole for ten minutes and go from there to the South Pole for another ten. That sort of thing. How do you do this without harm to the Human passengers or to Earth's magic?"

"The Sohi want the help of others in waking the magic of the Land," Lornix added.

Aran, hands waving and words tumbling out, told them about the University Penfield and Storng had been planning, and its similar mission. They talked another two hours about the possibilities. Faelen asked if the institutions might work together. He had apparently decided this would be his contribution to the Trow leadership.

After they had exhausted this conversation, Aran said, "I have a favor to ask of you as well. You may not even be able to grant it. But Storng used the Faraway as a storage area. He had a spell that allowed him to send things there and later retrieve them. If you come across a bunch of cargo containers where they shouldn't be, could I please have them? They will mostly contain Human objects, pretty useless to Trow. But they will also have his books and maybe other things since he had lived without a home for several years."

Lornix nodded. "Of course. But in return, I would appreciate the spell to accomplish such transport. It could be very useful in recovering the Faraway. I won't use it, but others can."

As Aran left through the mind-reading threshold, he thought, *my friends*. The time had passed far too quickly. With the adrenaline gone, and his mind churning with the possibilities two universities created, he hardly noticed the surrounding landscape on his way back to the portal.

Kimper looked exhausted when they met at the Faraway. She slept as he carried her to the portal. She tinkled merrily and zoomed about when she felt the Earth's sunshine again.

# Scene 2

### Aran (Silth)

Aran always thought of it as the *old colony*. It was the place where he and Shra had been flirting on the day his long journey began. It had had many names since then, the most recent being Raponcil, which meant *Restore Town*.

The Sohi had set up a school here for deprogramming the Newfies. Few times in the history of the three races had any religion been so severely disavowed as that of the Newfies; not only had the believers learned their objects of worship weren't celestial, but also, their gods had tried to kill the Newfies along with the Humans and other Silth.

Then, to make matters worse, the Trow told them their entire religion was based on a joke.

The Newfies were spiritually lost, their leader dead, and their world crushed. They met with counselors who told them they would be alright. The recovering Newfies knew this was a lie, told in charity. Then they met with the Sohi. The Sohi, who still recalled living through their own spiritual awakening, were helping them learn to think for themselves again, but also to be comfortable searching for meaning.

Besides the primary Silth religion, various Human groups had set up outposts in the town to share their perspectives. Thus, the town had become a beacon for others seeking to find themselves, and for scientists studying the Silth and the region. Lively discussion filled the cafes and schools that had opened in the area around the old colony.

Despite the many new Human and Trow structures, there were no longer any empty buildings where Aran could meet Merit. He also couldn't meet her in the canopy as they once had. It was tricky to transport into a tree, and her wings no longer worked. He'd chosen to meet her at the waterfall where he'd met with Nadara for the first time away from the Tiki Crew, partway between Raponcil and his home colony. He thought about moving the whole thing somewhere with fewer ghosts of girlfriends, but it was too late.

He tried to quiet his thoughts and to still his hands, nervously grabbing every little thing around him as though they had a mind of their own.

He was perched on a rock next to the waterfall when she appeared. She sat down and leaned against him.

"I've been thinking about your challenge to me. Who am I and what do I want?" he said.

"Don't. Don't think about it. Who am I to ask you to answer this when I can't answer it for myself?" She reached behind her back and moved her wings into a more comfortable position.

He held her hand and sought her eyes before lowering his glamour.

"It was a perfect challenge, and I know the answer. I know what I want. I know who I am. It doesn't mean my path is fixed. I don't think that's how it works. Things may change, but I feel more like I'm choosing rather than just being propelled by events."

They sat in the moonlight, listening to the waterfall. Then Merit moved to face him directly.

"Alright, tell me this revelation."

Her voice was gentle. Perhaps even slightly amused, he thought, as though she couldn't really believe that he had resolved her challenge. "Who has Heartless become? What will the shaman, not-shaman, harvester, singer, storyteller, diplomat, warrior, leader, and so on become now?"

"In all those things, what I enjoyed was finding an alternative way and showing others that way. Making and testing plans, bad as you may have thought them. The world has now presented me with an opportunity to do this as a way of life. The *worlds,* I should say."

"Well, you should say more than that, because that was just coati-scat crazy."

"Penfield asked me to replace Storng as his partner in starting a university here on Earth, for Humans, Silth, and Trow to study the aspects of their cultures. The goals would be to strengthen us all and to work on the problems of our shared futures. I would head the Story College as well. My involvement would be in setting the curriculum of the school and problem solving, but not management of the University. Penfield will do that. The college would be mine to run entirely."

"That's fantastic!" Merit's wide grin was bent a little by her scar.

"It is. But here's where it gets *interesting.*"

"Hmm," she said, the grin disappearing and her shoulders drooping. "It's the interesting part that's usually amuck. But let's have it."

"Faelen asked me to do essentially the same thing in the Land with him. He wants to set up a university for the Trow, mixing in Humans and Silth, to help the Trow think through their future, avoid the problems the Humans and Silth have had in building things, understand magic, and build leadership. My idea is, I want to combine the two universities and have them work together. They have overlapping missions, but not the same. They can share some programs, and each can have its own programs specific to its mission."

"And along the way, you can think and plan and change the world."

"Exactly, and tell stories. To students, who can't complain about my voice."

Merit stared into the crashing water for a moment, then, "It's a good plan."

"What? I'm sorry—the waterfall was too loud. Did you say something?"

"You'll never get me to say it again."

"If you wanted, you could teach as well."

"What would I teach?"

"What you've been teaching for years. Discipline. Leadership. Tactics."

"Ha! I'll think about it. The timing would be right. I resigned as warrior leader in my colony. I'm training my replacement. I'll consider it."

"And in all of this, I know my heart. I know who I am and what I want. But more importantly, I know I want to share the *wanting* with you. I want to know what you want and share our road. I love you." He leaned forward and kissed her.

They moved to the grass by the waterfall, the moonlight shining down on them, and she fell fast asleep. He stayed awake in case a cougar decided they'd make a tasty treat.

Later, when she stirred, he said, "One more thing."

"There's more? You've been busy."

"I have a gift from Faelen and Lornix, but I want to be very clear about it in the giving. I love you with all your scars and brokenness. I *need* nothing different.

"I know you are proud of the battles you've fought, and you always could have glamoured away the look of your arm or the scar on your face.

"The creature that provides me sight was also a present from Faelen and Lornix. It is a Quitquot, a living symbiotic like the orchids in those trees. It has been wonderful. I hide it because I'm still not used to the reaction of people as they see me."

He picked up a cloth-wrapped parcel beside him.

"They have bred this one for you. If you attach it, it will grow into your arm. It is what the Trow do when they need a part replaced." He handed it to her. "It will hurt a lot, an understatement, when you attach it, but then it will live on as part of you. Like this one on my face, it will still look different, but it will work just like an arm."

She eyed the lumpy cloth. "An amazing gift. Does it take them long to make something this specialized?"

"Several months."

"What caused them, several months ago, to decide they wanted to do such a thing for me?"

"Well, you know Faelen thinks you're special."

She ran her hand down the hather on his face. "Faelen thinks I'm especially dim, as I recall." She turned the package over in her hands. "Before I broke my wings, I probably would have declined this. But I'm feeling a little *too* broken right now, and this may be exactly what I need. I can always glamour it to be a stick of wood if I want." She leaned forward and kissed him. "I think I'll wait to attach it later when you're not there to hear me scream."

"So where to next?" asked Aran.

"You're asking me?"

"Yes, I'm exhausted from all this planning."

# Scene 3

Aran (Silth)

Aran had never experienced a dream like this. But he knew he *was* dreaming while he lay in bed with Merit. He felt her arm draped across him as he lay facing her, wings behind him. He felt her breath on his face. But in the dream, he was standing in a place he'd never been, a meadow in an opening in a jungle unlike any he'd ever seen. There seemed to be one of each type of tree, plant, or vine, in each case a perfect specimen. Animals moved in the shadows.

A wolf stepped out into the clearing, neither male nor female, just a perfect wolf. It stared at him a moment before slipping back into the trees. The silent trees. No birdsong, no rustle of a branch in a breeze, and no twig snap as the animals moved around him.

A being that seemed made of light floated from the forest. Pure, white light, standing about ten feet tall. It moved its limbs, but was too bright to look at directly, hard for Aran to discern details. The light being stood in front of Aran as though waiting for him to speak.

"Who are you?"

"Amandamont L'maothis Triltinibaz—" The being continued on through several unpronounceable words.

Aran considered this for a moment before asking, "What do I call you?"

"Amanda."

"What are you?"

"I am true Fae, the voice of the Earth, the Land, and the Third."

Its voice came to Aran like a remembered song in his head, not through his ears. It was all high notes and chimes.

"Why come to me in a dream?"

"We can only communicate with this world in that moment between life and death. Sleep is the small death. We can come as you fall asleep." Whenever the being spoke, it moved its limbs, but these became still otherwise. Inside its light there was constant movement—clouds of brighter light floating across light skies.

Aran knew—and he wasn't sure why—he had to ask questions. Amanda would volunteer nothing. But what questions?

"Why have you appeared to me?"

"Because Storng said to."

"Did Storng communicate with you in this life or after his death?"

"Yes."

Aran huffed his frustration. "What do you want to tell me?"

"The Earth has given you a reprieve. It had decided *all must go and we start again,* but then there was enough, so it decided *one more chance.* It is the Earth that has put one last clutch of Silth in the nests of parrots, and the Earth which has allowed the Silth to have babies, just like the Humans before them. You will not have long, and there will be no other chances.

"You must resuscitate the Earth and restore the Land. But there is not enough energy left in these places to accomplish your task."

"Then how can we succeed?"

"You must reconnect with the Third. This will supply the necessary energy. And you must take other actions." Aran's mind flooded with questions. But before he could ask them, they were in another clearing, one that he immediately recognized.

*I know this place.* He saw the three crates, still in the center but now covered in vines and almost obscured by the dense vegetation growing around them. He pushed his way through the small trees and brambles. Opening the third crate, he pulled out the blanket and wrapped himself in it. The memories in the first two crates had flowed smoothly, like stories remembered.

But for this one, there was little connection between one thought and the next. He found himself in a lecture about the difference between AC and DC electricity. Then he was back in Tokyo in the room powered by magic. Or was it magic as a form of electricity? The next stray memory saved in the fabric of the memory blanket was the recollection of reading that light could be a wave and a particle at the same time, and wondering whether energy might be magic and electricity at the same time. But all magic had a cost, so did that mean that all electricity had a cost too?

Another idea spread through the blanket weave. Tesla had thought that eventually, electricity would form into the world brain. What if he was right, and this was another example of a fractal? Was the Human brain, powered by electrical impulses, a fractal of the world brain, also powered by such impulses?

Finally, there was the *magic dampener,* the device the Tokyo Electric Trow had used to modulate magic to be used as power without destroying machinery. What was that device and how did it fit into the mix? Unlike the blankets in the other two crates, the memories in this one were few. He knew he was close to some connection between them that answered something, but he was unsure of either the question or the answer.

Then, with no transition, he was back in the clearing with the light being towering over him. Amanda pulsed brighter but said nothing.

"How do we reconnect to the Third?"

"You must complete your journey to become the *rainbow crow*."

"I didn't know I was on a journey… and I have no idea what a rainbow crow is."

The light being said nothing.

"How do I complete this journey?"

"You must find the passageway to the Third. You must follow it and re-establish the connection."

"Where do I find this passageway?"

"It is in the space between life and death."

Aran thought for a moment. "When I find the passageway, what do I do to re-establish a connection?"

"I do not know. The rainbow crow will know."

"What is the rainbow crow?"

"You must discover this yourself."

"Is this journey dangerous?"

"Yes, for you and anyone who accompanies you. You walk the path on the edge, life on one side, death on the other. But you have walked this path for quite some time."

Aran put his hands on the sides of his head as though trying to squeeze thoughts out of it. "What do I need to take with me?"

"Study the strengths and weaknesses of the rainbow crow."

From behind the light being, three light butterflies emerged from the jungle. They were the same butterflies, or at least the same type, that had come to Storng's funeral.

"Did you send those to Storng's funeral?"

"The Earth did."

"Where are we now? Is this the Third?"

"No, this is the Overlap, the place where all three worlds come together as one."

The light being faded.

"Amanda, can I contact you?"

"Perhaps. But only here, for now."

"Have I left out any important questions?"

"Most certainly." And it disappeared.

Aran awoke and as he lay there, the first of the missed questions occurred to him.

*How am I going to tell Merit?*

He looked at her as she slept peacefully next to him. He listened to her breathe, her breaths regular and comforting. He waited as his own pulse slowed and his breaths matched hers. *Perhaps it's time for Jules and Nadara to save the worlds.* He closed his eyes and was promptly asleep again, a deep and untroubled slumber.

# CHARACTERS

## *SILTH*

### ARAN
Storyteller, who became a shaman, also called Heartless

### SHRA
Aran's lover, deceased

### STORNG
Shaman, also called Storm Rider

### NADARA
Leader of Tiki Crew

### DON, KIRSTN, NICK, LOANA
Tiki Crew members

### MERIT
Battle leader, also called Dawn Defender

### CASIUS
Aran's brother, high priest of the New Faerie

### TEMKAA
Chief of the Congo Silth

### KRACKLE
Silth shaman from the Brazilian Refuge

### JULES
Leader of the Steamer Crew

### JABTAR
Head of the Shaman Council

### STEAMER CREW
Slatt, Tara (3 of 5), Abney (4 of 5), Blay (5 of 5), Ada, Vander, Valente a group of mercenaries

### TRANDAN
Aran's assistant

# CHARACTERS

## *HUMANS*

**JOCELYN (JOSS)**
Former manager of the refuges, now a UN employee

**KATE**
Joss's friend, manager of Costa Rica Refuge

**DR. BRANDON STRIDEMAN (TINY)**
Volcanologist

**ALEXANDRA PRUNA**
Major, Ecuadorian air force

**DIMBA TSAGO**
Congo Ranger

**REVEREND JEREMIAH TOBIAS**
International televangelist

**JOAO LUIZ SOUSA**
Brazilian ambassador to US

**CATHERINE PERCROW**
President of the United States

**DR. IRVIN PENFIELD, JR.**
US Assistant Secretary of State

**MARIA LUIS**
Caretaker in Brazilian Refuge

**TONHO**
Caretaker in Brazilian Refuge

**GENERAL JOHN COGBILL**
UN General

**GENERAL JOHN COGBILL (2.0)**
Son of General Cogbill

**FETU**
Tiny's friend and bodyguard

# CHARACTERS

## *TROW*

### FAELEN
Former general of Trow army, son of Xafar

### THEST
Current general of Trow army

### XAFAR
Former King of the Trow

### LORNIX
Sohi nurse

### TEGRAT
Speaker of the Sohi Will

### LIR, TETHRA, MANAN
Leaders of the Neirad

### DEMEST
Thest's deceased wife, killed by Silth using magic learned from Xafar's son Faelen

## *OTHERS*

### SHADOW
Tiny's dog

### KIMPER
Aran's flower fairy

### MACHO
Joss's dog

### STALBON
Merit's harpy eagle

# GLOSSARY

### COATI
A raccoon-like mammal native to Costa Rica

### COLONY
A place where larger numbers of Silth live; typically surrounded by villages, each centered on an extended family

### FAERIE DUST (FD)
The powdered, enchanted dirt which strips the ability to blip from Trow and Silth

### GLAMOUR
As a verb, the act of disguising the true appearance of a Silth or a Trow; as a noun, the particular appearance projected by a being

### HARVEST
The annual process of Silth gathering Human products for their own use

### HATHER
The hairlike feathers of a Silth

### THE LAND
The home world of Trow; also referred to as Faerie by some Humans and Silth

### NEIRADS
A band of Trow living beneath the ocean

# GLOSSARY

## SILTH

The progeny of Trow and parrots, about the size of a large parrot; humanoid, with the arms, legs, torso, and sharp features of a Trow, but with wings and the coloration of a parrot; the Trow call them Paerries as a derogatory term, but when they apply it to themselves, they mean it as a show of defiance

## SOHI

A band of Trow who have styled their society on the ancient Human Sohi.

## TROW

Called Faeries by Humans and Silth, but the Trow hate the name and use it to refer to lesser animals; a race of inter-dimensional beings who have been visiting the Earth since humanity's early days

Thanks for reading! If you liked the book and have a moment to spare, I'd really appreciate a short review as this helps new readers find my books. Reviews can be left on Amazon. You can check out the timing for the next book on the Facebook site @worldofpaerries and subscribe for information on the series as well as bonus material and news on the author at ww.worldofpaerries.com

If the world permits, I plan to continue with a Book 4 after a couple of other projects.

# ACKNOWLEDGEMENTS

My cover illustration was done by Gennady Sokolenko. Copy editing was by Annie Jenkinson. My thanks to Martha Slone, always my alpha and omega copy editor and more. Special thanks to my beta readers, they inspire me while showing me the guardrails. Also, thanks to Sparkfire Branding who do my final book setup. Thanks to Anastasia Storer, Jessica Brown, and Amanda Slone, who help me manage and create the social media, vlog, and marketing that is so much harder than writing a book.

Finally, I want to express my deep gratitude for the magic of the world in which we live, and its manifestation in wildlife and natural systems around us.

**A PORTION OF THE PROFIT FROM ANY SALES OF THIS BOOK IS DONATED TO A SANCTUARY FOR PARROTS WHO HAVE BEEN CAST OFF OR OUTLIVED THEIR OWNERS OR FOR HABITAT PRESERVATION.**

Made in the USA
Middletown, DE
14 August 2021